Beyond the Rain

Beyond the Rain

Jess Granger

BERKLEY SENSATION, NEW YORK

THE BERKLEY PUBLISHING GROUP
Published by the Penguin Group
Penguin Group (USA) Inc.
375 Hudson Street, New York, New York 10014, USA
Penguin Group (Canada), 90 Eglinton Avenue East, Suite 700, Toronto, Ontario M4P 2Y3, Canada
(a division of Pearson Penguin Canada Inc.)
Penguin Books Ltd., 80 Strand, London WC2R 0RL, England
Penguin Group Ireland, 25 St. Stephen's Green, Dublin 2, Ireland (a division of Penguin Books Ltd.)
Penguin Group (Australia), 250 Camberwell Road, Camberwell, Victoria 3124, Australia
(a division of Pearson Australia Group Pty. Ltd.)
Penguin Books India Pvt. Ltd., 11 Community Centre, Panchsheel Park, New Delhi—110 017, India
Penguin Group (NZ), 67 Apollo Drive, Rosedale, North Shore 0632, New Zealand
(a division of Pearson New Zealand Ltd.)
Penguin Books (South Africa) (Pty.) Ltd., 24 Sturdee Avenue, Rosebank, Johannesburg 2196,
South Africa

Penguin Books Ltd., Registered Offices: 80 Strand, London WC2R 0RL, England

This book is an original publication of The Berkley Publishing Group.

Cover art by Phil Heffernan.
Cover design by Diana Kolsky.

PRINTING HISTORY
Berkley Sensation trade paperback edition / August 2009

Library of Congress Cataloging-in-Publication Data

Granger, Jess.
Beyond the rain / Jess Granger.—Berkley Sensation trade pbk. ed.
ISBN 978-0-425-22926-2
I. Title.
PS3607.R36285B49 2009
813'.6—dc22 2009015904

147204767

To my husband, my hero, my very best friend.

ACKNOWLEDGMENTS

This book wouldn't exist without the love and support of my family. Thank you for all your encouragement and patience. You've been there for me, no matter what. I'm glad I could make you proud.

I'd also like to thank my agent, Laura Bradford, and my editor, Leis Pederson, for their belief in this story and their patience as I learn a whole new side of publishing. I'm grateful to all the staff at Berkley, from the cover artists to the copy editors and everyone in between. Thank you for your hard work and dedication.

And special thanks to Rose, my reader from the very start; Angie, my critique partner and friend; Julia and Melanie, who got me hooked on romance to begin with; Kate, for setting me up with Angie; Susan, for a pilot's insight; Kristie, for keeping me sane; and finally Heather, for being an advocate for Science Fiction Romance everywhere.

1

"DAMN IT, HATCH! THIS IS WAR. IF YOU CAN'T HANDLE IT, GET YOUR ASS BACK to the transport." Cyani slammed her back against the tunnel wall as the shattering explosion of a K-bomb shook the ground. Fine pebbles and dust crumbled over her head, illuminating the laser sights streaming from her team's eyepieces. She scanned the other men in the tunnel to see if any of them were beginning to panic. They couldn't lose focus.

"I'm fine, Captain," Hatch shouted back. He cringed as another blast rumbled in the distance. "Don't like tight spaces is all."

Earthlen, they could be so damn unpredictable.

"Keep control, I'm counting on you," she urged.

Hatch squared his wide shoulders. "I got your back, Amazon."

"I'm Azralen. Get your species straight." She brushed the

fallen dust off her shadowsuit and assessed the tunnel to see if their path had caved in.

"Wouldn't get it, Cap'. It's an Earth thing." He winked then focused on the holo-map projected in front of his left eye. "We have coordinates on the prisoners. Vicca found them."

"Good girl," Cyani whispered to herself as she touched her com unit to turn on her own holo-map. The tiny floating screen lit with brightly colored dots, indicating the location of each prisoner her fox had marked with her com collar. She just hoped the little ball of fur was safe.

The seven Union soldiers they were assigned to rescue huddled in a small cluster in a single cell near the supply storehouses, but Vicca had discovered an eighth humanoid. The unknown prisoner had been locked in the more secure section on the other side of the compound.

"*Shakt*, Vicca, not now," Cyani cursed as she pressed the recall button that should have sent her fox racing back to her. The blue dot on the holo-map jumped forward then remained still. It seemed her scout wasn't going to return.

"You stubborn little myhrat. You were supposed to stay with our prisoners, not find one of your own." Cyani flicked the sensor at her temple and the holo-map disappeared. Whoever the lone prisoner was, he had earned the sympathy of her wayward scout. She would have to go get her. She couldn't let the security codes in Vicca's collar fall into enemy hands.

"You two!" She pointed to her men. "Take the microbe packs and free our men. I'll go after Vicca and this lone one. Hatch and Tola, secure the passage back to the transport. Remain on UC-4 until further notice. That communication channel should still be secure. We meet no later than thirty-five fourteen, understood? I refuse to leave anyone behind on this spirit-forsaken chunk of rock." She stretched her fingers and pulled her sono from her side. Adjusting the eyepiece and ear set of her com, she turned back to her men.

"Comin' with you, Cap," Hatch insisted.

"No," she commanded. "You have your orders." The last thing she needed was to lose one of her men trying to retrieve her own damn fox. She had to do this alone. She worked best alone.

"I don't like this, Captain," Tola protested.

"You don't have to," she responded. "You're in charge, Lieutenant. Get everyone to the transport before treating any injuries, do you understand? Time is the enemy now."

He looked up at her, his swarthy expression as enigmatic as ever, but there was something in his eyes, something she couldn't acknowledge.

"Protect my men," she added, softening her tone. She had done her best to keep them safe in the five years they'd fought together. They were brave, smart soldiers, and she'd never forgive herself if she lost another man because of one of her orders. Losing three during the Felli campaign was bad enough.

Tola nodded as his hawklike expression hardened with resignation.

Cyani continued to the rest of her team, "Don't get caught. I don't want to fly into Krona to haul your butts out of an auction pit. Be careful." She took a microbe pack and hooked it to her belt. The men shuddered, but Hatch's black eyes turned to steel.

"You be careful, Cap. Azralen sell for a nice chunk of trillide on the slave market. You're twenty times more valuable than any of us." Hatch placed his large dark hand on her shoulder, even though she had made it clear several times she shouldn't be touched, ever. That strict rule of her culture had been beaten into her, and she still bore the scars.

She looked down at Hatch's hand, unable to chastise him. If they didn't make it out, such a brief touch was a forbidden comfort, but a comfort all the same. They were more than her men, more than brothers. Hatch patted her shoulder then motioned to Tola. "We'll be waiting for you."

"If I'm late, I'm dead. Now go," she ordered. "We'll meet in victory soon."

Cyani left the communication channel open as she flicked on her holo-map. The tiny map buzzed to life. The small blue dot that represented her stell fox remained unwavering beside a glowing orange dot marking the unknown humanoid.

"Whoever you are, you'd better be in some serious trouble, or Vicca's not getting her belly scratched for the next ten years," Cyani grumbled as she pulled herself up through a drain grate into the dark, iron-barred halls of the slave enclosure.

The assaulting smells of quar mold and urine made her eyes water. Holding the crook of her arm over her face, she scanned the area while trying to keep her breathing shallow. The terrible smell, the burning in her eyes, the darkness—she couldn't let herself be distracted by her memories. She didn't have much time before the Garulen discovered their defenses were down and powered the laser locks back up.

She rubbed the palms of her hands slowly on her thighs, then focused on the task at hand. The last thing she needed was to be killed or captured with her release from the war within her reach.

She pried open a dead laser lock with her flick knife and crept into the dim interior of the slave cells. The large stone blocks closed in around her, making her shudder. She stilled, waiting, watching. Water dripped on stone. The soft *plink-plink* echoed in the empty hall. With silent caution she crept farther down the passage.

K-bombs echoed outside like thunder but seemed distant from the interior of the small stone fortress. She set her com to high alert and scanned her surroundings. Cyani snuck along the walls to the cell door and turned the heavy latch. Pulling the door open with all her strength, she peered inside.

Warning, humanoid life-form encountered.

She flicked her holo-map off, so her eyes could adjust to the dim light.

Cyani stared in awestruck horror at the naked man chained to the wall. She felt her heart race as her stomach clenched in outrage and disgust.

Slave bands dug into his arms, waiting to inject him with whatever torturous poisons the Garulen needed to keep him submissive. As if that weren't enough to control him, chains bound his hands and feet so tightly that the cuffs dug into his blood-caked skin. Severe-blinders hooked into his temples, and his toned back and chest bore deep, ugly contusions from a recent beating. Though lean, he seemed in prime physical condition, not starved like most slaves. His knuckles swelled with open cuts and bruises, as if he had done some damage in retaliation during that beating. In spite of everything, an aura of power and menace clung to him.

What was he capable of? She crept closer to the wall, inching toward him. Her hand hovered over her weapon. She couldn't forget he was dangerous, a crouched wild beast wary and ready to strike.

Her heart raced, and Cyani felt a tingle rushing through her arms as her mind fought back the memory of lying beaten on the floor, listening to the mob chant in the halls.

She forced the dark echoes from her mind and focused on him. Who was she dealing with? What did they use him for? Was he a pit fighter? Or worse?

He clenched his jaw but remained silent. He *watched* her, even though she was certain he could see nothing through the smooth black plates covering his eyes.

Vicca trotted to the prisoner, her com collar blinking through her fur. The movement drew Cyani's attention, and she focused on her scout. The fox rubbed her head and shoulders against the prisoner's leg while her tail swished in indignation. Cyani had been irritated with her scout, but now she understood. She couldn't have left him there either. Every ounce of honor and holy righteousness that had been ingrained in her being refused to leave him to such terrible torture. She knew this darkness.

"Com, identify humanoid life-form." Cyani prepared the microbes to remove the slave bands while waiting for the report to sound in her ear.

Humanoid life-form has been identified. Species: Byralen. Gender: Male.

"I noticed," she muttered. She wasn't familiar with the Byralen people. "Ability to translate?"

Language: Unknown. Ability to translate: 0 percent.

"Great, this should be entertaining."

Culture: Unknown.

"That wasn't a request." Exasperated, she inched closer to the prisoner. "Any unusual defenses?"

Physical characteristics: Byralen can be identified by dark stripes over their shoulders and arms and streaked hair in varying common shades. Their irises contain a phosphorescent chemical compound and can change color at will, possibly used as communication. Byralen emit potent sexual pheromones when aroused, and their sexual fluids contain highly addictive properties. Byralen are strong and fast. Their eyes have the ability to hypnotize. Though not known to be aggressive, Byralen can be deadly when trapped or cornered. Remaining in the presence of an aroused Byralen of the opposite sex can cause altered states of consciousness. Recommendation: Avoid contact if possible.

"This is getting better by the minute. What are they used for?" she asked the com, though she had a fairly good idea what the answer was going to be.

Byralen are rare and actively sought as personal sexual slaves on Krona. They are used by the Garulen to produce illegal sexual stimulants and narcotics for the shadow trade. Their worth at auction: Nearly priceless.

"Fantastic. What did you get me into, Vicca?" Her stell fox pricked her large ears forward and blinked her ice blue eyes then curled her body around the bound foot of the Byralen. Cyani didn't want to think about what this man had suffered. The thought made her sick. Was he even sane? She turned her attention back to her fox.

"It's the stripes, isn't it? You are a sucker for creatures with stripes."

Vicca purred and swished her ringed tail.

"Com, establish perimeter. High alert." Cyani waited for the affirmative *beep* then crept toward the Byralen.

"I'm here to help you," she called to the man in the common language of the Union. As she moved, he continued to track her in spite of the blinders. "Hold still while I remove the slave bands."

She inched forward and touched his foot. He sprang from the wall, snarling, his large hands grasping for her.

With agility and instincts born from generations of her warrior matriarchs, Cyani leapt over his shoulder, then rolled to the right, out of the reach of his chains.

He thrashed in his chains like a Xalen tiger, growling low in his throat. The slave bands on his arms beeped and whirred. The red lights of the bands flickered in the dim light, signaling an injection. The Byralen let out a low moan and staggered on his feet.

"No," Cyani gasped. "What are they doing to you?" Cyani ran forward and caught the man before he collapsed to the ground. He winced as she lowered him to the floor. "I have to get you out of here. Com, switch to language of Garu."

Hoping her hunch would work, she removed the ear set of her com and attached it to his ear. He twitched and growled, but his body remained limp. She pressed the release buttons on the severe-blinders. The black metal unhooked from his eye sockets and fell from his face.

His irises were a dark and swirling mix of black, violet, and glowing red. She tried not to look him in the eyes, unsure if he'd use them to try to hypnotize her. Her skin grew warm and tingled with a strange electric sensation anywhere he touched her.

She fought the immediate urge to push him away. His touch shook her resolve. She could almost feel the sting of a teaching whip across her calves. She was being impractical. He was injured. She didn't have long to save him. He needed to trust her quickly.

"I'm trying to get you out of here," she insisted in a less patient tone than she would have liked. She didn't have time to waste.

Easing back, she tried to break her contact with him, but he grabbed her thigh. She waited for a response, desperately hoping he could understand her.

They remained motionless for a moment that stretched into an eternity.

BLINKING HIS BURNING EYES, SOREN'S VISION SLOWLY RETURNED TO FOCUS. His head pounded with the sickening tranquilizer polluting his blood.

A woman leaned over him, a soldier. He could see sharply in the dim light, but it would take a while to regain his sense of color. He needed to see the color of her eyes.

She tossed a dark braid of hair over her shoulder and studied the slave bands. Her face was hard but beautiful in a fierce way, and she wore some sort of machine that circled her eye. His head swam as he tried to think. A stabbing pain burst in his heart. He didn't want to die like this. What color were her eyes?

She spoke to him, her voice low and commanding, almost as unyielding and determined as her expression. A metallic voice rang in his ear through the contraption she had attached to him. The harsh Garulen language made him shudder, but he understood the words.

"Can you understand me? Do you know I'm not your enemy?" She leaned closer, her voice a controlled whisper. His vision finally cleared enough to see dark green shining in the strands of hair around her face. *Ckili moss, the color of ckili moss.* He knew that color. He remembered it. The rest of his vision sharpened. Like dawn after a storm, her eyes were clear bright blue.

Blue.

He swallowed a lump in his throat. It was completely irrational to try to read her eyes. He knew they probably didn't change color like his, but seeing blue in someone's expression after so long in the dark seemed to ease his suffering, even if it was only an illusion.

"Do you understand me?" she asked again, louder this time. He nodded as the warm brush of fur at his hand drew his attention down to the strange creature licking his thumb.

His sense of relief had been enormous when the warm creature first rubbed up against his ankle. At first he thought it was a silky rat. It wasn't a rat, but a very small fox, a beautiful thing with a snowy white face and mantle that deepened to a coat of rich red and black stripes with white socks. It swished its bushy ringed tail and leapt up on his stomach. The creature must belong to the woman.

"Thank you," he whispered to the animal in his native language. He hadn't spoken those words in longer than he could remember. The creature squeezed its eyes shut and purred.

"I need to get you out of here," the woman stated. She attempted to keep her voice low and calming, as if she were talking to an injured beast.

She *was* talking to an injured beast.

Soren shook the thought from his mind. Her urgency came through her no-nonsense yet beautiful voice. He had to help her, not get distracted by the drugs.

"There's a transport waiting," she continued. "Hold still while the microbes remove your slave bands. I'll work on the chains." The woman pulled a small box from the low-slung belt on her hip. The skintight dark gray and black suit she was wearing left very little to his imagination. He felt a familiar tingle race down his spine and stared at the ceiling.

The Garulen kept him on a constant regimen of stimulants so he would be ripe when they wished to harvest. It could get him into trouble now. He didn't need to be distracted by her either. She was his only hope. Who was she?

She opened the box, and tiny metallic creatures that looked like spiders crawled out. He stiffened and pushed closer to the wall as the creepy bots crawled up his arms. He wanted to scream, but the sound would not escape him. His terror paralyzed him as the metal creatures scuttled over his arms.

"Relax, they will remove the bands. Hold still."

Soren shut his eyes and forced himself to breathe as he felt the metallic spiders dig into his flesh and crawl under the slave bands. He screamed aloud this time, the sound coming out as a choked roar. He shuddered and tried to swallow his panic. Over and over, he remembered the hot burn of metal against his skin. He tried to pull against his chains, but the metal clinging to him cut deeper into his wrists. He willed himself to hold still, thankful for the tranquilizers. He would have harmed her in his panic without them. He dug his fingers into the palms of his hands as his body shook.

"What's your name?" the woman asked. He felt her hand on his. It was a weak attempt to calm him. He tried to focus on her.

He tried to answer but couldn't. He could feel the spiders digging through his flesh, crawling under his skin. He had to focus on her. He forced himself to watch her mouth, to keep his mind on anything but the metal creatures.

"Please tell me your name," she prodded again. She still wouldn't look into his eyes. She probably knew how he could use them. She didn't trust him. She shouldn't trust him. He reached for her, but she backed away.

"Stay with me. What is your name?" she demanded, as if her voice alone could shake him from his terror. He could handle the pain, but he couldn't control the panic he felt whenever metal touched him.

The bands on his arms beeped, then with a soft click, released their constant stinging pressure. The spiders crawled back into the box, leaving a creeping trail of his blood over his arms. Soren's head swam with relief as he took several hasty breaths to calm down.

"Soren," he forced through his burning throat. "I am Soren." The affirmation of his name helped calm his racing heart. For so long, his name hadn't mattered.

Her expression softened. "I'm Cyani, and that's Vicca," she said, pointing to the fox. "It seems she likes you, Soren."

With delicate care, Cyani opened one of the slave bands fully, extracting the ugly needles from his flesh. She winced at the shriveled skin beneath the bands and the deep bruises where the needles inflicted their endless torture. He was finally free of them. The thought confused him. The only thing that seemed real was his pain. His heart raced as he helped her pull the other band out of his arm.

"Captain, prisoners are free and en route to transport." Soren pulled the sickening machine from his ear and handed it to her. She took it from him and fixed it in her ear. He couldn't control his shudder. He had no way to communicate with her now except his eyes, and she wouldn't look at him.

Cyani stood, leaving him leaning against the wall.

She had to be quick. Time was running out. "Com, switch language, Union. Hatch, report."

"All seven prisoners freed and on transport, Captain. We received a perimeter warning. The Garulen have discovered that the defense system for the prison is down. Get out of there."

"Give me a minute. There's a Byralen here."

She pulled out her laser and focused on the cuffs at Soren's hands.

"Not to be rude, Cap, but you don't have a minute. We have to get these men out of here now!"

"I won't leave him!" The lock on one of Soren's cuffs snapped off. He yanked his hand free of the chains and held still as she worked on the other three.

"I won't leave you," she stated, even though she knew he couldn't understand her. She hoped he understood her intent. As his other hand came loose, she leaned to reach his feet. He caught her chin in his fingers and tilted her face toward his.

The sensation of his bare skin against hers shocked her.

The electric tingle pulsed over the skin of her face as all her senses seemed to heighten. She gasped as he forced her to look up. Fear raced through her as his red violet eyes turned a deep shade of aquamarine. She blinked, fascinated by the swirling color. Was he trying to say something to her?

The aquamarine glowed, cool, calm, *grateful.* She nodded to acknowledge she understood then pushed his hand aside and continued her work.

In seconds she had both his legs free. Vicca raced out the door, barking in urgency. Cyani wrapped his arm over her neck to help support him as they ran from the prison.

"Captain, our sensors have spotted an incoming stingship formation. We have to leave or the ship will be torn apart," Tola's usually calm voice snapped with panic.

Just then the power returned to the fortress. Sirens blared while red strobe lights illuminated the hall. They ran for the open gate without looking back.

Warning! Humanoid life-forms approaching.

Cyani ducked from under Soren's arm as she spun on her heel. She pulled out her sono and flick knife in a smooth motion, ready for the attack.

Four Garulen guards ran toward her with shock throwers and a shock net. Focused on her prey, she let them come.

The one to the left threw the shock net. Cyani ducked beneath it as it flew over her. She felt the energy of the net tingle through her skin as it passed her and landed over a crumbling stone.

She shook off the numbing sting in her muscles and leapt toward the leader of the group as she fired her sono at the one reaching for the net.

He fell dead.

The leader charged, his shock blast missing her head by inches. She spun, pulled her flick knife across his neck, then fired a shot at the guard to her right, hitting him between the eyes.

The low *whoam* of a shock thrower discharging propelled her forward as she twisted to avoid the blast.

The blast slammed into her shoulder, knocking her into the wall. The searing pain of the hit burned through her blood, followed by terrifying numbness. It spread through her body like ice in her veins as her muscles seized. She fought, but her brain couldn't make her arms or legs move. Her heart echoed in her ears as her eyes stared unblinking. The last guard stalked toward her with a greedy look on his hairy face and no concern for his fallen comrades.

A feral roar ripped through the hall as Soren slammed into the last guard. His movements seemed in slow motion in the incessant light of the strobe. He wrenched the thrower out of the guard's hands. With one powerful strike, he slammed the butt of the gun into the guard's face, crushing his skull.

The guard landed with a thud as Soren turned his glowing red eyes to her.

She gasped, helpless. It would take at least twenty minutes for the shock blast to wear off. More guards would come. They would be caught. There was no way out. They'd pierce her arms with slave bands, throw her naked on an auction block, and after her buyer raped her over and over, she'd be tossed into a fighting pit to kill, or die. She couldn't let that happen. What could she do? She was helpless. She had to fight. The ground felt cold against her cheek, just as it had when they had thrown her, beaten, into the cell all those years ago. She was a child then. She was just as helpless now.

Soren fell to his knees next to her and placed his bare hands on her cheeks. He lifted her head, forcing her to look at him as the electric sensation tingled in her skin again.

She couldn't move. She couldn't save them. He'd be captured and tortured again. It was all for nothing.

She tried to pull her head from his hands, but her body felt dead. His glowing acid yellow eyes roved over her face as he gently pulled her limp body into his lap.

"*Gnar hox*," he murmured in Garu, leaning his face closer to hers. Her heart thundered with fear as she lay against his warm skin. What was he doing? He caressed her cheek with the burning heat of the back of his knuckles. Her com automatically translated his next words. "Trust me."

He brought his face closer to hers, his breath whispering over her skin, her face alive with sensation. A rich, clean scent overtook her, like cinnamon and suka melon. She inhaled, fighting to avoid his touch. A desperate plea ripped through her trapped mind. This was forbidden. She willed her body to stand, to fight. Suddenly her fingers began to tingle.

His lips brushed over hers, a whisper of a touch. Her heart pounded in her ears as the unfamiliar pleasure of his caress flooded her mind like a terrifying drug. He kissed her, opening her mouth to his and stealing her breath.

What is he doing? They'll kill me for this.

Her body came alive in a rush of agonizing fire. Crying out, she arched her back and rolled away from him. Her limbs felt as if they had been asleep for hours. Each nerve screamed with life and stinging pain. She pushed herself up with one of her arms, curling her leg beneath her.

She flopped back to the ground, the right side of her body numb and unresponsive.

Soren crawled toward her and caught her around her waist.

"No," she choked out as her eyes watered. "Do . . . Don't."

"Hold still," he whispered, pulling her into his body. "I will help you."

He brushed her braid over her shoulder. The brief touch of his fingertips scored her with an agonizing rush of pleasure.

Cyani tensed, trembling in anger and gut-twisting anticipation.

Soren's hot mouth pressed against the nape of her neck. She moaned as a warm rush of sensation flowed through her blood. This was forbidden. She could feel the sting of the slicing whip against her legs. They would do more than whip her if anyone ever found out. Her body thrummed with energy as he poured hot, soft, painful, breathtaking kisses across the base of her neck.

"Enough!" she shouted, leaping to her feet. Stunned, she took a wobbly step to the side, staring in wonder at her hands as she opened and closed her fingers. The paralysis had completely left her body. *How?*

He looked up at her, unapologetic for his actions. "Better?"

What had he done to her? All of her senses reeled as she looked around. Her normally acute eyesight reached a new level. The darkest shadows revealed their secrets to her new sight. The stale, acrid smell of the prison choked her, but she could pick out her own scent, Vicca's, and Soren's, as if each was a tangible thing hanging in the air for her to grasp.

Soren rose, rubbed the back of his neck with his hand, then limped toward Vicca.

The alarm on her com went off with a relentless *beep*, throwing her back into the moment.

35:14.

She was out of time.

"Captain, we can't wait any longer," Hatch yelled through the link. "They're right on top of us."

The hiss of stingship blasts pelted the tunnel entrances. Her heart sank. She would not be responsible for their deaths.

"Get out of here," she shouted into the com.

"Cap?!"

"Go." She closed her eyes. "Tola, that's an order, damn it. Get out!"

"We'll find you, Captain," Tola responded. "Stay alive. We will return, and we'll get you out."

"We'll meet in victory," she answered. Though she did not say it, her mind finished the saying. *Or in death.*

Static buzzed in her ear then her com went silent.

Her head and heart pounded in unified pain as she closed her eyes and tried to dispel the panic rising like a tidal wave through her body. She was too late. They had to leave her. There was no way out. It was the right thing to do. It was what she ordered them to do. Her men would die if they didn't leave.

She heard the familiar roar of the transport engines.

Her hope sank as the ship lifted off the ground.

Soren grabbed her hand.

She let go of her breath and looked up at him. His eyes swirled with myriad colors, magenta flowing into warm gold and green. A strange sense of calm rushed through her body, easing some of the ache of the shock blast and allowing her to breathe. Her thoughts slowed and focused under the hypnotic effect of his eyes. They had to find another ship.

"Hurry," she gasped.

He nodded, then they ran after Vicca. Stingship blasts rained around them as they dove into the tunnels.

A large explosion shook the ground and Soren grabbed her, pulling her beneath him as he sheltered her from the falling debris with his body.

With her senses heightened, her body immediately reacted to his secure weight pressing down on her. His scent overtook her, and as she looked up, the debris around them seemed painted in iridescent color. She struggled to push herself out from under him. The computer had grossly misstated the nature of the Byralen's narcotic effect.

She had to clear her mind. She was a warrior. She had spent the last fourteen years in training. She was hard, cold. She had no attachments to anything or anyone. She would resist being distracted by him. Both of their lives depended on it.

Before the dust had time to settle, Soren leapt to his feet and pulled Cyani up with him. She blinked hard to clear her vision of the swirling colors dancing before her eyes. Hitting the map on her eyepiece, she ran after her scout, Soren following close behind.

"Com, find coordinates for any remaining Union vessel and plot on map." A bright yellow dot appeared on the map on the far side of the tunnel system near the old Hannolen ruins. Relief flowed through her veins like landing the last blow after a long sparring match. "Com, contact ship," she ordered.

Static hissed in her ear, broken by an incomprehensible voice.

"Union vessel, compatriots en route to ship. Do not launch until rendezvous. I repeat, do not launch," she shouted into her com, hoping the ship could hear her.

"Vicca, find path to Union ship," she commanded, as the fox tore through the darkness, her blue dot leaving a streak on her holo-map. She followed the path, her hope returning as Vicca's blue streak finally reached the yellow dot.

They ran blindly through the tunnels as the sounds of the war faded to silence. Afraid the Union ship would take off without them, Cyani pushed her aching body as fast as it would go. Her shaking calves burned as she ran through the tunnels, ducking the low-hanging rock. A broken shard of a metal brace ripped a hole in her shadowsuit as she passed.

Though Soren had to be in pain, he followed relentlessly. He stumbled once. Cyani pulled him to his feet, blood from the seeping wounds on his wrists sticking to her palm.

With every step forward, she stared at the yellow dot of hope in the darkness, willing it to remain on the planet until they could reach it.

She burst out of the tunnel system and slammed her back against the dark walls of the ruins.

"Com, scan for life-forms." She turned her head slowly, her holo-map peering through the old stone walls. No new dots. No warning. Only silence. Gripping her sono, she motioned to Soren to follow. Turning the corner, she stared in horror at the sight before her.

A Union ship rested on its hull, one side smashed against the wall and its wing broken and lifeless in the clearing. A rock spire had toppled and crushed the cockpit beneath the dark stone. Vicca barked at the ship as if she were angry it was wrecked. Through the static in Cyani's com, she could make out the ship's distress call.

The overwhelming shadow of hopelessness loomed over Cyani as she stared dumbstruck at the ship. She let her sono fall to her side and hung her head as an enormous weight pressed down on her shoulders.

She turned to Soren. He seemed to come to the same realization she did as his gaze slowly sank to the ground. His eyes faded from a bright rose to pure black.

They were trapped.

2

CYANI STARED AT THE HATCH DOOR HANGING FROM THE BENT HULL. IT SWUNG back and forth in the fan-wind like a hideously broken arm.

"*Shakt!*" Cyani placed her hands on her thighs to try to pull air back into her burning lungs. She rubbed her sticky palm against her thigh in a vain attempt to clean it. Her nerves raced, but this was not the time to give in to old scars in her mind. They were in the middle of a nightmare. They would have to find shelter and hide until the patrols in the ruins ceased, then lie low until her team could rescue them. Her tongue stuck to the roof of her parched mouth. They needed water, food, a place to rest. She needed to think. She needed to clean her hands.

"Come on." She forged a mental list of everything they would need to survive the next few weeks. She didn't have much time to gather supplies. The Garulen would swarm the ship as soon as they could.

She slid inside with Vicca at her heels. "Vicca, scout food, medicine, clothing, weapons, and com pieces." The fox scurried under a crushed vent column and disappeared. Dangling wires snapped with live current. Cyani tempered her urgency with caution as she struggled toward the cockpit.

She pulled herself upright near a piece of the shorn wall. The night opened up above her. The glow from fires painted the swirling fog of the atmosphere shield burning orange. The light flickered on the shining surfaces of the broken rocks like yellow moonlight glinting off volcanic glass. She climbed over a large chunk of the rock spire that had smashed part of the ship and slid back into the wreckage.

It took a moment for her eyes to adjust back to the dim light. Her heart dropped into her stomach. A young man slumped over the controls. His youthful face rested on the panel, blanched of its life. Dark empty eyes stared at her. A piece of the spire crushed his body while the last of his blood pooled beneath his pale cheek. Cyani sighed as she inched her way to his side.

She closed his eyes with a gentle swipe of her hand. "Rest well, warrior," she whispered, pulling his ear set from his body. She didn't know the pilot, but she felt deeply for him and sad that his team couldn't get his body out.

Cyani crawled back over the spire and slipped into the main wreckage of the ship. Soren stooped near the broken hatch, lifting large chunks of the spire from the collapsed corridor where Vicca had disappeared. Cyani let her gaze wander up and down his body. The lean but powerful muscles in his back flexed as he hefted another piece of stone out of the hatch. Heat blossomed in her face. For the first time since they escaped the slave cells, she noticed he was naked.

A tingle raced up her spine as her eyes drifted over the smooth indentation where his muscle wrapped around his side and slid down over his hip leading to . . .

"We should get you something to wear." What in the name of Ona the Pure was wrong with her?

He looked up at her, his eyes black and weary.

She lifted the dead pilot's ear set to her lips. "Com, switch to language of Garu." Walking toward him, she fixed it on him as quickly as she could.

Dark violet lights shone in the deep blackness of his eyes as he stared down at her. She wondered what the violet color meant. It seemed a common secondary color to the furious reds, fearful yellows, and dismal black that expressed his mood. She pulled her hand away from the com, but her fingers brushed his jaw. It flexed beneath her touch. An electric tingle rushed up her arm.

She looked down to avoid his dangerous eyes. "Does it work?"

"You mean the translator," he whispered, rubbing behind his ear, "or something else?" His voice turned bitter, almost accusing.

She turned from him as heat rushed to her head and burned her ears. She hadn't meant to stare. Leaning to keep away from the exposed wires, she backed toward the door.

"Clothing," she interjected as she ducked past him and slipped down the dark corridor. "We're searching for clothing."

His species gave off addictive pheromones. She couldn't let herself forget that. She shouldn't be too near him. "Vicca!" she shouted as a dizzy heat flowed through her blood. It was only a chemical.

Vicca barked from the back of the ship.

The fox had saved her once again.

She avoided looking at Soren as she pushed through the crushed hull. She could hear his footsteps, his quiet breathing so close behind her. The skin on her neck tightened, rushing with energy. How long would this last?

She swallowed the lump in her throat. She was too close to finishing her mission to let something as crazy as this ruin her chances of returning home to a life of peace.

This was her last mission as a captain in the Union Army. She was tired. While she could not, would not, let her weariness show, she hadn't slept well in years. Every time she closed her eyes, the world of her dreams seemed bathed in blood. Emaciated bodies walked through her memory like living skeletons, the soul stolen from their glassy, hopeless eyes. For five years she had battled the slavers and freed their victims. She had seen nothing but the vile repercussions of cultures greedy and vicious enough to feast on the demise of others.

She was ready for peace. When she returned to Azra, she'd take up her place in the temple and live a life of isolated meditation. No more blood, no more darkness, only clean, pure light. She wouldn't have to fear for her life anymore, but that security came with a price. Pressure built in her chest as she thought about the long years of lonely silence she would have to endure.

If she made it home alive.

"This ship, can it contact your people?" Soren asked, snapping her back into the moment. *Control*, she needed control of herself and her situation. Her head throbbed as the onset of a post-shock-blast migraine unfurled behind her right eye. At least the pain would keep her nerves focused on something other than him.

"The electrical system is badly damaged, but it's possible," she explained. "We don't have time to fix it. The Garulen will try to strip the ship of any technology they can."

"We have to find a safe place." His voice remained low, calm, even though his words sounded harsh with the choppy cadence of the Garulen language.

They scrambled through the hull to find Vicca hopping up and down on an overturned locker with a medical steri-cover in it. They also found a shadowsuit and skinboots.

Cyani shook out the loose-fitting medical suit meant to protect against biohazards. "Put this on for now. We'll see if we can clean you up before you put on the shadowsuit. We have to hurry." Cyani searched the med-bay and the supply lockers in the hall. She scooped various medical supplies into a sack, along with emergency rations, water, some tools, and some spare wiring.

"No," he stated.

She turned just as he dropped the baggy steri-cover on the floor.

"What?" She didn't mean to snap, but the migraine made her edgy.

"It's bright white. I'll be seen, and I won't be able to move." For as irritating as his logic was, he made a good but uncomfortable point.

"But you're naked," she felt obliged to point out.

"I'm used to it. I have no shame left." He shrugged as he gathered the rest of the clothing and tucked it under his arm.

Cyani ran a shaking palm over her face. He might be used to it, but she certainly wasn't. She didn't deserve this. "We aren't out of trouble yet. Let's get out of here."

They were working their way back toward the hatch when Soren paused.

"Is that the machine you used to kill the guards?" he asked, pointing to a weapons locker. She picked up a sono and held it to the activator on the wall. With a metallic *whirr*, it came to life.

"Do you know how to use one?" she asked.

He shook his head. "No, but I'm sure I'll enjoy figuring it out."

"It has to be imprinted to you," she explained. "Hold out your hand."

Soren's eyes glowed yellow again. He swallowed, his neck flexing, then held out his hand. Dried blood cracked on the rough skin of his palm. "This might sting," she warned. The truth was it did a hell of a lot more than sting. He huffed in a half chuckle as she realized her palm was covering the wounds on his wrists, wounds he had probably willingly inflicted on himself by pulling on his chains in spite of the torture of it. He didn't fear pain. No, something else about the weapon bothered him.

He flinched as soon as metal touched his hand, but held perfectly still as it activated and glowed bright white. It was Cyani's turn to wince as she remembered the burning pain of an imprint. Slowly the weapon cooled, but the sulfur glow in his eyes did not.

"You're the only one who can fire it now." She kept her own gaze fixed on the weapon, not wanting to think about all the things his reaction revealed. Instead, she pointed at the trigger on the grip of the sono. "This one makes things dead." She touched the button on the top. "And this one keeps them alive, barely."

"Good to know," he mumbled, his eyes fading to black again.

She scooped up Vicca and hopped out of the hatch.

Scanning the area with her holo-map, she rubbed Vicca's ears then placed her fox on the ground. "Vicca, find shelter with water and secure perimeter." Vicca melted into the darkness.

Cyani collapsed against the broken wing, leaning her head back while Vicca did her job. The shattered ship loomed over her. It echoed the desolate feeling in her heart. She let her eyes drift shut for just a minute. The aftermath of the fight washed over her, sapping the strength from her body and will. She felt crushed, as if every muscle had been beaten with a stick wielded by an Earthlen gorilla. Her heart thumped with slow, painful beats as her nose and eyes stung, and the stabbing pain behind her right eye made her dizzy and nauseated.

What was she doing? How were they ever going to get out of this? How would they even survive the next few weeks? A solid hand squeezed her shoulder. She instinctively pulled away.

"Are you okay?"

"Soren, what did you do to me back there?" she asked.

He sighed with a look of resigned disgust. "I still have Garulen drugs in my blood; they make me very potent."

"*Potent?*" She raised one eyebrow.

"Sweat, saliva, other things . . ." he muttered. "How should I put this? They affect the nervous system."

"Well, that's an understatement," she grumbled. "What happens when the drugs wear off?"

He scratched the back of his neck and shrugged his shoulders. He didn't want to talk about this. It made his skin crawl. When the drugs wore off, he would have real problems.

Soren watched her closely as she sank to the ground, crouching with her rounded hips over her heels.

"I can't let you touch me like that again." Her voice sounded soft, a mixture of exhaustion and sadness. "Do you understand me? You can't touch me, and you can't hypnotize me like that."

He remained silent. *Why not?* She was clearly a fierce and well-trained fighter, but sometimes touch was the only link to sanity. Touch was all that reminded him he was not alone during the long, slow years of his torture. She looked so terribly alone. The night had taken an unbearable toll on her. She rested her head on her crossed forearms, pulling herself into a loose ball. She could use some comforting; they both could.

Even in such an exposed position, looking as if the world had just crushed her, she held her weapon in one hand, and an easy readiness clung to her as tightly as her clothing. It only took her a moment before she lifted her head. She rose from the ground like a young tree that would grow in strength until nothing could move it. Once again the iron power and deadly resolve she carried so easily settled on her strong shoulders.

He shook his head. She had killed three of his tormentors with lightning speed and agility. She was amazing, like a night cat—fast, efficient, and deadly. And yet, as he looked at her now, there was a vulnerability about her. She was not immune to their situation, warrior or not. She wasn't immune to him either, in spite of what she said.

"We should move," he suggested. "We're exposed here."

Her eyes flicked over his naked body again. A tingle flowed up his spine. He certainly wasn't immune to her.

She pressed two fingertips into her brow, squeezing her eyes shut as if in pain, then opened them and looked around.

"Wait here," she whispered, the mechanical device circling her left eye glowing in the dim light. "I think Vicca found a place for us."

She slipped into the ship once again, embodying the night cat she reminded him of.

Soren lifted his weapon and turned in a slow circle as every sound echoed in his wary ears. He didn't like being exposed. Why was she going back into the ship? They needed to find safety, quickly. She was wasting precious time. After only a minute or two that felt like an eternity, she leapt up out of the cracked hull of the ship, skidded down the broken wing, and broke into a furious run.

What did she just do?

He chased after her, the soles of his bare feet burning after the long run on the jagged stone of the tunnels. She wasn't the only one suffering from exhaustion. He felt ready to collapse with her. Only one thing kept the pain from overwhelming him. He was free.

She had no idea what she'd given him, but he was acutely aware of what she sacrificed to do so. He wouldn't be taken again. He wouldn't let them take her. He'd die first.

They darted from between the crumbling buildings of a ruined city. Craters from bomb blasts scarred the jagged streets. The cracked stones seemed darker than the recesses of the night sky as the creeping shadows stretched away from the light towers.

The war-ravaged walls of the ruins formed a tangled labyrinth of stone, with spires reaching up as tall as great oaks. No plant life survived anywhere, not even a withered weed creeping out of a crack or moss on damp stone. Soren shivered. He was a grower, a caretaker of life. He didn't belong in this place.

He turned to Cyani, only to see her dive behind a wall.

"Guards," she hissed between her teeth. He ducked down and ran to her. Pressing into the shadow of the wall, he grasped the weapon she had given him.

Cyani hovered her hand over his, stilling his fingers on the weapon without touching him. She shook her head, pointed to her eyes, then pointed at the road.

Soren watched, his heart racing with the rage flooding through his blood. He would see them dead.

A pebble rattled along the road as the foot of a Garulen guard came out into the light. Soren shifted onto the balls of his feet and tried to raise his weapon, but Cyani stopped him. His fury burned like acid. He wanted to leap out and rip the monster apart.

"We can't kill them. They'll know we're here. Close your eyes; they're glowing. Don't move," she ordered, but her words barely penetrated the thick red haze of his hatred.

He growled low in his throat and balanced his weight, preparing to leap, to strike, to kill. He would feel their hot blood on his hands instead of his own.

"Soren," she snapped in a hushed whisper. "Don't."

Just as he was about to unleash his fury, a searing pain sliced in his side and shoulder as he fell back into the shadows.

Cyani's long limbs wrapped around his body in an impossible tangle as her face came close to his. She pressed her warm palm over his eyes, blinding him.

No! He would not be blinded again. *Never again.* He reached through the pain of her twisted hold and ripped her hand from his face.

She'd pay for that.

He pushed forward and kissed her.

She gasped in shock, and he took her breath, took her power, her stubbornness, her control. This was his. Blight her, blight them. She didn't want to be touched? A rot on it, he'd show her a touch. He'd make her feel it until she ached.

He kept his eyes shut and controlled the darkness as he used the sweet taste of her unyielding lips to keep the rage at bay. With adrenaline as a catalyst, he absorbed the deep pleasure of her body heat, and felt the violet spreading in his blood. The rush of color made him feel powerful. For the first time in his life, he drew it out of a woman—it hadn't been injected into him.

The heavy *thunk* of boots on stone rang in his sensitized ears, followed by a soft shuffle, and a grunt.

"Road clear," the Garulen guard shouted to his unseen squad.

The rhythmic fall of marching feet echoed through the ruins.

He continued to kiss her as the foul scent of the guards faded away, trailing toward the ship, but he softened the caress. The violet warmed him, eased the pain. He had never imagined he would feel it without fear and shame. Her hold on him relaxed as he inhaled the sweet scent of her body awakening to him. Her lips softened for only a moment as the tension eased from her limbs. As soon as she released her hold on him, he reluctantly released her from the kiss.

She blinked at him, her blue eyes foggy and confused. One soft lock of her dark green hair fell forward over her eye. Suddenly her pupils narrowed, and she pulled her fist back.

He caught it before she could land the blow.

"How dare you," she challenged, her voice breathy and sexy as silk.

"What?" he asked, forcefully shoving her fist down. Without the connection of the kiss, his anger returned in a flare of red. "Never bind me again."

"I saved your life," she protested as she sprang to her feet.

"I'm saving my sanity," he growled as he stood.

"You almost got us killed, or worse, captured," she accused. "You of all people should be helping me, not losing control."

"I barely—"

An explosion to rival the worst of the bombs shook the ground beneath their feet.

Soren ducked, but Cyani didn't even flinch.

"What was that?" he asked.

"I detonated the ship," she answered. "Now get up."

"What?" he shouted at her.

"I set the auto destruct sequence for the ship. I don't think we need to worry about those troops anymore."

Exasperated, Soren watched her wipe her hands as if she hadn't killed their only hope of escape and an entire squad of Garulen in one fell swoop.

"I thought you said we could use the ship to communicate with your people," he accused. "Now, how are we going to escape?"

"We could use the ship to communicate. That's why I had to destroy it. Union technology cannot fall into the hands of the Garulen. That is our primary order. It's the only advantage we have over the hairy, ignorant genetic rejects." She began to walk away, but he grabbed her by the shoulder. She snatched his hand and twisted it away.

Soren burned with his rage. "I don't care about the Union or their rotting technology. All I care about is getting off of this blighted rock, and you destroyed our only hope."

"My men will come for us. We just need to survive until they get here." Cyani turned away from him again. He picked up his weapon from the ground, half tempted to use it.

"How long will that take?" he snapped.

"They won't be able to unscramble the atmosphere shield for about three weeks," she said over her shoulder, like their situation didn't concern her at all.

"I can't wait that long," he protested. The drugs in his system would be gone long before they were rescued.

"Patience." She studied the little glowing square floating in front of her eye. "We just have to wait."

She had the luxury of waiting. He didn't. Time had deadly consequences. If they didn't escape soon, there'd be no hope for him. His body would rot on this lifeless rock. He stalked off through the ruins, driven by the urge to get away from her, away from everything.

"Where are you going?" she protested, jogging after him.

"I'm going to Vicca," he growled.

"You don't have a holo-map. You don't know where she is." She tried to reach him, but he surged ahead of her.

"Keep your infested technology. I can smell her." He ignored her, ignored his pain, and ignored the new spectrum of light he could see after the kiss.

He reached a wall that had fallen back onto another, creating a small triangular entrance leading into deeper shadows.

Soren squeezed through the hole and felt his way down a flight of steps into a dark chamber. Water trickled nearby. He tried to let his eyes adjust as tiny blue lights from Vicca's collar flew at him with a joyful bark. He caught her and struggled to keep her down as she squirmed in his arms.

A velvety tongue bathed his face as he sighed and stroked her soft back. "It's good to see you, too," he whispered to the fox.

Cyani entered, carrying a lamp that illuminated the room and the chip on her shoulder. She could chew on it for all he cared. He was still angry. Their shelter was nothing but four crumbling walls and a broken pipe hanging out of the far wall. Water trickled out of the pipe into a worn crack half clogged with mud. Vicca jumped down and circled Cyani's feet.

"Very good girl," Cyani praised. The fox placed her paws on Cyani's knee and panted. "Com, analyze water for purity and harmful contaminants."

Cyani leaned against the wall near the stream of water and let it wash over her hands. "The water is safe, but it might not taste very good." She gave her hands a quick rub on her pants then retreated to the darkest corner and pressed the heels of her palms to her eyes.

The water could taste like pilt rat droppings, and he'd be

grateful for it. He dragged himself to the pipe then looked back at Cyani, but her eyes were closed. Half of him wanted her to just leave. The other half wanted her to look at him.

He stepped under the tepid water and let it drizzle through his hair and over his skin. Placing his palms on the cool wall, he leaned his forehead against the hard stone and took several long, slow breaths, waiting for his heart to slow. With one hand he gently rubbed his arms, washing away the dried blood from the slave bands and his chains.

Pain and humiliation still clung to him; it had dug under his skin, crawled into his bones. He didn't think he would ever get it out. He let his rough hands slide over the skin of his arms, embracing the warm pleasure of cleaning his skin through the burning sting of washing his deep wounds. At the same time, he felt revolted by his state of arousal, like his own body betrayed him.

Soren watched the blood and filth slide down in dark streams in the water. No matter how hard he rubbed, he couldn't wash away the wounds; he never would.

His traitorous blood flowed hot in his veins. He felt heavy, aroused. For the first time it wasn't solely the drugs. The deep tug in his abdomen gave him a new pain to ponder.

He just wanted to feel clean again.

A tiny curled lichen clung to a crack beneath the pipe. He gently touched it. *Life.* There was life here. He was not dead yet. He nudged the crack with his damp finger and exhaled on the tiny symbiotic plant. Two different beings, each one depending on the other to survive. How did it live in the darkness?

He would help it grow.

Cyani opened her eyes and saw Soren standing naked under the pipe with his back to her. She watched the water drip down the golden skin of his back, tracing his muscles with tiny rivulets and washing over the dark bands of skin crossing his shoulders and his darker bruises.

Once again a tingling wave of anticipation started deep in her abdomen and flared out with a slow, aching pulse. She exhaled and forced her eyes to the floor. She was an untouchable. She shouldn't react, couldn't let herself react. But then, no one was standing behind her wielding a teaching whip if she did. The feeling frightened, and worse, excited her.

She watched him out of the corner of her eye. She had seen plenty of naked male species during her service, but they had all been starved slaves barely clinging to life. She had never seen a healthy one. Why was she so unsettled? Was it him, or her?

She pushed to her feet as heat flushed her cheeks again. She needed to secure the perimeter. Who was she trying to fool? She needed to get far away from Soren. She had to protect herself. The bloodline of her ancestor Cyrila the Rebel was notorious—talented, but notorious. She had to resist the rush of satisfaction that spread through her chest each time she did something she shouldn't. She had been fighting it for half her life. It was a battle she had to win. She'd be killed if she didn't.

Ducking under the fallen wall, she eased out of their sanctuary and checked for light that would give them away. Convinced that they were well hidden, she explored the ruins, placing sensors for her com so she could monitor their surroundings from the safety of the room.

She craned her neck to see the top of an old Hannolen temple. The cracked columns still stood proud, holding what remained of the open roof, after countless raids. Finding a handhold, she braced her foot against a column then shimmied up the crumbling structure as if it were one of the towering trunks of a great jungle tree on Azra. She swung onto the roof then crouched to assess their surroundings.

She could see the slave cells. They were part of a larger storage structure. An orange glow indicated a fire in the storehouses. She smiled, pleased with the plumes of smoke rising from the shadows.

To the left, about one hundred fifty standard meters away, she watched a stingship land on a flight strip.

Satisfied that they were far enough from anything the Garulen would find interesting, she climbed back down the column, checked the sensors, then started down the flight of stairs. She paused just before entering the room.

"Please be dressed," she whispered to herself.

Soren still had not moved from beneath the stream of water. *Shakt.*

She turned to leave the room again, but compassion stirred deep in her heart and she felt a painful ache for what he had suffered while enslaved.

"You okay?" she asked, trying to avoid the terrible thoughts of what he must have endured. She stepped over to the bag she had scavenged from the Union ship and pulled out the ERBs. She had only managed to grab twelve of the dry and tasteless ration bars. "Are you hungry?"

His sigh was nearly silent, but Soren's shoulders rose and fell in one slow motion. She looked down at the rations and turned her back, giving him some privacy so he could dress. He deserved some dignity.

"These rations aren't exactly thrilling for the senses, but they are nutritious. There isn't much . . ."

"Thank you, Cyani."

She jumped as his voice whispered so close behind her. She hadn't heard him cross the room. He took one of the rations from the pile and peeled back the wrapping. She tucked the rest of the bars back in the bag and glanced at the pipe. A small speck of lichen hung out of a crack. It wasn't there before, was it?

Reluctantly she dared to look at Soren again.

By the mercy of the Matriarchs, please be dressed!

Soren stood in the meager glow of the flare lamp. Water dripped from the light and dark streaks of hair clinging to his neck and shoulders. His bare torso glistened, while the fabric of the shadowsuit clung to his legs, clearly outlining every lean muscle. Great, clothes didn't seem to help that much. The annoying weak feeling in her legs remained. He took a huge bite out of the square cake of protein and carbohydrates and chuckled. "What are these? Dried mud cakes?" he asked. He took another bite. "They're still better than what I've been used to. Are we safe now?"

"Yeah. They won't look for us here. I don't think they even know to look. I've placed sensors all around the area. I can detonate them from here if I need to." She handed him one of the water sacks.

He ate in silence, taking long draws of water from the sack. He would pass it back to her on occasion so she could drink, too.

“Who are you?” he asked after a long silence.

Cyani shifted. They hadn’t exactly had a proper introduction. “I’m Captain Cyani, team leader of the Union Army, Eleventh Patrol.” She placed her palm over her heart then extended it to him in the Union greeting. He just stared at her hand.

“You take it,” she whispered.

He placed his palm on his chest then brought it to hers. She squeezed it. The battle was over for now. It was time to rest and get to know her new compatriot.

“That’s a strange greeting.” His eyes turned a warm brown flickering with gold. It seemed the fight had drained out of him as well.

“How do you greet one another on Byra?” Settling on the floor, she crossed her legs, and Vicca hopped into her lap. The fox curled into a tight ball, tucked her face under her bushy tail, and purred. Soren eased back on his hip, his long legs spreading out like a trill cat lounging on a branch.

“Soren of Eln. It is my honor to know you.” He pressed his palms together then opened his hands up and out until his palms lay flat before her.

“You don’t touch?”

He shook his head. “On my planet, there are . . . Touching is sometimes complicated. There are social implications.”

She felt her face flush.

“I’m sorry. I don’t know much about your people. I think I like your greeting better. There are social complications to touching for me as well,” Cyani admitted while absentmindedly rubbing her calf. It felt good just to talk to someone. She had often set herself apart when her men got together and teased one another. She had longed to be a part of that circle. She hoped they were okay.

"How will we escape?" he asked, his lids lowering over his dark eyes.

"We'll wait for my team." She didn't want to bring this up again. Her heart was just beginning to return to a normal beat.

"What's your alternate plan?" he asked. "You don't strike me as the type to sit and just wait. Especially when we have limited resources, our enemy surrounds us, and rescue is unlikely."

She had enjoyed the brief reprieve from her worries. She should have known they would not leave her for long. He was right. She would have to try to think of something. Just not right now.

"Right now we need to rest. You don't look well. How long have you been held captive?" she asked him, longing for that flicker of companionship again.

"I don't know. I was just entering the beginning of my maturity when I was taken. I had seen seventeen or eighteen growing seasons. I can't remember."

"How old are you now?"

He glared at her, his eyes flashing red. "I don't know."

Cyani hung her head. She didn't want to anger him again. She couldn't take the consequences. Her lips still tingled.

Cyani activated her holo-map. The sensors she had placed glowed green. "Com, set perimeter sensors at five standard meters."

"We could hide on a transport ship," he suggested.

"And we'd end up on Krona. I'd rather take my chances here, thanks," she huffed. "At least the Garulen are stupid. The Kronalen are scary."

"We have to do something." His exasperation seeped into his voice and his orange eyes.

"We're going to rest," she stated. "We're going to save our strength. If it gets you off my back, we can figure out a plan tomorrow. The way I see it, there are only two ways off this rock. Either we fly out on one of the Union ships during the next raid, or we fly out on one of the Garulen's."

"So all we need to do is steal a Garulen ship," Soren suggested as he settled down on the floor next to the wall. He rested his head on the cold stone without flinching.

Steal a Garulen ship, sure, one guarded by a whole battalion of troops. It would be easy.

3

SOREN GASPED AND CHOKED. HE COULD FEEL THE LIQUID PUSHING DOWN HIS throat. Hot metal burned his skin. His pores wept sticky sweat. His mind screamed over and over, trapped in his paralyzed body. He thrashed against the drugs and the blackness.

His head hit something hard.

Soren opened his eyes. He couldn't see. The darkness surrounded him.

"Lakal!" he shouted into the black. "Lakal, where are you?" He sat up and twisted his body, searching for any sign of life.

He could move.

He tried to stand. His body felt heavy, weak. His head spun as he stumbled over something and slammed into a hard stone wall. Where were his chains?

"Lakal?"

Then he remembered. He remembered the hiss of the slave

bands injecting Lakal with poison, the look on his friend's face as Lakal realized the Garulen were killing him.

Soren collapsed to the floor and pulled his limbs in to his chest to try to soothe the ripping pain there. Lakal had fallen. Soren had cradled his friend's head as life faded from Lakal's bright copper eyes. "This is not the end," his only friend whispered as his last breath left his body.

It was my fault.

Soren slammed his fist into the floor as he shivered against the cold stone.

The Garulen killed Lakal, and it was his fault.

In his dark misery, he could have sworn he felt the warm, calming influence of Lakal's power.

"It's not going to work this time," Soren muttered to himself in the cold, empty room. Lakal had been tasked with keeping Soren on a mental leash. Soren would have hated him for it, except he knew it ripped Lakal's soul out every time he had to take Soren's free will. Extractions were terrible for both of them, what Soren had to physically endure and what Lakal had to suffer mentally because of it. That pain bonded them as brothers. After a while, Soren tried to protect Lakal by enduring extractions willingly, but in the end they both decided Lakal numbing him was best. Lakal would often try to use his power to comfort him. Soren never let him.

A high-pitched bark echoed against the chilling stone.

Soren started and turned toward the noise. Three bright blue lights scampered toward him, then a warm ball of fur crashed into his chest.

It took him a second to remember what had happened. "Vicca," he called in relief as his waking mind caught up with the present. He was free. Her warm tongue bathed his cheeks as he tried to wrap the wriggling creature up in his arms and smother her in his gratitude. He was free. Lakal did not die for nothing.

"Soren!" Cyani called as their small shelter flooded with light. Soren had to close his eyes against the brightness, but quickly squinted so he could see her.

The watery light of the lamp caught in the dark tendrils of hair framing her face, making them glow with deep green life that reminded him of the gardens of his home. Her large blue eyes were wide with worry as she rushed toward him.

"Are you okay?" she asked, kneeling at his side. She had ripped off the sleeves of her clothing to bind a wound on her arm. He caught her hand and brought it closer to examine the strange markings on her forearms. He needed to touch her to absorb the chemicals in her skin. Her touch eased his sickness and his grief. She tried to pull away, but he held fast.

Her skin was naturally tinged pale blue from elbow to wrist. A tattoo of a flowering vine danced around the edges of her unusual coloring. It was delicate, playful and feminine, a complete contradiction to his cold warrior. With a forceful tug, she pulled her wrist from his hand.

"You left me," he mumbled. "I woke alone." He didn't mean for it to sound like an accusation, but a small part of him stung from an irrational feeling of betrayal.

Cyani hesitated, then briefly touched the back of her hand to his forehead. "You're burning up."

"I'm fine," he dismissed, letting his head fall back on the cool wall.

"Soren, you have a fever." She reached for her bag and

pulled out a small machine. She brought it closer to him, and he slapped it out of her hand. It skidded over the floor and came to rest near a pile of stones.

Cyani's expression darkened from concern to irritation as she scowled at him. "That's a diagnostic tool. It won't hurt you."

"I'm not sick," he countered as a wave of chills racked his body.

"You're not?" she asked in a very patronizing tone.

"*Asylal en eham.*" He looked up at her, knowing the machine in her ear couldn't translate his words. *I am dying.* It was as simple as that.

"Now is not the time to play games." She crossed her arms.

He shrugged, refusing to speak. He wasn't in the mood to spar with her. He knew she had to do things on her terms, but he didn't feel like speaking to her. He slowly stroked Vicca's head as he stared at the lichen clinging to the crack near the pipe. It had grown to be three times its original size. A tiny swell of pride eased the dark anger in his heart.

"Soren." Cyani's voice sounded soft, almost pleading, but in a reserved way. "Please tell me what's wrong. I want to help."

Soren sighed. It was the first time she had given him such a concession.

"I'm in withdrawals." He couldn't bring himself to admit anything more than that. A lingering doubt remained in his heart. If she knew there was no hope for him, would she abandon him? He couldn't take the chance. Even if he was dying, he didn't want to be alone.

She looked at him with dawning comprehension. "The

Garulen drugs, they caused the violet color in your eyes, didn't they?"

She should have realized it earlier. It all made sense. His eyes had been showing less and less violet. The drugs were wearing off.

"In essence, yes," he responded, looking disgusted again.

"What are the symptoms?" she asked. She needed to know how to make him more comfortable until he pulled through this. When she heard him shout from her lookout position outside their shelter, the sound had chilled her.

"Fainting, dizziness, erratic fever." His voice trailed off. She got the feeling he was holding something back. He scratched Vicca under the chin as the fox filled the empty room with a loud purr.

"What can I do?" She had to help him. She knew what it was like to suffer alone. She couldn't inflict that on another. Several flickering colors sparkled in the deep blackness of his eyes, including a brief flash of violet. What was he contemplating? His dark gaze slowly wandered down her body, sending a fiery tingle racing down the backs of her legs.

"Talk to me," he answered as his eyes rested on Vicca. She released the breath she had been holding. She was afraid he would ask for something else, something she couldn't give him. "Talk to me until this fever goes away," he added.

She settled in next to him. He leaned against her shoulder. She initially leaned away, then relaxed. If a little human contact comforted him, she could give him that. Azra was light-years away, and physical contact with him no longer gave her the rushing electric sensation. She hung her head. She was only sitting next to him. It meant nothing. A little part of her smiled at the small rebellion. Cyrila would be proud.

"What does *Lakal* mean?" she asked.

He took a long, deep breath, and let it out slowly. "Lakal was a man, my friend, my keeper. Before the Garulen enslaved him, I had to be blinded and chained all the time. It was that way for years. Once they had Lakal, they used him to control me. After Lakal came, they took the blinders off, and I only had to be chained by one leg. He fed me, cleansed me, cared for my health, those sorts of things."

"How did they use him to control you? Did they threaten his life to force you to obey?" Cyani knew the power of such a threat.

"His kind have mind abilities." Soren shifted and looked away from her. Cyani decided not to press him. Psychic abilities weren't common, but they were well documented in several races. She wondered what the nature of Lakal's ability was, but Soren didn't seem to want to talk about it. Mind control was a terrible thing.

"What happened to him?" she asked instead. Her heart felt like it was sinking into a bog. She didn't need his answer. She knew.

"We tried to escape and they killed him." His jaw set as he stiffened. "Without Lakal keeping me tame, they couldn't control me, so they were going to sell me off to some unfortunate Kronalen leech." He shook his head. "That's why I'm here on this blighted outpost."

"When did this happen?"

Soren shrugged one shoulder in a resigned way. "I think it was four days ago, but I lose a lot of time when I'm blinded."

"I'm sorry," she whispered, and she meant it. She thought about the men she had lost in battle. The weight of their deaths seemed imprinted on her soul.

"What about you?" Soren asked as he rubbed his arms and shivered. "How did you end up here?"

"It's part of my training to become one of the Elite." She wished she had a blanket to give him, but she had nothing but her own body heat. She didn't think it would be enough.

"What are the Elite?" he asked through gritted teeth.

"They are warriors who rule my planet. We have to spend five years in battle. This was my last mission for the Union Army. I was going home." She *would* make it home; she had to believe it. The promise of peace was a thread of a delicate web she couldn't break.

"So you'll become a leader of your planet?" He leaned closer to her and stretched out his legs. She knew what he was doing, and she wouldn't let him get any closer. She was pushing her comfort levels enough.

Cyani let out a derisive snort. "No, I won't ever have power. I'll just be a religious figurehead."

"Why?"

"They don't trust me." She smiled to herself, though her bitterness clawed at her.

The Grand Sister had never trusted her, and the others learned quickly that ratting her out anytime she even contemplated breaking a rule earned the Grand Sister's favor. The Grand Sister intentionally started her out in the bottom ranks of the Union Army. She had to spend five years bathed in blood behind enemy lines instead of clean and righteous in tactics meetings like the rest of the sisterhood.

"Why don't they trust you?"

Cyani laughed a slow, angry laugh under her breath, and Soren let the question drop.

"Do you enjoy it? The battle?" Soren asked. He looked at her again with a disturbing intensity. "The kill?"

"I am good at it," she admitted. "That's all." She felt strangely empty inside. The bare cracked stone seemed to press in around her. Why was she putting up with this incessant questioning? How many times had she asked herself the exact same things?

"How many have you killed in this war?" he asked.

Cyani looked him dead in the eye. "I don't know."

"Outside of it?"

Cyani felt her stomach drop as the blood rushed from her head. Could he read her mind? No, he was just pushing her. She clenched her fists, fighting the urge to wipe her palms. It was happening again. The terrible memory claimed her anytime she let her guard down against it. She could almost feel her hands sinking into the foul mud. It oozed between her fingers as the pain of the high-hawk's blow lanced through her head.

Then she remembered agony, hard fists and boots pounding her half-starved body. The sunlight burned her eyes, blinded her as they threw her into a pure white cell. She left a dark smear of blood and grime against the wall as her beaten and broken body slid to the cold floor. Her tears fell on her mud-caked hands.

The crowds shouted in the Halls of Honor. "Murderer! Execute her!"

Cyani snapped out of it and sprang to her feet. "Why are you asking me this?" she demanded. "Don't you trust me? Do you think I'm dangerous? That I'm going to hurt you?"

Soren watched her, the way a cat contemplates a cobra. "You are a predator. I just wanted to know what kind."

"And what kind am I?" she snapped.

"A wolf," he answered in his low, calming voice. "You follow your pack. Loyal, noble"—he paused as he looked at her—"beautiful, definitely a wolf."

Cyani stared down at the floor as she pulled her braid over her shoulder. If she was a wolf, she was at the bottom of her pack. "And you don't mind being stuck in a cave with a wolf?" she asked.

"It is better than being stuck in a cave with a wounded old bear," he answered with a half smile.

Cyani crossed her arms. Tension drained out of her as she felt a comfortable humor return. He reminded her of Tola. Her second-in-command also knew how to defuse a volatile situation. She rubbed her itching hands. "A bear, huh? You aren't that fat."

"I've been hibernating," Soren teased as he stroked Vicca's snowy belly.

Cyani sat again, crossing her legs once more. "You're familiar with wolves and bears. Is Byra a deciduous planet?"

"We have old forests, cool weather, and lots of rain. It is a very fertile place. Well, except for the people. How do you know what wolves and bears are?" he asked.

"They are common creatures found on several planets, just like humans and platypuses," she answered with a shrug.

"How is that possible?" A furrow creased his brow.

"The Gatherers spread us around." She picked up a pebble and flicked it toward the wall.

"Who are the Gatherers?" he asked, curious. His world didn't deal much with others, and Lakal didn't seem interested in contemplating the mysteries of the universe during their enslavement. They were too focused on staying alive and trying to escape.

One thing they did talk about was what they would do if they ever saw their homes again. Lakal never doubted that he would find his way home and drink melon wine by the fires with his people again. Soren hadn't been so optimistic, but Lakal did his best to keep Soren's hope alive. It died with his friend.

"Soren, are you listening?" Cyani asked, nudging him with her elbow.

"I'm sorry." He'd have to let Lakal go. He was gone, and nothing would bring him back. Cyani mattered now. He returned his complete attention to her. "What were you saying?"

"The Gatherers were an ancient alien race, similar to humans. They died out from a genetic disorder long before recorded universal history. According to legend, they gathered species from planets and planted them on new worlds, forcing species to adapt and evolve. The current theory is they were searching for a cure to their disease in the genetic codes of other living things."

"That's interesting," Soren mused. "So you and I?"

"Different breeds of dog," Cyani answered with a subtle grin.

"What's a dog?" he asked. The machine in his ear was unable to translate it.

Cyani laughed outright. "A domesticated wolf."

"Why would someone want to domesticate a wolf?" he teased. His chills abated and he took a deep breath.

Different breeds of dog. Was Cyani compatible with him as a mate? A flicker of hope flared in his heart. He didn't think it was possible for any species other than his own to balance his blood, but if what she said was true, he had a chance to survive.

But what good would that do? His long imprisonment destroyed any chance he had of a normal healthy life on his own world. If he had stayed on Byra, his lifegarden would have reached its maturity. It would have been able to sustain him and his mate and children for the rest of their lives. Without him, it would be as withered and dead as he felt inside. He had nothing. Even if he made it home alive, he had no future there.

At least he could be buried in the soil of his home. The roots of the crown trees would embrace him as his body nourished them. His spirit in death would help the trees reach new heights, and through their feathery needles, he could feel the gentle rain once more. He would become part of the garden of a young nephew struggling to weave an intricate web of life. His spirit would aid the boy. He would make the pakka vines bloom and the sweet honey melon grow. In that small way he would continue on and bring life to the next generation.

Everything in his life had been wasted. He didn't want his death to be wasted, too.

The situation left him in a quandary. To die with honor and in peace, he would have to touch her enough to keep himself alive and convince her to help him return home. That only left him one option. He would have to seduce her, and that would be as easy as seducing a prickleback.

He rubbed his eye. It burned with fatigue even though he had just woken up.

"How long was I sleeping?" he asked, trying to turn his thoughts to something other than the perplexing mating habits of pricklebacks. The fever seemed to be breaking. He felt exhausted and drained, like he hadn't rested at all.

"You were only asleep about two and a half standard hours. I was out watching the Garulen troop movements. I'll leave Vicca with you in case you wake again."

"Is there a way to teach the machine my language?" he asked. It was such a simple thing, but he couldn't stand to hear the language of the Garu any longer.

Cyani sighed, then reached out and took the machine. A shiver raced down his spine as her fingertips skimmed over the shell of his ear.

Heat pooled in his blood, soothing the ever-present ache of his chemical dependency for only a moment.

She removed her own com then placed his in her ear. She gave the com an instruction in her language. After a moment, she pulled it from her ear, and handed it back to him.

He fitted it back onto his ear with a shudder. Most of the time he didn't think about the com, but no matter how useful the tiny machine was, he hated the feel of it.

"I've set the program. When you want to start it, say, 'Com initiate Garu to Byra learning program.' When you want it to stop, just say 'end program.' All you have to do is repeat the words and sentences it says in Garu in your native language. The computer will do the rest." She sighed then rubbed her eyes. They looked puffy and red.

"Have you slept?" he asked, reaching out and taking her hand. He would not let her back away from him. As soon as he grasped her, she began to withdraw, but he had caught her in his snare.

"I'm busy, Soren. You're the one who needs to rest. I'm fine," she protested, looking down at his hold on her. She could probably break his fingers, but he knew she wouldn't just yet.

"Have you eaten?" He drew her closer as the tension in her hand hummed like the strings of a guilla.

"We have to conserve our food. We are going to be here for a while." Her eyes widened with confusion as he pulled her closer. He didn't have much longer before she figured out what he was up to.

"I won't let you sacrifice any more of your health or strength." He closed his eyes for a moment, gathered his will, then opened them again.

Cyani gasped in shock, but her gaze was caught in his. He could see the glow of his eyes reflected in the clear pools of hers. A look of wonder, then panic, flashed across Cyani's face before her long dark lashes drooped low over her lovely eyes.

"Sleep," he whispered, as the tension drained out of her body and she collapsed on top of him.

He sighed as he pulled her closer to him. He cradled her head in the crook of his arm and tugged the tie off the end of her braid. He gently loosed the plait until her rich hair spilled like emerald silk over his arm. She would be as spitting mad as a red-ruffed badger when she woke, but he didn't really care.

"Com, initiate Garu to Byra learning program," he muttered as he held her close to his side.

He pressed his lips to the top of her head and inhaled the sweet scent of her hair. She unconsciously trailed her hand up his chest until it rested near her mouth, and snuggled into him like a sleepy kitten.

Soren looked down and laughed as Vicca rolled on her back, stretched her paws up into the air, and let her little pink tongue loll out of the side of her mouth. He loved the little fox. She had saved him.

Now would her master choose to do the same?

4

CYANI'S BODY SLOWLY PULLED HER TOWARD WAKEFULNESS. DEEP GREEN SURrounded her like a warm blanket. She could hear the soft rush of cool water tumbling over stone and rich laughter followed by the squeal of a child at play. She fought the urge to open her eyes.

A musical chanting lilted in the background, followed by a bark, something clicking along stone, and the furious scratching of a fox trying to run on a hard smooth surface.

"Com, end program." Soren's distorted voice rumbled in her ear. She cracked open one eye. Her thumb came into focus right in front of her face, resting on a warm expanse of smooth golden skin.

A tingle rushed down her spine as her waking mind put two and two together.

She lifted her head and looked around. Horrified, she stared into Soren's dark green eyes, his face only inches from hers. Her hand splayed out over his chest, and the pressure of his palm in the small of her back pressed her hips to his thigh.

"Did you sleep well?" he murmured, his dark voice deep and husky.

She smacked him hard on the chest and rolled out of his embrace. Leaping to her feet, she turned and glared at him.

Vicca trotted in front of Cyani, dropped a small stone near Soren's hand, and barked, the fox's thick tail swishing back and forth in excitement.

"Vicca, not now!" Cyani scolded. The fox lowered her ears and curled into Soren's side.

"You're mad at me. Don't take it out on her. We were playing." Soren leaned forward and stretched, seeming oblivious to the fact that she was about to release a torrent of curse words in four different languages that would make a Fellilen patrol pilot proud.

"Mad?" Her voice squeaked, but she didn't care. "I'm furious. How dare you?"

"How dare I *what*?" he asked, blinking up at her. "How dare I take care of you?"

"Don't look at me, Soren." She turned her shoulder to him then focused on the bag on the other side of the room. She crossed the room to it and fumbled with the contents, looking for her sono.

"Cyani?" She halted her search. His voice sounded too close for her comfort. "Tell me honestly you don't feel better, that you are not thinking clearer, even if you're angry."

"I'm thinking clearly all right," she said, turning on him.

"I'm thinking I'd clearly like to break your nose." She watched his eyes sparkle vivid green, glowing in the dim light. Bursts of bright lavender danced in their depths. She forced herself to turn away from them, afraid he could use them to hypnotize her again. His eyes had far too much power over her, even when he wasn't intentionally holding her in a thrall.

With a frustrated jerk, she pulled her hair over her shoulder. The truth was, she did feel like herself again. Her body seemed looser and stronger, her focus complete, and her eyes no longer burned from exhaustion.

"What does green mean anyway?" she asked so she wouldn't have to admit out loud that he was right.

"What are you talking about?" He stared at her as Vicca circled his legs with the rock in her mouth.

"Your eyes turn yellow when you're agitated or frightened, black when you're sad, red when you're angry. What is green?" She bunched her hair together and tied it in a loose knot.

"My eyes are green?" His voice sounded strange.

"I'm not in the mood to play, Soren. Why would I say they were if they weren't?" She thrust her hands on her hips and tried to glare at him without looking him in the eye. It didn't work. Instead she focused on his mouth. She shivered as she remembered how it felt pressed against the back of her neck.

He rubbed his jaw as a smile spread over his face.

"Well?" she demanded.

"Green is happy." He stooped to pick up Vicca's rock.

"What?!" Cyani slammed the palm of her hand against the wall. Her face flushed with heat. "Now I *am* going to break your nose."

"I'm sorry you're angry, but I'm not sorry about what I did, so get over it." His jaw set and he rose to his full imposing height. She tilted her chin up just slightly in defiance.

"We are stuck in a pit on a rock in the deepest cesspool of space. What in the name of Fima the Merciless are you so happy about?"

He dropped his attention down to her fox. Vicca danced in a circle on her hind legs, and he flicked the rock up the tunnel. She raced after it, her back legs slipping on the stone.

"Let me think," he began, his tone entirely too sarcastic for her liking. "I'm able to speak my native language for the first time in longer than I can remember. I spent the night warm and comfortable with a beautiful and courageous woman instead of blind and shackled to a wall. I feel strong. And Vicca taught me this amusing little game." His smile widened. "It was a very good night."

For the first time, Cyani noticed he was not speaking Garu. "Com, assess ability to translate for language Byra."

Language: Byra. Ability to translate: 78 percent.

"How is that possible?" she whispered. "It should take months to program that level of proficiency."

"The com is a very fast learner." Soren shrugged as Vicca trotted back into the room with the rock.

"I don't believe it." She stood in shock. There was no conceivable way for the com to reach that level so quickly. Did it already know Byra? But then why couldn't she access it earlier?

"If I never hear or speak that filthy language again, I will die a happy man." He flicked the rock up the passage again.

"Soren . . ." Cyani rubbed the bridge of her nose between her eyes.

"What?" he asked, turning his attention fully to her.

"Do you have any idea how angry I am?"

"Rot, Cyani, listen to yourself," he admonished. "I helped you. I did nothing but help you. Your problem is the only creature you trust is Vicca." He scooped up Vicca and held the fox out to her. "Be angry all you want. I'm sure you'll never forgive me." Sarcasm dripped from his words as he thrust Vicca into her arms.

Cyani stood, shocked, as Vicca pressed her silky head under her chin and purred. Realizing she was gaping, she snapped her jaw shut. No, he couldn't be right. That wasn't it. He was wrong. She wasn't that isolated, that afraid.

"That isn't it at all," she argued, gently dropping Vicca to the floor.

"No? Enlighten me." Soren crossed his arms, seeming so strong and sure of himself.

What was bothering her, really? She had slept deeply using him as an enormous male pillow. Was it the contact with him that bothered her? *No, yes . . . No!* She didn't want to think about her attraction to him. She needed to deny it, needed to keep her distance. Unwilling to discuss the fact that he made her feel like a woman, she turned the argument back to the beginning.

"I told you I didn't want you to hypnotize me and you did it anyway."

"I see." He still didn't seem concerned.

"Do you see? Do you really, Soren?"

"I see more than you think I do. You're upset that I disobeyed orders." He tilted his head and shrugged one shoulder. "I'm not one of your soldiers, Cyani."

"I'm trying to save our lives . . ."

"Which is why I'm trying to look out for your health, but you won't eat, and you wouldn't sleep. This is not a training exercise. You do not need to prove to me how strong you are." His voice rose, and her heart pounded loud in her ears. "I know how strong you are."

Cyani froze. His words struck her as deeply as a shock blast to her heart. He thought she was strong? If only he knew how terrified she really felt. She wasn't strong at all. No, any moment she would give in to her dark thoughts and the pressure of their situation would crush her.

"You betrayed my trust," she whispered, once again avoiding thoughts best left in the dark.

He took a step toward her. "I didn't realize you gave it to me," he murmured. His scent, it reminded her of sunlight on leaves and the scent of pike flowers on the wind. It enveloped her as she dropped her gaze to his feet and tried to swallow the sudden lump in her throat. She didn't want him to come any closer. The slightly spicy fragrance of his skin made her feel dizzy and hot. She reminded herself it was only the chemicals, nothing more. She needed to ignore it.

"Don't touch me," she warned.

"Is that an order, Captain?" His whispered voice floated over her. She closed her eyes, trying to fight the burning she felt deep inside her body. She could hear the whip cracking, the Grand Sister's hard voice, the agonizing silence of the other Elite every time she entered a room. She was so alone. His fingertips brushed over the tingling skin of her cheek.

She took a step back, turning from him. He pushed forward in step. They continued the dance until her back pressed against the cold wall.

"Look at me," he demanded in a husky whisper.

She refused, keeping her eyes firmly on the ground.

"Blight and rot, Cyani, look at me." He reached behind her ear, weaving his fingers into the hair at the base of her skull. He cradled her face in his warm and gentle palm, and slowly tilted her face up. She wanted to grab his hand and twist his fingers, but something in her resisted. She let the forbidden touch linger as she opened her eyes, daring him to hypnotize her again.

"I didn't want to hurt you," he murmured, "but you don't listen to me."

He leaned forward. His face was so close to hers she could feel the prickling tingle of anticipation in her lips.

"If you don't listen to me, I can't help us," he continued. He lifted his chin slightly, still not breaching the agonizing gap between them. His eyes glowed with violet fire. "I've been helpless far too long. I need to be a part of this."

Burning with heat, with want, she battled the urge to lean into him, to touch him. Her thoughts turned into a jumble of noise in her head, a constant humming underlined by the frantic beat of her heart. He bunched his hand in her hair beneath the knot, the pressure of the hold firm and commanding. She was tired of fighting. And tired of feeling so isolated.

His fingers loosened their grip, and he slowly pulled away from her. She opened her eyes and fell forward, taking a step to balance herself as she watched his retreat. Confused and irritated, she pressed her lips to the back of her hand to try to stop them from tingling. What was he trying to do to her?

Soren looked down at the floor then turned his attention to Vicca as he crossed the room. She trotted after him, with her rock in her mouth. He stooped to pick up the shirt of his shadowsuit.

Cyani fell against the wall, shaking. The sudden chill of the air felt like ice after the warmth of his body.

What was she doing? Had she completely lost her mind? Suddenly relief that he had not kissed her rushed through her. She did *not* need this. She didn't need to battle his addictive nature. And she was still mad at him! Wasn't she?

"Soren, how can I trust you if you can control my mind?" She watched as he pulled the shirt of the shadowsuit over his head. The slightly shimmering black material stretched taut over the muscles in his chest and arms. She couldn't help staring as each of the defined muscles of his abdomen disappeared under the black fabric. Covering up his chest was a shame. Cyani rolled her eyes. It was official. She had gone insane.

She waited for a response, but he didn't seem anxious to give her one. Instead, he reached up and ran his fingers through the streaks of reds, browns, gold, and black in his hair then tied it back in a ponytail with a shredded strip of fabric.

"I can't control your mind," he finally admitted, pulling on the cuffs of his shirt. The uniform made him look like a warrior, not a slave. She felt a tremor of arousal shiver through her limbs.

"What do you mean?" she asked.

"*Hypnosis* is a strong word for what I can do," he explained. "I can only do three things with my eyes. I can communicate what I feel, whether I want to or not; I can calm someone who is frightened or agitated, sometimes holding them in a thrall; or I can send a person to sleep. That's it. I can't make you do what you don't want to do, unless you don't want to sleep.

Only then do I hold any power over you." He took a step closer and looked her in the eye. "I can't control you, Cyani." He reached out to her, but let his hand hover near her shoulder before letting it fall to his side. "I don't want to."

Cyani didn't know what to say. Her heart pounded in her chest as a tremble raced down her arms. Of all the things he could possibly say to her, that was the one capable of disarming her. Her body was one thing. He was emitting hallucinogenic pheromones. She couldn't control her body's attraction to him, but she thought she could control her mind. Why did he have to say something like that? Something that resonated so deeply with her most private thoughts. She was always under someone's control, always under her own. Damn him.

"Now, how are we going to steal an enemy ship?" he asked, wrenching her from her reckless thoughts.

"Do we have to talk about that now?" she protested. She needed to get away from him, to check the sensors, do something. Her moment of weakness blossomed into sharp thorns of irritation. It was the only way she could defend herself.

"Fine, have you eaten?" he asked.

"Soren!" she snapped. "You are being . . ."

"I know what I'm being," he admitted, reaching into the bag and tossing a ration to her.

She snatched the ERB out of the air with a strike of her hand. "We have to conserve our food. We don't know how long we'll be here. I'm not that hungry." Her stomach chose that moment to betray her with a growl. One of Soren's dark brows arched.

"You can't hypnotize me and make me eat," she challenged.

"No," he answered, "but I can refuse to eat until you do."

"Fine." With an angry rip, she opened the ration and took a bite out of it. "Are you happy now?" she asked with her mouth full. Damn his green eyes, of course he was happy.

She sat on the floor and tore a chunk of the ration off and tossed it to Vicca. She batted it around the room like a toy. Soren laughed and sat down next to her, peeling open a ration of his own.

"Our escape," he continued.

Cyani sighed and rubbed her forehead. She had had rashes less irksome. "Before you knocked me out, I scouted the area thoroughly," she began. "There are two working flight strips, but both are very heavily fortified. We can't penetrate them."

"How many men?" Soren asked.

"At least four hundred." She calmed down as they talked logistics. In that brief moment, he really reminded her of a soldier.

"You mean you can't take out four hundred men?" he teased.

She found herself smiling before she could stop it. She hadn't been free to smile since she was a child. "I'd have to count on you for at least a hundred."

"I don't think I can take out one hundred armed guards," he admitted, "though I would certainly enjoy trying. I bet you could handle the remaining three hundred, though."

Cyani shook her head in disbelief. His teasing reminded her of her brother. Cyn had an inappropriate sense of humor as well. She missed her twin so much. Every time she thought about him, she felt a sharp stab of grief. She just hoped he was safe.

"The transports aren't as heavily guarded," she mentioned.

"But we'll never be able to outrun a stingship in one. The only hope for stealing a ship lies beyond the warehouses." She took another bite. Hopefully when he realized they wouldn't be able to steal a ship, he would stop bothering her about an escape plan.

"What's back there?" he asked.

"Two broken stingships and a badly damaged flight strip," she answered. "I doubt either ship is capable of flight, or the Garulen would have shown more interest in them. They might not be able to get through the rubble from the bombed warehouses."

"Can Vicca find a way through?" He stroked Vicca's arching back as she sent the chunk of ration skittering across the floor with a swipe of her paw.

"You aren't going to let this drop until we check it out, are you?" she accused.

"I have to get off this asteroid, Cyani," he confessed.

"Why?" She needed answers, and she needed them now.

Soren rose and began to pace along the far wall. Vicca followed relentlessly at his heels. "The fever I had, my dizziness, the fainting, it's going to get much worse."

"What is going on, Soren?" His pacing made her nervous. He reminded her of a Xalen tiger again.

He looked like he wanted to answer but didn't.

"Out with it," she demanded.

"I am not in withdrawals from the drugs. I'm in withdrawals from myself," he admitted without looking at her.

"I don't understand."

"My body needs a certain hormone in my bloodstream for my nervous system to work properly. The drugs the Garulen injected in me forced me to produce that hormone—it's what they used to make their narcotics. On my planet, we produce the hormone when we have physical contact with our spouse. The hormone makes us fertile, but it's such an important part of our systems, my body can't work right without it."

"So on your planet, you need to remain in the presence of your mate to stay healthy?" she asked.

"Yes," Soren answered. "But the Garulen corrupted my system. They poisoned me with the stimulants. Now without them, my body isn't producing the hormones I need."

"So you need to return to your planet and find a mate. Otherwise, you'll continue to be ill," she concluded. She finally understood his desperation to escape. She needed to wait for her men, but she owed Soren her life. If he was unconscious with fever, she wouldn't be able to get him to whatever location her team chose as the rendezvous, and returning here for him would put her men in danger. *Damn it.* She had no choice. They were in this together.

"I can't stay here, or I'll be useless." His eyes darkened once again to black.

"If you reach your home, what then? What do you have to do to find a mate?" she asked.

"She has to choose to stay with me in my lifegarden."

"*Lifegarden?*" She had never heard the term before.

"My home," he grumbled.

"That's it?" With his species' dependency on their mates, she assumed there would be a little more pomp and circumstance involved.

"We're a simple people."

She sighed. "We have to get out of here." Cyani crossed the

room to stand in front of him. He stopped his pacing and watched her with a resigned expression on his rough face. If he needed to escape to stay healthy, then they had to try. He'd be no good to her while ill. "Get your boots on. We have work to do."

5

THREE DAYS. THREE DAYS OF HIDING AND SEARCHING, AND NOTHING TO SHOW for it. They were running out of time.

Cyani climbed over the debris of the collapsed warehouse, taking care not to disturb anything. Thin wisps of smoke snaked up from the rubble from the K-bomb blast that had destroyed the structure. They'd been trying to find a path through the warehouses with no luck. Their food was running out, their clean water was already gone, and Soren's symptoms seemed to be getting worse. The fevers burned hotter and lasted longer each night.

The patrols in the ruins had also increased as the Garulen contained the main fires, and now all efforts had turned to salvaging what they could.

They had to escape.

Cyani felt a sharp pang of regret. Part of her would miss this place. She mentally kicked herself for even thinking that thought, but when she thought about her future, all she could see were long years of silence and isolation. The past three days, while frightening and frustrating, had been fun.

For the last fourteen years of her life, she had met with only scorn. She had no friends, no one to talk to but Vicca. She hated the other Elite, but she had no choice. Putting up with their dung was the only way to stay alive and save Cyn.

Even if she succeeded in becoming one of the Elite and the Grand Sister kept her promise to raise her brother out of the deadly slums to the security of the high cities, she'd never see him again.

"Are you coming?" Soren called back to her. He looked concerned as he watched her from his perch on a broken wall.

Soren made her feel real. He was witty, smart, and mentally strong. He liked to talk, but he also liked to listen to her. No matter how bleak things looked, he never gave up, and he never complained. In the Halls of Honor she often felt like she was a walking statue. She existed, but nothing more. Now she felt alive.

In three days, she had talked more than she had in a decade, mostly making plans or sharing observations. Often they talked about Vicca. While Soren remained as elusive and occasionally irksome as the day she freed him, she found herself eager to hear the sound of his voice. She could smile, even laugh without fearing a reprimand. The strange freedom didn't sit well with her, and she tried to hold back in spite of Soren's goading.

If she made it out alive, things would have to change, or she would become addicted to these things that were forbidden to her. Maybe she already was.

"Cyani, are you okay?" He hopped off the wall and walked back to her.

"I'm fine. Just thinking. Let's go." She forced herself to focus and followed him into the crumbling building.

Sliding under a slab of wall, she pulled herself up on the other side.

There was some evidence of digging at the base of the warehouse. The Garulen seemed focused on trying to clear a collapsed doorway into the structure. Normally they posted charges to clear debris. There was something inside, something delicate they didn't want to destroy, and they wanted it back. If they wanted it bad enough, more troops would arrive. They didn't have much time.

Vicca had discovered a way through the building to the damaged stingships beyond, and hopefully this one was passable. Cyani watched Soren crawl under a section of the collapsed roof and feared for him.

It was dangerous going inside. The building could crumble at any moment, and he was not well.

A shiver of dread slithered down her neck. She couldn't shake the feeling he was keeping something important from her.

She followed him into the hole, crawling deeper into the heart of the destroyed warehouse. The ominous creak of a metal support beam slowly bending under the pressure of the heavy roof echoed through the cavernous space. The sound chilled her. If a beam failed, another section of the warehouse could collapse. She squeezed through a narrow slit in the stone ahead of her and found herself in a dark room. A dim glow from Soren's flare lamp flickered beyond a pile of broken crates.

Something clattered to the ground, and the light behind the pile of crates flickered. Vicca barked urgently, her sharp call echoing in the darkness.

"Soren?" Cyani called. He didn't answer.

A guttural cry filled the room, punctuated by Vicca's frantic yelps.

"Soren!" she screamed, pushing herself into a run as she heard a loud crash in the chamber beyond.

She wheeled around the crates, slamming into a large pile of rubble as she turned another corner. With her heart thundering in her ears, she leapt to the top of the heap, her adrenaline riding her hard.

Soren lay on the floor, his body stiff and contorted. He wasn't moving. Matriarchs help her, he wasn't breathing!

She flew off the rubble heap and knelt by his head. Vicca ran around them yelping in alarm.

"Soren?" She brushed her palm over his cheek, but his jaw remained clenched, his lips pulled back in a macabre grimace. With his eyes pure white and lifeless, he lay twisted, his hands clenched up, frozen, grasping at nothing.

She watched in horror as his skin paled before her eyes. His lips turned purple. He wasn't getting any air.

"Soren, snap out of this. You can fight this . . ." Her panic rose like a storm within her. The sound of Vicca's terrified yelp faded into nothing as the thundering heartbeat in her ears blocked out everything else. She reached down and pressed a palm to his chest. She couldn't feel his heart, and his lungs didn't pull in any air.

"Come on, Soren," she ordered. He couldn't die like this. She ripped open the clasps of his shadowsuit and splayed her hand out on the bare skin of his chest to try to find his heartbeat. It stuttered, then pulsed frantically into her palm.

His chest contracted, forcing the air out of his lungs as froth bubbled up out of his mouth. He puffed, choking air into his lungs through the liquid. She inhaled as well, unaware that she had been holding her breath, but the rush of relief was all too brief.

The spasms began.

Cyani lifted Soren's head onto her thighs, and held on tight to his jaw as his body twisted and shook. His head jerked, slamming back down onto her thighs as spit bubbled from between his lips. His eyelids fluttered and his eyes rolled back. She held his head so he wouldn't slam it into the stone floor. It was the only thing she could think to do, the only thing she felt she could control. She tried to remember her emergency medical training, but she had nothing, could do nothing.

She closed her eyes, but she couldn't escape the sharp metallic scent in the air, or the sound of his limbs slapping against the hard stone floor. She wanted to scream and scream to somehow release the stark terror eating away at her as his saliva dripped onto her hands. Instead she let out a helpless gasp and continued to hold on to him, refusing to let go.

His contortions ended almost as quickly as they began and his limbs stiffened once more. She held still, cradling his head in her lap, hoping his labored breathing would not cease again, and the ordeal was finally over.

"You have to pull though this," she whispered, her voice raw and choked. "Please, Soren." After everything he had suffered, he didn't deserve a slow and tortured death. The others she had lost had been swift; she couldn't think before she knew they were already gone. This was too slow, teasing her with time, tormenting her with the need to do something to save him.

She felt the tension drain out of his muscles as his body slowly relaxed. With a low moan, his breathing eased, though it rattled in his chest.

Cyani shook all over, feeling weak and battered as she brushed his hair from his face and tried to wipe the saliva from his mouth.

His throat swallowed, and he tried to lift his head then relaxed against her thigh. His breathing sputtered in his chest as he fell into a deep sleep. He snored. She let out a choked laugh through her clenching fear.

She sat with him for what seemed like hours, helpless, exposed. The Garulen could come at any minute. She prayed more desperately than she ever had in her life, but his life, his death, was no longer in her hands.

She needed control. She needed more information. Was this part of his withdrawal?

"Com, find source files for the general information on species Byralen," she said, desperate for something to focus on.

Six files identified.

"Com, list files . . ." Cyani stroked his hair, smoothing his brow with her palm. The Elite and their rules could go suck on it. In the dark, alone and terrified, the girl she had been resurfaced. In the ground cities, you cared for one another or you died.

She chose to listen to a log entry from a Union Army lieutenant regarding a freed Byralen captive. The rest were medical reports, and would be harder to follow.

Accessing file: During a raid on a Krona shipping colony, our team discovered a strange specimen among the slave population. He had been separated from the others, fitted with severe-blinders and immobilized. The com was unable to give us any information on the captive. I filed his physical descriptions during the medical examination. The captive displayed extreme aggression at first, but soon succumbed to feverlike symptoms.

After forty-eight standard hours, the captive suffered from fainting spells. He seemed weak, in spite of medical efforts to stabilize his condition. The captive was either unwilling or unable to communicate. During his quarantine he often destroyed the objects in his room, focusing most of his aggression on the bed. After seventy-two hours had passed in observation, the subject's fainting spells progressed to seizures.

Fifty-four hours after the seizures began, the subject died in quarantine. Medical examinations were inconclusive as to cause of death, but determined this species as the source of the Passion drugs filtering into the illegal market.

Cyani felt her heart drop into her stomach. The prisoner had died. No, she shouldn't jump to conclusions. The Byralen could have died of anything.

"Com, project medical reports on holo-screen." Cyani quickly scanned the reports, three different Byralen, two males, one female, the same symptoms, different time lines, fevers, fainting, seizures, death . . .

Cyani's hands started shaking uncontrollably. She crossed her arms, pinching her hands in her armpits, but the tremor just spread to her whole body. This was all for nothing. He was going to die, and there was nothing she could do to save him.

And he knew it.

Why didn't he tell her?

Cyani swallowed convulsively.

Finally his eyes blinked open, his irises pure white. He stared at her, his gaze bleary and confused.

"Cyani?" he whispered.

She felt a tear slip over her cheek as she tucked an inky lock of hair behind his ear. "I'm here. You're safe now."

He pulled away from her, struggling to his hands and knees. She let him go, unsure of what to do. He heaved, vomiting on the floor, then swayed. She pulled him back away from the mess and let him rest his head on her lap.

Reaching his hand around her side, he clung to her waist, his whole body trembling. She smoothed his hair and sang, a silly lullaby her father used to sing to her when she was a little girl and suffering from nightmares.

She could barely force the tune out of her constricting throat, the words a jumble of half syllables she didn't have the strength to speak. Her voice sounded raw, felt torn, as she did her best to comfort him.

Slowly the shudders ceased, and he fell asleep in her lap. She let him rest, grateful for the quiet peace after such stark terror. Vicca whined as she licked his face, then curled up against his chest. Cyani rubbed her fox's ears.

"I know, girl," she whispered. "He scared me, too. Now I need you to guard us." Vicca gave Soren's hand a final lick then scampered off.

How long did he have?

The beginning of the seizures was the beginning of the end.

For the first time, she looked up at the room. The light of the overturned flare lamp flickered against the dusty rubble.

A strange machine stood untouched by the disaster all around them. It had to be some sort of medical table. It was large enough for a full-grown man to lie inside, and two doors closed over the body. One of the doors hung open, revealing shackles on the table beneath, and a sort of harness for the hips.

"Mercy of the Matriarchs," she whispered, realizing what she was seeing. It had to be the machine they used to make the drugs from Soren. She stroked Soren's hair again. No wonder he had a seizure.

Closing her eyes, she leaned over Soren. He murmured something and snuggled deeper into her lap, his strong hand snaking beneath her shadowsuit to cling to her bare waist.

He coughed and then lifted his head, his black eyes glassy and confused. He trembled, letting his head loll back down onto her lap.

"Do you need some water?" she asked, reaching for the supply sack. She wished she had something better to give him than the bitter and dirty-tasting drain water.

He nodded slowly, his brow crinkled. "What happened?" he whispered.

"You had a seizure," she answered, trying to keep her voice calm and controlled. "It looks like it's over now."

He shook as she handed him the water. His eyes swept around the room, pausing on the bile then fixing on the machine. They flashed bright yellow, glowing in the darkness.

"Soren, listen to me," she demanded, reaching out and turning his face to hers so he would look her in the eye. "It's over now. It's over."

"It will never be over." The resignation in his voice broke her heart.

"I'm going to get you home. I swear it to you." She swore it to herself. If that sickening machine had convinced his body he had to mate, she would get him to his home planet so he could have a real partner and a hope for survival.

The corner of his mouth twitched and he turned back to the machine. He stared at it a long time. "It doesn't look how I remembered it."

"Stop looking at it. I'm getting you out of here, right now." Cyani stood and helped him up. He swayed on his feet.

"It won't do any good," he mumbled. She looked up into his eyes as they faded to black once more.

"Why didn't you tell me these withdrawals are fatal?" she asked. Her voice sounded soft, lost, even to her ears. How could she sound so vulnerable? How could she *feel* so vulnerable? He was the one fighting death; why was she so deeply terrified?

He shrugged his shoulders. "What could you do about it?"

Nothing, she could do nothing.

Unless . . .

Glancing around the room, she noticed one of the crates still intact. "Com, scan contents."

The com projected its readings on the holo-screen, and her heart flipped in her chest. It seemed where there was smoke, there was fire. She recognized the chemical compound from the Byralen medical reports.

"Soren, what would happen if you were to take the drugs they made from you?"

Soren looked down at Cyani, confused and still feeling ill. What was she saying? His eyes fixed on a single crate half buried in the pile of rubble he had climbed over.

"Soren?"

He tried to think, tried to answer her question, but his mind still felt thick and unresponsive.

He swallowed as he stared at the crate. A sinking feeling twisted in his sensitive stomach.

"What would happen if you were exposed to those chemicals?" Cyani insisted.

"My body would respond by producing the hormones I need," he admitted. The bitter irony of the situation was almost as bad as the sour taste in his mouth.

Cyani leapt from his side. She ripped off the top of the crate and plunged her hands into the white foam inside. Slowly she extracted a small metal case. She walked back over to him and opened the case. Inside were four tiny vials of amber liquid. He knew how they were used. He had heard the Garulen guards talk about rubbing it on themselves, then raping slave after slave. His mouth began to water, and he had to take several deep breaths to settle his churning stomach.

Cyani's enormous blue eyes reached up to his in hope. He put his hand over hers and shut the case.

"I can't use those."

"Why not?"

"You wouldn't understand." He stumbled as he tried to walk to the far side of the chamber toward the small tunnel under the collapsed roof. What if he became aggressive? What if he hurt her?

"Soren," Cyani shouted at him. "These could save your life."

He turned back around and looked at her. Sure, they could prolong his suffering, but for how long? Could he make it home? Perhaps it was all hopeless, and even his death would be a waste.

"Cyani," he said, his voice coming clearer now. "I think it's best if you leave here without me."

"Don't," she responded, shaking her head as her bright eyes narrowed in anger. "I'm not going to let you give up."

"Do you know what that person suffered?" he yelled, pointing at the case in her hands. "Do you know how many days they had to be strapped in that thing and tortured to create that much?" He didn't lower his voice as he pointed at the extractor. "I can't use it!" He let the tension fall out of his shoulders and lowered his eyes to the floor as another wave of nausea hit him and his head began pounding with a sharp ache. "It might make me dangerous to you . . ."

"These probably came from you," she reasoned. "It's only right they should save your life. And even if they didn't come from you, wouldn't it have been easier to endure knowing the end result helped one of your kind live to see your home once more?"

He looked at her again, her beautiful eyes shining in the darkness. A lock of her hair fell over her brow, making her seem small and alone. How could he leave her?

In the last three days, he felt like he had lived a whole life. Just being free, comfortable, clean—they were such little things, and she would never know how much she had given him. In that short time, she reminded him of a broad-wing coming out of a long sleep in a chrysalis. When they would talk, he caught glimpses of the woman she tried to hide beneath the mask of a soldier. She was warm, mischievous, driven, competitive, and intelligent. He couldn't leave her alone, not when he could help her get out of this pit.

"I said it before," she murmured, her voice low. "I'm not leaving here without you."

He stepped up to her and cradled her cheek in his palm.

For the very first time, she didn't pull away. She turned her face into his palm, her long lashes feathering over the sensitive skin on the pad of his thumb.

"I don't want you to have another seizure, Soren," she whispered, her breath caressing his palm. "It was awful, and I don't want you to die."

He sighed as he took the case from her hand. She won. He looked at it then gripped it tighter. She won.

He let her go. "I don't want you touching me after I use this. I don't want you addicted to me, and I don't know how I will behave . . ."

"How about if you try anything, I kick your ass?" She smiled at him. He prayed she could if it came to that.

"Deal," he whispered, opening the case and removing one of the vials. "Go on ahead, Cyani. I don't want you to see this. Start working on getting us out of here. I'll be okay."

"You'll use it?" she asked. He supposed she had a right to question him. He had given her little reason to trust him in their time together.

"My eyes will glow bright violet. Don't let me touch you as long as they're violet. Do you understand?"

She nodded then reached out to him. He backed away.

"Go," he commanded. "Just go."

6

CYANI SQUIRMED THROUGH A TIGHT FISSURE IN THE WALL. THE STINGSHIP BAY lay directly in front of her. She couldn't help looking back at the small opening. Soren would be alright. She had to believe that. At least Vicca was with him.

She sent up a quick prayer to the Creator that the drug would buy them some time. Cyani kept low, wary of her surroundings. Following the shadows of the destroyed warehouses, she crept toward the stingships.

The ships loomed over her, their form neither sleek nor compact. They were segmented, with the cockpit connected to the weapons bay by a ring of metal. The main body of the ship swelled behind it like a giant abdomen with the energy converters dangling beneath it like spindly legs. The ship reminded her of an enormous insect, a wasp ready to devour anything in its way.

They were not ships designed for intergalactic flight. They were patrol ships, but the Garulen had modified them to use as scout and defense ships. They'd be able to get them to the next star system—if they were lucky—but there was no way a stingship could make it all the way back to Azra.

One of the ships listed toward a crater, its energy modifiers crushed beneath it. The other remained perched on its landing posts. Without energy modifiers, the ship near the crater would never take off, so Cyani jogged toward the one still on its feet while keeping a close eye on her holo-map.

Wheeling open the manual hatch at the tip of the ship's abdomen, she pulled herself up into the large bay. Garulen technology latched onto the familiar Fellilen panels and control ports of the cargo bay, looking like a technological fungus.

Cyani scuttled through the narrow ports until she reached the cockpit. Using her com, she tried to hack into the Garulen system using the old security code her team had used to breach the atmosphere shield.

"Work, damn it," she cursed as she waited for the computer to accept the old code. "Come on, come on, come on."

The display screen lit up several lines of Fellilen programming code.

Yes.

The ship hadn't been linked into the main computer system since the attack. That would be a problem. They didn't know the new code to breach the atmosphere shield. Turning on the ship's minimal functions, Cyani began a diagnostic.

"Com, scan ship for fuel levels, exterior damage, and life-support system failures."

Unable to determine fuel levels. Exterior damage report: One vertical modifier damaged beyond repair. Ship maximum speed and launch ability compromised. Energy modifier shield strength compromised. Life support: Temperature controls functioning, atmosphere controls functioning, pressure controls functioning, gravity controls damaged, ability to function compromised.

"*Shakt*," Cyani muttered under her breath. Moving to the power controls, she tried to get the fuel level diagnostic up and running. She just needed to know if they had enough to get off the ground and boost over the crater on the flight strip. The energy modifiers would take them the rest of the way.

Overall, it wasn't that bad. She listened to the com list the ship's functions working at maximum capacity. The only other compromised system was communications, and the ship had no failed systems. It could have been worse.

Cyani watched the holo-map as two blue dots ran toward the ship. Her heart raced with a sudden flood of relief, but her mind remained wary. Soren warned her he could be dangerous. She couldn't forget it.

She listened to the low grinding squeal of the hatch shutting, then boots echoing through the silent ship. Climbing down the ladder from the cockpit, she turned to meet Soren as he entered the weapons bay.

Cyani gasped before she could stop herself. His eyes radiated light so bright, she couldn't see his pupils. The swirling red violet burned through his thick lashes, and cast the room in a faint purple glow.

"How do you feel?" she asked, widening her stance just in case. There was a hard edge to his jaw, a tension in his body, like a fault line about to crack and unleash a devastating quake.

The corner of his mouth twitched as his gaze slowly traveled down her body then returned to her face. "I'll survive," he muttered. "What do we need to do?"

"We have three problems," she said, keeping a wary eye on him without looking directly into his eyes. In her heart she knew he wouldn't hypnotize her, but she didn't want to take that chance. She had heard stories of the drug he had taken driving humans mad. "The first problem is I can't determine how much fuel is in this ship. The second problem is we don't have the security code to breach the atmosphere, and the third problem is the Garulen will know something's wrong as soon as we power the ship up."

"Then let's begin with the first problem." His voice was low and controlled, but his body still exuded sexuality. "Is there another way to determine the amount of fuel?" His scent was much clearer now, much more potent. Cyani felt a strange fluttering in her stomach, and turned to the weapons bay deployment panel. Iridescent colors danced over the panel. That could be distracting.

"I'll take a look at the fuel sensor, see if it is something I can fix." She glanced at one of the Garulen panels attached to the wall. "Do you read Garu?" she asked.

"No, I can only speak it."

She sighed. She would have to handle weaponry as well, though he might be able to manage the voice commands once they were in the thick of things. She slid past him and jumped down the tube into the main bay. She needed to find the service panels for the fuel cells.

Soren followed. He stood on the catwalk of the bay with Vicca rubbing her cheeks against his heels as if she were in heat. A warm shiver slid down her neck. *It was just the chemicals.*

"I've activated the minimal functions of the ship's computers. I don't think that will draw attention, but it might. Can you take Vicca and stand guard? I've got a bad feeling." She ripped off a panel on the wall and stared down at the fuel input connectors. One of them was fried to a crisp.

"About the Garulen, or me?" His voice sounded dark.

"I'm going to have to retrieve a part from the other ship. I need you to watch my back," she countered, avoiding his question. "Are you able to handle this?" she asked, staring him in the eye for the first time. The intensity of the emotions that burned there nearly stopped her heart—anger, desire, guilt, and pain. He was doing his best to maintain control under the influence of the drug. Cyani noticed his hands shaking just slightly.

"I'll handle it," he confirmed, letting the red in his eyes seep into his voice.

"I need you to keep us safe. If a guard unit does come around, burn off a little of that energy . . . got it?"

He smiled for the first time, the red in his eyes flaring. "Perfectly, Captain."

Soren led the way out of the stingship. Cyani followed, watching him carefully as he went. Occasionally he would pause and shudder then continue with the same steeled hardness that had troubled her when he entered the ship.

He reminded her of a volcano, silent, trembling, ready to unleash chaotic violence. What had the drug done to him? It had worked so quickly. Was this only the beginning of the terrible war raging in his bloodstream?

SOREN SWUNG HIMSELF OUT OF THE HATCH AND LUMBERED ACROSS THE stingship bay then crouched behind an overturned canister. Vicca sat at his side, her ears upright and alert.

He watched Cyani run across the field, her powerful muscles shifting under her shadowsuit like the sleek body of a cat on the hunt.

His shoulders tensed as another dizzy rush of pleasure throbbed through his body. It made his head ache just behind his temples. She was so beautiful. She had no idea she was so beautiful. She only saw herself in one light, and it was a very harsh and unforgiving light.

He had to protect her. He owed her that. He couldn't let himself be distracted by his growing attraction. He could think about that later, if he thought about it at all. In his current state, with the drugs working to restore his unnatural hormone levels, he had to be careful. The Garulen were right to keep him chained. His own culture was right to keep the breeding men isolated. He was dangerous.

He watched Cyani disappear into the wreckage of the second ship and breathed a sigh of relief. Focus was the key to control. He turned his eyes to the horizon then slowly scanned the stingship bay, watching, waiting.

Vicca stood and lowered her head. With her whiskers pushed forward, she twitched her nose and swished her tail. The lights on her collar blinked red. The fox looked up at him and growled, then focused on a gap in the heaps of rubble that had once been huge warehouses on the far side of the broken stingship.

"What is it, girl?" Soren asked as he grabbed his sono. Vicca growled again, then whined and slipped behind a half-destroyed wall. Soren followed, watching the gap. A tingle raced down his spine.

The collapsed warehouse exploded with a boom that echoed through the bay and punched the air out of Soren's lungs. He ducked, wrapping his arms over his head as debris rained down on him. A metallic groan filled the bay, followed by the jarring cacophony of metal crashing against stone.

Soren looked up in time to see the wrecked stingship lurch on the edge of the crater then plunge down the slope, rolling onto its back like a dying roach.

He didn't have time to worry about Cyani. The hull seemed intact, and she could handle anything. His attention fixed on the four Garulen guards crawling out of the hole created by the blast.

With swirling dust and debris in the air, he had the advantage, but he needed to strike quickly. Deep, burning rage and desperation drove him forward. Hormones flooded his system. They made him possessive, violent, and deadly.

"Vicca, find Cyani," he ordered. The fox sprinted through the debris toward the overturned ship.

He crept toward the group of Garulen, concealing himself in the clouds of dust. He was able to sneak right behind them. He steadied his hand as he lifted the sono. Tensing, he prepared to fire.

A voice crackled through static. "Scout unit one-four-seven, position and status . . ."

One of the Garulen soldiers pressed his hairy palm to the plate of armor on his chest.

"Route clear through warehouse seventeen. We are in the stingship bay. One ship damaged beyond repair. The other looks damaged but functional."

"Bring ship's systems up . . . Report damage . . . Half an hour."

The guards turned their backs to him, and Soren struck. He fired three blasts at the leader of the group. The guard spasmed then collapsed as the other three guards stared in shock.

Soren took aim and fired a volley of blasts, taking down another guard.

The other two sprang into action, firing shock blasts at him. He ducked behind a pile of debris as the shock blasts crashed into the heap, destabilizing the pile. The rubble crashed toward him and he leapt out of the way.

Charging the guards, he let out a feral scream and allowed his eyes to blaze with his fury. The guards froze, their meaty jaws gaping in transfixed fear. One stumbled backward, tripping over a chunk of stonework.

Soren fired on the one still standing, just as the guard brought the shock thrower to his shoulder. Soren's sono hit the guard on the chest, but not before the low *wham* of a shock blast hummed through the air.

The blast hit him in the gut as he stumbled forward toward the last guard. Soren screamed a second war cry as he surged through the bone-chilling pain and numbness. He collapsed on the last guard, fixing his fingers over the creature's exposed throat.

The guard let out a strangled gasp as Soren forced all his fury into the waning strength in his hands. His muscles contracted, paralyzed by the blast.

Slowly the life drained out of the guard. Soren closed his eyes and let the numbness wash over him.

He didn't know how long he remained paralyzed. He was too high on the stimulants to remain incapacitated for long. His body screamed in pain as it began to wake again.

A raspy little tongue bathed his face. He shook his head and lifted his bleary eyes to Cyani. She looked confused.

"What in the name of Fima the Merciless happened out here?"

Soren glanced at the bodies scattered around him. "I killed them," he choked out of his parched throat.

"I see that," Cyani responded. "You are going to have to get up on your own, because I'm *not* kissing you."

"Rot. Are you okay?" he asked, pulling himself to his feet. He bent over, resting his hands on his knees to fight the swelling nausea in his sore abdomen. He knew she was only teasing, but even the thought of her lips touching his made his blood flow white-hot in his veins. As soon as they were safe and the drugs waned, he'd find a way to kiss her until he couldn't breathe, and he wouldn't let her back away.

"I'm fine, a little bruised. I need more time to remove the fuel indicator, or we'll have no way of knowing how much power the ship has."

"We don't have time. This scout group is supposed to get the ship linked and enter a damage report in just a few minutes. If they don't answer, this place will be crawling with half the Garulen army."

Cyani kicked a small rock, sending it skipping across the bay. She pinched her eyes closed and rubbed her palm on her shirt.

Even under such intense pressure, he found her enthralling. He felt the sudden rush of arousal and stilled, knowing he needed it to live, but worried that his attraction would distract him, or threaten her. A blight on the drugs for making him so aware of her at a time like this.

"This is a huge risk," she commented.

"I'm willing to take it if you are."

Cyani turned to the ship. It was their only hope. She'd have to depend on her faith in the Creator. Her fate was in his hands.

Hand.

Inspiration struck suddenly as she looked at the dead Garulen soldiers.

"Soren, do you speak Garu well enough to convince them you're one of them?"

"I believe I do," he answered with a puzzled expression.

"Good." Cyani pulled her knife from its sheath. "Which one was the leader?"

"Soren pointed to the body farthest from them. She bent down next to it, removed the forearm shield, and with one smooth strike, chopped off the body's hand at the wrist.

"What are you doing?!" Soren shouted. "You can't defile a body like that. It's unholy."

"We can ask for forgiveness later." Cyani tested the flexibility in the fingers. "He doesn't need it anymore, and we do. Come on, I have an idea."

7

"HOLD THIS." CYANI TOSSED SOREN THE HAND AS THEY CLIMBED INTO THE cramped cockpit. He fumbled trying to catch it and flung blood across the display screen.

"What am I supposed to do with this thing?" Soren scolded, holding it out by the tip of one pasty finger.

She threw herself into the pilot's seat and reached for the controls, checked her com sensors and the ship's diagnostics, then looked for anything she might have missed. As soon as they powered up the ship, they'd have no time for anything but escape.

"Garulen communications systems are activated and maintained by palm scans to prevent intelligence leaks. When I power up the ship, press the hand to that panel over there and pretend to be the hand's former owner. Are you with me?"

Cyani swung around in the chair. Soren dropped his gaze

to the hand, looked over at the communications panel in front of him, then a slow smile spread over his face. "I'm with you."

"Good. Whatever you say to the central command, I need you to get two things from them. We cannot leave this rock without the code to the atmosphere shield. Tell them the gravitation generators have been damaged and we must take the ship out of the range of the asteroid's generators to assess the nature of the damage."

Cyani turned the chair and tried to reach each of the five control pedals for her feet, but the seat was set for the stocky legs of a Garulen pilot, not her long limbs. Her knees banged into the control panel each time she tried to reach the high pedals.

"Is that true?" Soren interrupted.

She felt along the bottom of the chair for some sort of adjustment lever.

"Is what true?"

"Is the gravitation system damaged?"

Cyani sighed as she threw her knees wide to reach the pedals with her toes.

"Unfortunately, it is true, and their computer will confirm it. We're in for one hell of a ride. Are you ready?"

Soren nodded. "What was the second thing?"

"What?"

"The second thing you needed?"

"Fuel levels."

Cyani felt her gut drop as she mentally prepared herself for flying the ship. Placing her hands on the control globe before her, she took a deep breath and pushed the globe forward, bringing the sleeping ship to life.

Soren visibly tensed as the lights in the cockpit flared on the console. The ship let out a low rumbling moan that settled into a droning growl.

Cyani watched him out of the corner of her eye, hoping the shock blast and his technology phobia wouldn't trigger another seizure in spite of the drugs he had taken. She needed him. Even if she could speak fluent Garu, which she couldn't, the Garulen didn't let women in their ranks. Who was she kidding? She just needed him.

A tinny voice rang through the cockpit. "Receiving damage estimates, status report . . ."

Soren placed the oozing hand on the control panel and pressed it to flatten the palm.

"Don't forget to ask about fuel levels . . ." Cyani whispered. Soren glared at her.

"Ship in functioning condition, unable to determine nature of gravitation loss. Request authorization to test gravitation generators outside shields." Soren pulled the hand off the panel and looked over to Cyani.

She nodded, but found she had nothing to say. Each second ticked by, swelling to the length of an eternity as the crackling static remained devoid of a response.

Vicca jumped into Soren's lap and sniffed the hand with interest. He shoved her away.

"Soren, strap in for plan B," Cyani warned, preparing to stand on the emergency thrusters. They would have to fly in and destroy the shield generator. It was suicide.

A string of code scrolled through the console screen. Cyani released her breath as her head swam with relief. It was the new shield code, their ticket to freedom.

"Good work, soldier," she whispered.

The static broke.

"Flight permission granted, stand by for escort."

Cyani snorted, placed her hands on the globe, and positioned her feet for takeoff. "I have no intention of waiting for an escort. Are you ready?"

Soren pressed the palm to the panel again. "Flight permission acknowledged. Request information on fuel levels. Fuel indicator is ill-functioning."

Soren winced at his sudden lapse in vocabulary and shrugged a hasty apology.

"Fuel levels adequate for mission," the voice answered, but there was a questioning tone in the disembodied voice.

Soren pulled the hand off the console.

"*Adequate?* What was that supposed to mean?" Cyani huffed.

"Good enough for me. Let's go." Soren grabbed Vicca, tossed the hand, and pulled the flight harness over his shoulders, locking it into place.

Cyani worked the stabilizers with her hands as she ignited the thrusters. "Hold on, this should be interesting."

With a surge of power, the ship took off, dipping low over the crater in the airfield then surging up toward the milky atmosphere shield.

Sirens screamed in the cockpit. Cyani blocked them out as she focused on her task. She had to power the energy converter and jump into macrospace before their "escort" arrived.

"Warning, breach of flight permissions. Stand by for escort." The computer scolded in a blaring monotone.

"Really? I hadn't noticed," Cyani ground out between her clenched teeth as the ship sliced through the shield.

The whole of the universe opened up before them, the stars brilliant in their intensity.

Cyani fought to place her feet on the top pedals as she simultaneously plotted their coordinates and initiated the energy converter.

Just then, an alarm blared and the sensation of weightlessness overcame Cyani. Soren shouted in shock as Vicca floated out of his lap, transformed into a giant ball of fluff with scurrying legs.

"Hold on!" Cyani yelled as she banged her fist against one of the panels.

With a loud resonant hum, the energy converter initiated. Soren grabbed Vicca, trying in vain to shove floating hair out of his face. He clutched her to his chest, determined to hold the panicked fox.

"Cyani, they're coming," Soren shouted over the alarms.

Snapping her attention back to their situation, she noticed the readout of the two stingships coming up fast on their tail. A blast shook the ship just as the gravitation generators came back online. Cyani slammed down into her seat.

More blasts rocked the ship, shaking loose an overhead panel that swung from wires above them.

"Hold it together, baby, we're almost there," Cyani muttered as she watched the bar indicating the ship's interdimension energy potential slowly rise. Once it hit green, they could leap macrospace.

Using evasive maneuvers, she tried to avoid fire from the stingships behind them. A blast shook the ship. Cyani couldn't avoid another hit. They had locked on.

The macrospace indicator flashed. Pushing forward with

all her strength, she launched the ship into the dimensional fold, while fighting against the surge of g-forces pressing her back into her seat.

With a gut-turning lurch, the ship settled into her stride and everything went still. A high-pitched *beep* punctuated the silence, adding a slow staccato to the low hum of the energy converter.

Soren turned to look at her. She took a deep breath and rubbed her palms as the stress of the launch caught up to her. Her head pounded and her fingers felt shaky and weak.

"Did we make it?" Soren asked. Vicca scrambled out of his hands. She grabbed the severed hand and disappeared into the hold.

"For now. There's no way to communicate with, or fire on, a ship in macrospace."

"And the ship?"

As if on cue, the hull shuddered before settling again.

"She's holding together," Cyani answered as she tried to fix the loose panel back into place. "Barely."

Soren reached for the latch of his harness.

"I wouldn't get up just yet. It seems the gravitation generators are giving us all or nothing. They'll probably fail again . . ." Cyani slammed her palm against the loose panel, and it seemed to lock into place. She kept a wary eye on it just in case.

"Vicca!" she called. The fox didn't return.

"How are you holding together?" Soren asked. He reached out to touch her bare arm. He couldn't help himself. Instead of a wild rushing need to possess her, he felt a burning desire to protect her. He pulled his hand back. He was still dangerous.

"I've been better," she commented while rubbing her bruised knees. "This isn't over. They know where we're going. They could read the computer coordinates. They'll be right on our tail as we come out of macrospace, and they aren't the only ones."

"What do you mean?"

"I programmed the ship to take us to the nearest star system in Union-controlled space. We'll be dropping out of the dimensional fold near an undeveloped world. The Union has a spaceport on a moon in that system."

"That's a good thing. They'll be able to help us."

"Perhaps. The Union might take out a couple of ships following us, but that's not what I'm worried about. We are in a Garulen ship, and there is something wrong with the communications system. I don't know if the Union will recognize us."

"Great," Soren muttered. "Could things get any more difficult?"

"I don't want to tempt fate." Cyani resumed her fight with the chair. She twisted a knob under the seat of the chair and it dropped several inches, relieving her knees.

Sheer exhaustion seeped into her bones, making her body feel like she was on a gravity five planet or higher. She managed to lift her hand long enough to check the gravitation generators. Unfortunately, they were working fine. It was her body that was betraying her.

"Are you okay?" Soren asked.

"I'm fine," she snapped.

"No, you're not."

"Damn it, Soren. Is now really the time for this conversation?" She slammed her palm down on a panel, leaving a dent.

He crossed his arms.

Cyani clenched her teeth. Her mind reeled with words, but none of them seemed to string together into a response with any more substance than "Go suck a rankock." She swallowed her anger, realizing that showing her irritation only proved his point.

"Could you make yourself useful?" She focused on the panel before her, checking her coordinates and preparing the ship for the drop out of macrospace.

"Doing what?" Soren grumbled. He shook his head as if he pitied her.

Tension pulled her strained muscles tight through her neck. She forced her muscles to relax and acknowledged that his little shake of his head was a sign that she won this round. He was letting it drop, for now. Unfortunately, she knew it was not the end of things.

The gravitation generator dropped out again.

"When do we slow down?" Soren asked, gathering his hair in his fist at his nape. Vicca barked from somewhere in the hull. Then the generators kicked back in. The sudden sense of falling invaded more than just her heart.

"Vicca, get your fluffy butt back here," she shouted.

"I'll get her," Soren offered, unstrapping his flight harness.

"Leave her. She'll be okay. We're approaching the other side of the dimensional fold." Focusing on what was to come, Cyani put her feet on the pedals and her hands on the controls. "Com, link to transmitter and broadcast Union distress code five."

The ship trembled and groaned as it began the drop out of macrospace. Cyani initiated the shutdown of the energy converter as the ship came alive with noise and light once more.

The viewscreen blazed with color as they streaked past an outlying aquamarine planet in the star system.

Warning: Union ships locked on target.

The cockpit flooded with red light as Cyani whipped her hands over the globe, spinning them off to the left, hoping to duck behind the moon of the planet.

The ship lurched twice as the energy waves of two more ships dropping out of macrospace crashed into their hull.

"Damn it, Vicca. *Come!*" Cyani screamed as she twisted the ship around in a dizzying spin that swung the moon before them in a dancing loop around the viewscreen.

The blaring noise in the cockpit blended into a jarring hum in her mind as she used the moon's gravity to swing them down and around the planet, racing to the bright yellow and blue gem in the distance.

A red flash lit across the viewscreen.

Warning: Energy converter reaching critical potential. Event imminent.

"*Shakt*, why isn't it shutting down?" She banged her fist against the controls again, watching the red line slowly grow. The energy converter latched to the belly of the ship was about to explode.

"Hang on!" Spinning the ship toward the Union patrol, she flew past them as a volley of fire rattled their small cage. With a steady hand on the controls, she headed straight toward the Garulen ships that had followed them into macrospace.

Reaching above her, she punched a series of codes into the

computer. "Com, jettison converter," she shouted above the blaring sirens.

She held their course steady, her eyes trained on the Garulen ships growing on the viewscreen. She slowed the ship, and with a gut-twisting lurch, the ship released the converter.

She nearly stood on the pedals, pushing the auxiliary engines into overdrive as she flipped them straight back and over, then twisted around until the tiny planet that offered their only hope of salvation swung into the viewscreen once more.

"View, 180 degrees." The screen switched so Cyani could see what was happening behind them. They needed enough distance from the converter. It glowed like a tiny white and orange veined ball of blue fire in the blackness of space.

"Hold on, keep it running, baby," she whispered to the ship as the Garulen ships tried to pull up to avoid the converter.

With a flash of brilliant white, the converter exploded. The cockpit went still for a fraction of a second, then the deafening *boom* rocked the ship. The force of the energy wave shook them with a ferocity that beat Cyani into her seat, the straps of her flight harness battering her shoulders and waist.

The ship tumbled out of control on the energy wave, cartwheeling toward the planet.

"View, zero!" she screamed as the view switched, not that it did her much good. She fought to stabilize the ship, battling with the controls as the brilliant star, the heart of the system, blazed through the screen.

Turning their nose up and out, she managed to stop the spinning and roll the ship back toward their goal. Checking the sensors, she didn't see the Union ships. Hoping the energy wave tumbled the Union ships as well, she stood on the thrusters again, determined to power them to safety.

Warning: Fuel levels are low.

"*Shakt!*" Cyani slowed the ship and pulled the nose toward the horizon as the planet loomed before them. She surfed the edge of the atmosphere for a minute before dropping the ship through the fire into the embrace of the planet.

"We overshot the Union outpost. I'm going to have to bring the ship down in the middle of nowhere." She spared a glance at Soren, who looked pale as death. "Where is Vicca?"

"I don't know."

Her heart dropped into her boots. She didn't have time to worry about her fox. They were going to crash, and they were going to hit hard if she couldn't slow them down. The ship screamed through the planet's atmosphere, red fire licking over the viewscreen.

The sweeping plains of the planet rushed toward them as Cyani tried to level off and bring the ship to a hover before dropping them to the ground. Her ears popped with a sharp pain that lanced down into her throat as the ship wobbled through the air. Using the force shields as a buffer, she dipped them low to the ground. The right thruster gave out.

A strange, paralyzing calm came over Cyani as she closed her eyes. She didn't hear the metal crushing around her, didn't feel the shattering glass abrade her skin.

She remembered her mother's eyes, bright gold; they'd shone in the darkness that constantly surrounded them. Now that she knew Soren, Cyani couldn't help associating the catlike gaze of her mother with fear. Her mother never showed fear—did she feel it? Would she be ashamed that her daughter felt it now?

She pictured her brother's boyish face, his dark green eyes and waving iridescent black hair, so like their father's. His smile, that ever-present about-to-start-a-fire-that-brings-down-the-world smile. He was her twin. She had never known a moment of existence without him. Even if his presence was only in her heart.

Is this what it is like to die?

Are these the things people think about?

"I'm sorry," she whispered.

The bone-crushing sound of the ship's destruction shook her as the cockpit ripped away from the rest of the ship and tumbled across the savannah.

THE BLACKNESS SURROUNDED HIM. SOREN TRIED TO STRUGGLE AGAINST IT. He had to escape it.

I have to escape.

Panic rose in his heart like a wild animal. He thrashed against his restraints, the pain in his body nearly unbearable.

Then, like a cool breeze on his face, the familiar, overwhelming sense of calm stole through him.

"Lakal?" he whispered.

It couldn't be. Lakal was dead. Lakal couldn't be controlling his fear, but he'd known that mind-touch for years. He would never forget the feel of it. It was Lakal. He was near.

"Lakal, are you there?" Soren called. He felt the flush of hope and joy rush through his heart.

If he could feel Lakal, it could only mean one thing. He was dead, too.

How could death be so painful?

Soren groaned as he opened his eyes. Crushed and ripped metal surrounded him, pressing against his side as he hung suspended in his flight restraints.

They'd crashed. He was still alive.

The pungent scent of scorched earth and metal reached his nose as an ominous black liquid seeped from one of the crushed control panels. Flecks of blood spattered over everything.

"Cyani?" he called, turning his head to the side in spite of the sharp pain in his neck.

She lay lifeless, a dark stain of blood seeping through her hair.

"Cyani!" He ripped at his flight restraints. Fear tore his heart and lungs like a starving wolf at a carcass. He worked his body free of his restraints, and pulled his leg out from the crushed metal. A jagged edge ripped through the muscle of his calf, but he didn't care. His heart pounded so fiercely, he could think of nothing else but the terror of losing her now.

Sunlight burned through a large hole in the twisted wreckage as Soren carefully unlatched Cyani's flight harness and brushed bits of broken glass from her hair. He could feel her faint breath against his cheek.

Placing a palm on her breast, he felt her heart beating. It seemed weak to him, unsteady, but she was alive.

"I'm going to get you out of here," he promised. "We're going to make it."

With tremendous care, he lifted her out of her seat, and managed to pull them both through the hole.

The intensity of the sunlight seared Soren's eyes. He

squinted at a sea of grassland. Small fires burned around the wreckage of the ship, making the heat in the dry air undulate.

The wreckage had gouged a huge chunk out of the red soil, creating a decent fire barrier. Soren limped to the shaded side of the destroyed cockpit. Hot blood poured down his leg, but he ignored the burning pain as he cradled Cyani against his chest.

"We are going to get through this," he whispered to her. "I promise."

Once again, he felt the calming touch of Lakal. It simultaneously confused him and kept him focused. He looked up, scanning the endless grasses, then placed Cyani on the ground with delicate care.

Peeling off his shirt, he tore strips of the material to tie over the deep cut on her brow and bandage his leg.

"Wake up," he ordered. "I need you to wake for me."

She didn't open her eyes, but her breathing hitched.

Soren ran his fingertips over her face. "Don't leave me," he whispered. "I can't do this without you."

He bent over her and brushed a kiss on her forehead, then over her lips.

"I can't," he murmured against her lips. He kissed her deeply, pouring his fear and his desperation into the caress, hoping it would wake her. With the drugs in his system, his kiss had to be potent enough to wake her. Her lips felt too soft, too yielding. It terrified him. She had to wake. She had to. Any moment she'd open her eyes and slap him.

He pulled away, careful to watch for any sign that she might recover. She sighed. Her eyelids fluttered, then remained closed.

Soren looked up at the endless blue lavender sky. There was nothing else he could do. In that moment, he felt more alone and helpless than he ever had in his tortured and chained existence.

Calm. He couldn't panic. Cyani needed him.

On the breeze he heard a faint yelp.

"Vicca," Soren gasped.

Half limping, half hopping on his good leg, he struggled over the ripped soil to the largest hunk of fuselage.

"Vicca!" he called as loudly as he could. A desperate bark echoed inside the ship.

Soren squeezed through a tear in the hull, and blinked in the shadowy darkness of the wrecked ship.

"Vicca, come," he called.

The fox whined in pain.

Using the sound to guide him, he lifted a large sheet of metal beneath a mangled control panel.

The fox struggled toward him, but one of her front legs was badly broken, the bone pushing through the skin. She collapsed, yowling in pain. Blood stained her fur pink, and her bright eyes looked glassy and distant.

"Easy girl," he murmured to her, scooping her up out of the wreckage. "I've got you. You're going to be okay."

She whimpered as she struggled to lick his face then settled on licking his bloody hand. Holding her as gingerly as he could, he fought his way out of the wreckage and limped back to the place where he left Cyani.

She remained unconscious.

Feeling his heart drop into his stomach, he placed the fox next to her master.

A shadow rippled over the golden grasses. Soren looked up. Large black birds circled overhead.

What was he going to do?

Stumbling away from Cyani and Vicca, he cried out to the endless savannah before him.

"Help me," he shouted. "Someone, please . . ." He collapsed to his knees. The sunlight seared the bare skin of his shoulders. "Help me," he whispered, not in the language of his captors, not in the language of his home, but in the language of his lost friend. Why did he speak Makkolen? He didn't have the energy to think about it. The language comforted him, made him feel less alone. It always had.

He lifted his head. An overpowering sense of urgency rushed through him. He had to move. He knew which direction. He didn't know how, but he knew.

Soren dragged his broken body through the swaying grasses, compelled by a desperation that seemed outside of him. He squinted into the bright sunlight. Ahead, a naked, emaciated man walked away from him, strolling easily through the tall grass. Deep brown ringed spots covered his bony back, and his ragged hair shone red in the blazing sun. He seemed hazy in the heat rising off the ground, surreal. The man looked back over his shoulder toward Soren and smiled.

"Lakal?" Soren gasped in disbelief.

The image shimmered and changed as the starved slave's body grew with strength and vigor. Clothing appeared on him, and his hair swept up into an intricate braided pattern. He nodded to Soren then turned back to his path. Rich, warm laughter echoed over the empty plain as the man sprinted away, disappearing into the waving sea of gold.

"Lakal, wait," Soren shouted after him. It couldn't be. His heart felt like it was about to burst from his chest. All his pain, confusion, and guilt felt like a storm within him. He must be delirious. Death was coming. He had to save Cyani. He pushed himself to his feet, and in spite of the tearing pain in his leg and blistering sun on his back, he managed to run.

Tears streamed out of his burning eyes as he jogged forward. Soren could taste the bitter blood in his parched mouth as he limped along, losing strength.

"Where are you?" he called. He no longer cared if he was sane or not. He desperately needed his friend. "I need your help. I can't let her die."

He crumpled into a heap on the ground. With determination born of pain, he tried to pull himself back to his feet, but he couldn't. "I can't let her die," he whispered again, clenching his hands on the hot, hard ground.

A low growl rumbled through the grasses.

Soren lifted his head.

The bright amber eyes of a white lioness stared directly into his. Her tongue slowly swiped over her large jowls, displaying her deadly fangs.

Soren managed to struggle into a low crouch. The lioness's rumbling growl rolled through her throat as she stalked closer.

Soren gathered his will and projected the light through his eyes.

He took a deep breath as the lioness collapsed in a deep sleep. He heard a rustle behind him.

"*Lhiri!* What did you do to her?" a strange voice demanded. He spoke Lakal's language. Confusion stunned Soren for a moment.

Suddenly pain ripped through his scalp as he felt himself pulled up to his knees by his hair. The cool touch of sharp stone at his throat forced him to hold still.

"Who are you, and what are you doing here?" the stranger demanded. Soren felt the push to answer, along with a forced blanket of paralyzing fear. It was not his fear. He did not fear death. It was a projected feeling. And this time it was not Lakal, but another like him. Another Makkolen. The man was another Makkolen.

"Help her, she's dying," Soren gasped.

"Who?" he demanded.

"At the ship."

Pain exploded in his head as a hard blow crashed into the back of his head, and the world turned black once more.

SOREN WOKE SLOWLY. HIS HEAD SPUN, AND HE COULDN'T MAKE OUT HIS SURroundings through his blurred vision. He was someplace cool, not dark, but shaded and sheltered. He felt the heavy influence of calm in the room. Every thought came slowly, carefully into his mind. He was not alone.

"Ah, you wake," a deep voice commented. Soren tried to make out the speaker, but could barely lift his head. "Drink this, as much as you can bear."

He felt a hand lift his head and cool liquid spill over his parched lips. Soren drank deeply before he could fight the powerful influence enough to be suspicious. The tangy drink unfurled within him. His body began to heat from the inside out. His vision cleared, and much of the pain lifted.

Sitting beside him was a man with a broad, kind face and patient sienna eyes.

"Cyani," Soren choked out. "What did you do to her?"

"Drink, regain your strength." The man tipped the bowl again to force Soren to drink. "Your woman is sleeping in the hammock above you. Our animal healer is taking care of your strange dog-cat. She was badly injured. And my son is taking care of the bites on his hands, for he was also injured by your dog-cat." The man chuckled. "She is very willful, quite difficult to influence, and my son did not approach any of you in the most compassionate manner. He apologizes. This is a place of peace. We will not harm you."

Soren took the bowl and struggled to his knees. He couldn't think of anything until he saw Cyani. He pulled himself up to the edge of the hammock from the soft bed of blankets and pillows on the ground beside it.

Cyani slept peacefully with her dark green hair spilling around her bare shoulders. Soren reached out and stroked her hair, then let his hand trail over a dark bruise on her jaw. She sighed, but did not stir.

A translucent sheet of cloth draped haphazardly over her creamy flesh, barely masking her nudity. His gaze swept over each smooth curve of muscle, lingering on the soft rosy shadows of her nipples.

The hair rose on the back of Soren's neck as the hormones in his blood raged with sudden fire. He turned on the other man in the room, his instincts demanding he drive him from her.

The man stood to an imposing height as the room suddenly filled with an overwhelming sense of ease and peace. Soren's possessive instincts didn't put up much of a fight against the influence of the telepath. The man within him didn't want to.

"Easy," the Makkolen murmured as if he were talking to a feral predator. "We have not harmed your woman, and I have not touched her. Lai," he called.

A woman stepped into the small room. Tall and regal, her long copper and gold hair fell in waves of fire around her proud, spotted shoulders. She wore a gauzy dress that clung to matronly curves and left little to the imagination. Around her neck hung an intricate web of a necklace composed of tiny carved beads. A bonding necklace, Lakal had described them to him. The necklace was far more beautiful than he had imagined.

The woman assessed him slowly, then stepped in front of the man and elegantly sat on an animal skin in the center of the room. She folded her long legs underneath her and continued to watch him with knowing eyes and a cool, intrigued expression.

"This is Lai, my queen. She's been caring for your woman. Now, I have questions for you." The man sat on a stool next to his mate, placing his large hands on her bronzed shoulders.

"I apologize," Soren offered. "I'm more beast than man."

"Well then you are lucky that we are adept at taming beasts," Lai said through a smile. "You're in shock. Don't apologize. You've done no harm. Drink. The kiltii water will help you heal quickly."

Soren took another deep draught from the bowl as he looked around the small one-room clay hut. Soft light filtered in through a red cloth hanging before a small window. The heady aroma of afternoon sun on the dried grass roof infused the air with rich spice that surrounded him like a lingering fog.

Painted figures of men, women, and animals danced over the walls in bold patterns of black and white, while a lush, deep green vine clung to the clay. Delicate white blooms released a citrus fragrance that perfumed the sweet, clean air. One blossom remained curled tight in a neat bud. Soren breathed on his fingers then touched it. It opened in greeting.

He looked down at his hands. They were clean—even his nails had been scrubbed. His whole body felt cool and fresh, his hair damp, his wounds dressed with white cloth. He finally noticed he was naked once more, with a thin sheet twisted around his waist. He was so used to existing in a state of nudity, he hadn't even noticed.

"Who are you?" Soren asked the man. His dark auburn hair faded to gold at the ends of long braids woven intricately into a headdress of dried grass. Fading silver brushed his temples, but his strong bare chest bore no concession to age.

"King Lirkam," the man answered, circling his hand in a way that implied Soren should drink even more, even though his gut felt swollen with the water. "Who are you, star flyer? And tell me how you managed to carry the soul of one of our warriors home to us."

"Star flyer? I don't understand." Soren's head was spinning. This was Makko; they had landed on Makko.

"You're not one of the dark swarm, though you came here in their ship. You wore the clothing of a star flyer." The king rubbed the shoulders of his queen as she reached up and covered his hand with her own. He was talking about the Garulen, the dark swarm. Star flyers must be the Union.

"I'm not a star flyer," he tried to explain. "I was a slave, taken from my world by the dark swarm. A star flyer saved me. We escaped. We landed here."

"Your woman is the star flyer. I see." The king rocked back on the carved stool he perched on. "How do you speak our language?"

"Another slave, taken from here by the dark swarm, he was my friend, my brother. Lakal."

The king nodded, but the queen looked stricken. "My son saw a spirit on the plains. He followed it and found you."

Soren knit his brow. While he had talked much with Lakal about their homes, they rarely discussed death. It always felt too close to them. "I don't understand."

It was the queen who offered an explanation. "Our spirits have the ability to attach to those they love. Your friend led you here, and you carried him home. He is free now. For that we're in your debt. What is your name, brother?"

"Soren," he said, spreading his hands in greeting, then touching his fist to his heart, mouth, then forehead in the way of the Makkolen. His mind was reeling. How was this possible? Unless . . .

He'd continued to feel Lakal's presence after his friend's murder. Lakal insisted it wasn't the end with his dying breath. What force brought Vicca to his dark prison and kept her there? Why had Cyani decided to try to land here? Had Lakal's spirit guided all of these things?

He shook his head in wonder and disbelief as he looked up at the ceiling. The heavy weight of his guilt for Lakal's death eased, replaced by the bittersweet longing of missing his friend. He could bear that ache.

"About your woman," the king mentioned, changing the subject. "Her injuries were severe. You must force her to drink as much of the kiltii water as you can through the night until she wakes."

"She's not my woman," Soren tried to explain, but the king waved a dismissive hand.

"I've had purple eyes myself," he chuckled, leaning forward and kissing his mate on the hair. "My daughter has agreed to stay with her sister for a time so you and your woman who is not your woman may remain in this home until you are well."

"What role will we play here then?" he asked, trying not to let his suspicion darken his voice. He knew these people had no means of contacting the Union. They were stuck here, for better or worse. Their only chance for survival rested in the hands of the king.

"We shall see." The king stood and motioned to clothing left on a bench near the door. "These are for you. Bear them with honor and strength. You are welcome here as one of my family." The king pushed the heavy cloth hanging over the door aside and stepped out into the burning sunlight beyond. The queen followed, leaving him alone with Cyani.

He turned to her and brushed his hand over her silky hair.

She was all he had left. He'd care for her until she was well, then they'd do what they'd always done—find a way to survive.

Gratitude mixed with his fear as he dipped a small bowl into a squat, carved vessel filled with the kiltii water. Easing down on the hammock next to Cyani, he surveyed the contents of a large wooden platter laden with roasted meat, fruit, and crumbling flat bread. The hammock swayed with his added weight, rocking them gently.

He cradled her head in the cup of his hand so he could tip water past her full lips. Closing his eyes, he tried to focus with the violet spreading through his blood. He could feel it, the bright fire. His heart raced as he tried to fight back the beast it stirred within him.

The water dribbled over Cyani's lips as she remained limp and still.

There was nothing hard or cold about her now. He held his breath as he let his gaze wander over her body. The sheet had fallen away from one of her soft breasts. He stared, unable to stop himself. The violet rush of arousal coursed through his blood. His head throbbed with it while his muscles felt loose and tight at the same time. Great glory, his fascination consumed him. Like an addict, he couldn't stop staring at her. Before he was taken, he had lived alone in his new garden. The only women he'd ever seen were his younger sister and his mother, and he'd never seen a woman naked.

Men were comparatively ugly. Where he was hard, she was all soft, pale skin and smooth, flowing muscle. The lines of her body reminded him of drifts of gentle snow. Never in his life had he ever seen anything more beautiful.

Hard and aching, he let his gaze slip down one long sleek leg that had pushed out from under the sheet. Her calf bore the same striking blue hue as her forearms, and the dancing vine meandered below her knee and around her ankle, just as it did with her elbows and wrists.

The sides of her leg carried slashing scars, whip burns. He had seen enough scars like them in his captivity. He traced the edge of one. Her leg twitched, and he withdrew his hand. What had she endured to become such an efficient killer? Was it ever really in her nature? With tender care, he covered her as best he could, tucking the sheet over her shoulder.

He forced himself to concentrate on the dark and ugly bruises staining the creamy skin of her shoulder and hip. He unwound a bandage from his wrist so he would have a bit of cloth to dip in the water and bathe her.

Frozen with shock, he stared at the wounds on his wrists. They'd been caked with cracked scabs. Now smooth pink scars wrapped around his wrists. As he watched, the bruises from his shackles dissipated like a dark cloud pierced by the sun.

He took another long drink of the water then ripped off the bandage on his calf. The flesh knitted together, mending the fresh wound right before his eyes. He had never seen anything like it.

She had to drink.

"Cyani," he whispered, leaning closer to her. He could feel the heat of her naked skin through the thin sheet that barely separated his body from hers. "Cyani, wake for me."

He drank the water then kissed her soft lips. With delicate attention, he caressed them with his teeth, his tongue. He had to make her respond to him, only enough to drink.

With his body screaming at him to cover her, enter her, sink into her until he no longer knew himself, he leashed his passion, focusing on breathing life into her instead.

"Wake," he whispered against her lips. "Drink for me."

She moaned.

He quickly lifted the bowl to her swollen lips and poured the water across them one more time. This time she drank.

Relief rushed through him as warming and powerful as the magical water. He forced her to drink as much as he could before releasing her and sliding off the hammock.

The tension in his body thrummed as he tried to cool off. He dipped his hands in the water and rubbed them over his face and shoulders. He shouldn't touch her like that, no matter how right it felt. He couldn't touch her again until she woke. He didn't know how far he would go, and that frightened him.

Once again, he cursed the drugs in his system. At least he'd never have to bear them again. They were lost now, crushed somewhere beneath the wreckage of the ship. His only means of survival swayed in the soft hammock, asleep and unaware of how much he needed her.

9

THE AIR SMELLED DIFFERENT THAN SHE REMEMBERED.

"Cyani?" a familiar voice asked. It was him.

"Soren?" She blinked and tried to sit up, but a slicing pain lanced through her temple. With a groan she fell back. The whole room swayed. No, she swayed. She watched the thatched grass roof above her swing back and forth as she pulled herself up again. She was in a hammock? Where were they? What happened?

Soren leapt up from the corner of the small red-clay hut. He dropped a plank of food and scooped up Vicca.

"Vicca!" *Oh, thank the glorious Matriarchs she's alive.* Cyani grasped for her scout, her relief pounding in her aching heart. A hard clay cast wrapped around Vicca's front leg, but she was alive. How could Cyani ever make it without her? With furious energy, her fox licked her nose. Cyani buried her face in her little girl's fur, so desperately grateful that she had survived.

"Careful of her hip," Soren cautioned as Vicca curled up on her chest and purred so loudly, Cyani could feel the vibration of it in her toes. "We were all soundly beaten in the crash, but she's healing fast."

"What happened? Where are we?" She fought to remember, but the last thing she could recall was coming in hard for a landing on the wastelands of Makko. How did she end up clean, sheltered, and—oh merciful Creator, she was naked.

She clutched at the thin sheet wrapped around her bare flesh and tried to sit up in the hammock without losing her only protection from Soren's smoldering blue violet eyes.

Soren rose slowly. She barely recognized him. The thick streaks of color in his hair gleamed in the warm light seeping through a small window. The front had been twisted and intricately braided to hold his hair from his face. No longer covered with filth, his golden skin glowed, his stripes rippling over powerful muscles beneath a woven red vest. His scabs and wounds from the shackles and bands had disappeared, leaving pale pink scars in their wake.

Her eyes followed the smooth muscles of his abdomen down to the waistline of a loose leather kilt slung low around his lean hips. It fell to just above his knees. A bandage wrapped around one strong calf, but it didn't seem to hurt him as he pulled a stool carved into the shape of some sort of ape to the edge of the hammock. He sat next to her, placing the tray of food on his lap.

"How are you feeling?" his low voice rumbled. It sent a shiver down her spine as an uneasy tingling raced over her skin. He tenderly placed his palm on her forehead then slid it back over her hair.

"I . . . uh," she stuttered, sinking back down into the hammock. He was potent before. Now he was beautiful, beautiful and dangerous as the Xalen tiger he reminded her of. "I feel fine."

No, she wasn't fine. Keeping her distance from him had been hard enough when he had reminded her of a wounded soldier. Now he looked like some pagan god. She felt her control slipping away, like sand between her fingers.

"What do you remember?" he asked.

"The energy converter exploded, but I managed to steer the stingship to Makko. We crashed in the middle of nowhere."

"Not exactly." Soren smiled as green sparkled in his dark eyes. "As it turned out, we landed near this village. Lakal was from this planet. The tribe has welcomed us here as their guests."

Cyani adjusted her ear set. She couldn't believe what she was hearing, and she couldn't find her eyepiece. She needed it. It was a small barrier, but a barrier all the same. "You speak their language?"

"Yes. You must be hungry. The plant they use to heal works miraculously fast, but it stimulates the body into using massive energy and resources. I've done nothing but eat since yesterday afternoon." Soren lifted the plank of food so she could reach it.

"How long have I been unconscious?" *And naked*, she wanted to add, but decided against mentioning her nudity.

She picked up a large chunk of juicy meat and tasted it.

Heavenly. It tasted so good, she didn't even bother to question what animal it came from.

"For a day and a half."

By the glory of Ona the Pure, she was in trouble. She had to think about something else.

"How is Vicca healing? Will her leg be sound? And what is wrong with her hip?" Cyani asked between bites of meat and tasting a strange blue fruit. Her hunger writhed like a living thing. She couldn't stop eating. Vicca tried to steal the piece of fruit from her fingers. Cyani smoothed her hand down Vicca's striped back to keep her down.

"Her cast should come off the day after tomorrow, and her hip is just sore from being dislocated. She'll be fine. You managed to get us all off that asteroid alive." Soren held out a chunk of meat to the fox.

Cyani huffed through a half smile. "Barely."

Soren chuckled. "What do you know about the Makkolen people?"

"Not much. They're primitive, but they're highly prized slaves. They're worth more than me, though less than you, I'd imagine. The Union doesn't know why. We only know that in spite of our presence in this star system, the Garulen, and occasionally the Kronalen, try to raid this planet." Cyani continued to pick things off the platter, feeling relaxed and comfortable.

There was an easy feeling in the atmosphere, a feeling of happiness floating over everything. It didn't make sense. She tucked Vicca up closer to her breasts as she crossed her legs in embarrassment. She should not feel so at ease, but she did, and that contradiction put her on edge.

"The Makkolen are more powerful than you think," Soren explained. "The Union has dismissed them because they don't use technology. They don't need it. I don't think they want it. They're perfectly adapted for their world. They're proud of their traditions and their planet, but they are by no means defenseless."

"Explain. Does this have to do with their psychic ability?" She focused on Soren, trying to maintain her concentration when her body wanted her to ease back into a comfortable sleep. Her eyes slipped over his smooth chest, no longer marred by dark bruises. Maybe she shouldn't focus on Soren.

"Yes." Soren picked up a roasted bird leg. At least, she thought it was a bird leg.

"They can control minds?" Cyani tried tucking herself deeper into the hammock.

"Not exactly. They influence emotion. They can project whatever mood they want on any higher order creature they come in contact with."

"I don't understand." They could affect people's moods?

"They can make you feel happy, sad, calm, irate, afraid, whatever they want, even if it's irrational. This talent has made them powerful animal tamers. It's the only way to survive on a planet like this, overrun with fast prey and dangerous predators. The slavers use them to quell uprisings, and"—Soren scowled—"keep valuable property submissive."

"That's what your friend was forced to do to you, isn't it?" Cyani asked as gently as she could. She felt sick for him. What a terrible betrayal both Soren and Lakal must have borne, and yet they still forged a true brotherhood.

"Yeah, the extractor wouldn't have worked otherwise.

When they killed him during our escape attempt, they killed their only hope of controlling me. That's why they were trying to sell me to Krona. They weren't strapping me into that extractor again without someone losing their life, even with the tranquilizers." Soren picked at a bit of meat hanging on the bone.

"Why tell me all of this?" Cyani asked.

"I'm afraid with your superiority complex, you'll dismiss the power they wield," he admitted. He placed his hand on hers. She stared at it, but for the first time, she didn't try to pull away. His electric touch was the only thing that seemed familiar and real to her. "You were concerned that I could control your thoughts through hypnosis. These people can, Cyani. We are guests of the king and queen, but . . ." Soren looked like he was torn by something. "Don't underestimate these people, and stay close to me."

Apprehension slithered down her shoulders. How could she trust people who could control her mind? What choice did she have? The foggy haze of comfortable humor stole back into her mind. It was wrong; she shouldn't be lighthearted. It was these people's influence. She recognized the manipulation, but she was too tired to block it out.

"I do not have a superiority complex," she protested, then reluctantly pulled her hand back.

Soren laughed.

"I do not!" She picked up a chunk of rind and flicked it at him.

"Fine," he placated in a taunting tone. "You have a goddess complex."

"Enough, you're impossible." Cyani grinned. "I can't help

what I am." The easy feeling in the air was infectious, and for now, she decided it wasn't worth the effort to fight it. "Soren?"

"What is it?" he asked, sobering immediately.

"You got the three of us here on your own, didn't you? Vicca and I, you saved our lives." She looked up at him as his eyes darkened to an even deeper blue violet.

"I had some help." His ears flushed as he looked away from her.

"Thank you." She reached out and almost touched his shoulder, but stopped just short of her fingertips brushing his skin. She drew her hand back in and curled it against her chest.

"It was nothing," he mumbled.

"*Now* who is the one who can't accept praise?" she teased, and smiled at him.

Soren stood and placed the platter on the stool. Without a word, he crossed the room.

"Are you strong enough to dress?" he asked with his back to her. He picked up a bundle of clothing and carried it to the hammock.

She felt dizzy, tired and sick, but the promise of the security of some real clothing was too much for her to ignore. She tucked Vicca into a nook in the pillows and carefully swung her feet out of the hammock.

She stood slowly, but the spinning wave of blood rushing from her head stole the power from her legs, and her knees buckled. She nearly blacked out again. It was too soon.

Soren caught her and pulled her into his powerful body.

Ona forgive me, she silently prayed. Cyani clung to the warm muscles of his arms as her bare breasts pressed against his addictive skin. A soft pull throbbed in her breasts as her nipples tightened. The sheet slipped lower, barely hanging on her hips. It was the only thing separating her naked body from the electric power of his.

This was too much contact. Overwhelmed by him, she stood frozen, horrified and mystified at the same time.

The air burst into swirling color around her as his touch alone brought her into the next level of consciousness. She couldn't breathe, couldn't think as she stared up into his blazing violet eyes. He held his breath as well. His body hummed with tension, the vibration of it trembling under her palms. She could see it in a quivering, hot indigo aura around him.

Not knowing what to do, she stood there, clinging to him. She would have fallen without his firm support. Mercy of the Matriarchs, now she knew why this was forbidden.

Damn this blood.

She let her hand slip down his arm to brace against his forearm, and she breathed in. His scent enshrouded her in sweet promise and carnal spice.

He eased her down onto the stool as she wrapped her arms around her breasts. Even that touch was nearly too much to bear as her body felt heavy and flooded. An aching throb pulsed deep within her core, urging her to move closer to him, to dance to some primal beat common to all women. More than anything, she felt a longing to be complete that came with an awareness of how empty she was inside.

She was going to die.

She trembled. Her hair slipped over the sensitized skin of her shoulder. Overwhelmed, she felt her consciousness slip for a moment. She tried to gather her strength. Fainting was out of the question.

Soren slipped behind her, and with tender care, lifted one arm away from her heavy breast. She couldn't fight; she was too tired, too weak to resist. She closed her eyes and let his hand guide her body.

She felt soft but stiff cloth slide over her arm and wrap around her back as Soren tucked her arm back around her exposed chest, and pushed her other arm through the hole of a vest sleeve.

Her relief overwhelmed her as she clung to the edges of the tight vest, and pulled them closed over her naked breasts. She didn't dare open her eyes as she felt Soren's fingertips brush her as he laced it together with a strip of leather.

Cyani let herself breathe as she slowly opened her eyes. She looked down at the vest pulled tight over her chest. It stopped at the top of her ribs, leaving her midriff exposed. A black pattern of interlocked animals snaked over the shoulders and down around the edge of her breasts, making them look round and full, pressed together above the low-cut neckline.

Soren shook out a thick skirt, made of many layers of floating red, orange, and cinnamon cloth. He wrapped it around her waist and the stool, and buckled it with a carved wooden clasp on her left hip. The skirt fell away from her leg at the slit, exposing her skin from her calf to her hip up that side.

She had never worn clothing that had left her feeling so naked. Weak and shivering, she felt like her mind and body had just practiced branch-falls through the canopy.

"Are there any undergarments?" she asked, pulling the sheet out from under the skirt as Soren carefully strapped a sandal around her ankle. His warm palm cradled her calf as his fingers brushed over her tattoo. A shiver raced up her spine and ran down her arms. This was all too much. No one had ever cared for her. When injured, she had to tend her own wounds. The reverent way he met her needs made her feel so humble, and no longer alone.

He chuckled as he turned his glowing gaze back to her. It had dimmed, but not by much. "I don't think the Makkolen have a word for *undergarments*."

"How are we going to get out of here?" she asked, her head still reeling. At least the iridescent colors had faded from the room. She looked around the small, comfortable space. A rumpled bed of furs and pillows rested on the floor. Soren must have slept there. The thought comforted her. He had respected her space while she was unconscious.

Near the bed, a lush vine grew up and into the red-clay wall by the door. It bloomed with white star-shaped flowers, very similar to the ciera vines tattooed on her arms and legs. Several tendrils of the vine grew up toward the roof on one side, but on the other reached down toward Soren's bed. On that side, the blossoms coated the vine, bursting from every centimeter of the dark foliage.

"We're not going anywhere until I'm sure you're completely healed," he said as he brought her a bowl full of water. He picked a couple of blossoms and dropped them onto the surface before handing her the bowl. "Drink this," he insisted. "This vine has extraordinary healing properties. You'll feel hot and hungry, but the last of those bruises should fade away." He reached out and touched her jaw with the tips of his fingers then let his hand drop.

Cyani drank the cool, flavorful water. The more she drank, the more she craved, as wave after wave of soothing heat rushed through her body. She felt stronger, her head clearer, but ravenously hungry again. Choosing a round yellow fruit from the plank of food, she took a hasty bite straight through the rind. As she choked on her mistake, she pulled the rind out through her teeth.

"What was the condition of the ship?" she mumbled with her mouth full. Her com didn't have enough power to transmit to the nearby base, but if the power supply to the central communication system was still intact, she might be able to send a distress code. If that failed, perhaps she could integrate her com signal into a beacon, but she wasn't sure if that signal was strong enough to reach the Union forces either.

Soren took a deep breath as he picked up Vicca and reclined on the bed of furs. He let Vicca drink from a bowl as he rubbed her back. "I don't know what state the ship's in now. The cockpit separated from the rest of the wreckage. The hull was crushed. There were grass fires all around. It's probably burned."

"What happened to my eyepiece?" she asked.

Soren frowned, his dark expression saying far more than his colorful eyes. "It fell off. I'm sorry I was too busy trying to revive you to save your blighted eyepiece."

"Take it easy, I'm just trying to assess our situation," she defended, wiping some sticky juice from her chin. "What do you have against my eyepiece anyway?"

"I can't see your face when you wear it." He picked up a large oblong nut and crushed it in his hand.

"Soren?" She slid off the stool so she could look him in the eye.

"What?"

"Where are the drugs?" she asked.

He let out an aggravated breath and fed the crushed nut to Vicca. "I don't know."

"How long will the drugs in your system last?" She tried to keep her tone soft and comforting. He was on the edge, and she didn't want to push him over.

"Another three or four days, then they'll probably be at the same level they were when you first found me," he admitted as he let Vicca lick the remains of the nut off the palm of his hand.

"And how long would you survive after that?" She needed to know, and she hated to know at the same time.

"I don't know. Days, weeks, it depends." He tucked Vicca into a nest of pillows by the wall and stood. He studied the vine as the small white flowers seemed to turn their faces toward him.

"We need to return to the ship." She pushed to her feet, trying to hide the sudden rush of dizziness that nearly overcame her. She had been in worse shape. She could do this. She had to. "If I can send out a distress signal, the Union forces on Delta Eighty-four's base can rescue us, and we can get you home. In the meantime, we can look for the drugs . . ."

"Enough," Soren commanded as he towered over her. "We're not going anywhere. Vicca is injured, there are dangerous beasts on the savannah, and even if we find the wreck, there's nothing left of the ship that can help us."

Cyani stood and glared up at him as she stepped toward him. "We have to try."

He placed a hand on her shoulder and ran it over the dark bruise marring her skin. "We have to heal."

She shrugged her shoulder away from his touch. His eyes flashed his dark gray disappointment. He selected a mottled scarlet and ginger cloth from a bench and let the silk flow through his hands. He shook it open then brought it around her back. With careful attention he placed it on her head, and wrapped the sides over her shoulders.

"It will protect your skin from the sun," he explained. "Come on, I want to introduce you to the king and queen. They've been very anxious about your health."

Cyani adjusted the shimmering drape so it covered her bare shoulders and her cleavage. Unfortunately it wasn't long enough to wrap around her midriff. She placed a self-conscious hand over her belly button and stepped toward the door.

On Azra, the Elite were only allowed to expose the bare skin of their arms in public. Everything else had to remain covered. With her current costume, very little wasn't exposed. She felt like any opponent had a clear target on her deepest vulnerabilities. A shiver raced over her shoulders. Soren was one thing. They had nearly died together, and he was the closest thing she had to a friend. If he had seen her exposed, the unease she felt at the thought was tempered by her trust in him. An entire village of strangers staring at her exposed body was something else entirely. Their conversation about escaping wasn't over, but she would let it drop, for now, as she tried to figure out a way to protect herself. "Yes, I'd like to meet the queen and thank her for her generous hospitality and for healing Vicca."

Soren drew back the cloth hanging over the doorway and led her out into the sun.

It took a moment for Cyani's eyes to adjust to the bright light. She could feel the heat seep into her sore muscles. For the moment, it felt soothing, but she was glad for the shawl. After too long, the sun would be blistering hot on her skin.

She blinked as she studied the large village. A bright cacophony of voices and animal grunts, squeals, clucks, and roars blended together like a verse of foreign music. A large wall made of red mud and tall spikes of timber surrounded the squat little huts and the two large lodges on either side of the village.

Towering old trees with dark dry leaves and gnarled limbs shaded a garden and several animal pens. Soren led her toward the far end of the village as she turned this way and that, trying to take everything in. She'd never seen a place so foreign. The canopy of her rainforest home was sterile and white. The leaves and light of the canopy seemed ethereal. This place was raw and untamed. Bathed in shades of fire, it burned with primal instinct.

The huts circled a large clear area, with a carved altar in the center flanked by four enormous totems. Cyani wanted to get a closer look at the tangled carvings, but Soren pulled her toward a large hut on the far side of the courtyard. Were the carvings of people? They seemed to be wrestling.

A fat-bodied bird with stumpy black wings scrambled across their path, trailed by a gaggle of sun-kissed children with red gold hair and leopard spots dotting their necks and shoulders.

Cyani smiled at them. They froze in their tracks and stared at her, full lips agape. Their golden brown eyes lit with curiosity as they watched her.

She withdrew her gaze from them, only to find the rest of the village slowly coming to a standstill as all eyes turned toward them.

"Soren?" Cyani squeezed his tingling palm tighter. She could handle entire squadrons of enemy combatants, but she couldn't handle the natives' piercing eyes. She felt completely naked and exposed. She didn't belong here.

"They're just curious. They've heard about you from the women who tended you, but this is the first they've seen you. You look very exotic to them." He pulled her closer to his side and placed a palm on the small of her bare back. "And very beautiful," he whispered in her ear. She waged a war in her own mind about which was worse, his hand covering her skin, or having the small of her back exposed. For the moment, she tolerated his touch—she needed it. He was safe.

A little girl skipped to Soren and stopped just inches from him. "Your lady star flyer is awake, Brother Soren?" she asked. "Where is her necklace? She is very pretty. Why does she have kiltii flowers on her arms?" Cyani's translator caught the words and repeated them in her ear, but she didn't understand them completely.

"Her name is Cyani. Why don't you introduce yourself?" Soren suggested as he mussed the child's hair.

The little girl studied Cyani with big brown eyes. She blinked once, then threw her dusty hands over her mouth and galloped away, squealing in laughter.

Cyani felt her face flush as she noticed the other Makkolen. A group of young women whispered behind their hands as they watched her. She hated that. The other Elite would whisper about her, too. What were they thinking? How would they judge her? She couldn't silence these women with her skill in battle. Here, she had no power. The hot gaze of a young male burned into her from the shade of a tree. A trickle of fear slid down her spine. She knew that look.

"I think I should go back," she whispered to Soren. He stood like a rock next to her.

"Sounding the retreat?" he teased.

Cyani glared at him. He stood taller, embodying the pagan god of the wild again. The blue flickered brighter in his eyes. What did blue mean?

Cyani turned as a woman and a man walked toward them. Two white lions with pale ringed spots flanked them, the female near the woman, and the enormous male beside the man. Cyani watched the woman approaching with a mix of curiosity and recognition of one of her kind. Power and control rested on her elegant spotted shoulders with the ease of the gauzy dyed cloth draped around her neck. Her copper hair faded to gold at the tips, and she watched Cyani with bright sepia eyes that held wisdom far beyond her years.

The queen smiled. Though she carried the air of authority the Grand Sister displayed back in the Halls of Azra, she didn't seem touched by the hardness or raw ambition of Cyani's leader. The queen exuded comfortable confidence and an aura of warm grace.

The king reminded Cyani very much of her father. He seemed to have an easy good will that masked iron strength and resolve. Cyani lowered her head as a sign of respect for both tribe leaders as they came to a halt.

"Welcome to our home as one of us," the king greeted in a booming voice that carried over the entire village. A crowd of onlookers gathered in the shade of one of the trees. "We honor you, star flyer, and our brother Soren for your aid to those of our kind. What is ours, is yours."

The king raised his arms above his head, and a loud cheer erupted from the villagers.

The queen stepped forward and took Cyani's hand. "What is your name, child?" she asked as a warm smile crinkled the edges of her eyes.

"Cyani," she answered, knowing the queen would not be able to understand anything else she said. She suddenly felt her heart slow as an almost drugging sense of calm stole over her. She fought it immediately, turning her mind and her will toward her training. She repeated the chants of the ancients over and over in her head.

"Easy," the queen explained. "My name is Lai, and you are frightened. I wish to help."

"She is a warrior, my queen," Soren interjected. "She commands many in battle with honor and conviction without fear. The unknown is unsettling to her, as she prefers control over herself and her situation."

The sense of calm dissipated, and Cyani took a deep breath. Grateful for his intervention, she stole a brief glance at Soren. "Thank you for your aid, and your generosity," Cyani offered to the king and queen. Soren translated and she continued. "Your world is very new to me."

"Then I will introduce you to our tribe, so you will know us." The queen smiled again and reached out to take Cyani's hands. Cyani tensed, but didn't pull away at the contact. It probably wasn't wise to offend her benefactors. She did her best to return the open smile.

She glanced at a black plume of smoke curling into the bright blue lavender sky. "Is that where the ship wrecked?" she pointed at the smoke.

Soren didn't bother to translate her words. She whapped him lightly across the bicep to get his attention. "Soren, ask them. Is that where the ship wrecked?"

He let out an impatient huff and addressed the king.

"The fires still burn in the grasslands. They could be worse. Tonight a storm will come. It should quell the flames."

She had to return to the ship. She couldn't wait. She would strike out once the sun set. She needed to get a message out to the Union forces. It was her only hope. She couldn't stay. She'd search for her eyepiece and the Garulen drugs and return before Soren even knew she was gone.

10

SOREN WONDERED HOW MANY DIFFERENT WAYS CYANI COULD HIDE HER NAvel as he watched her struggle through the attention and curiosity of the tribe.

He'd never seen her like this. It both concerned and amused him. She'd always been guarded, but now she reminded him once again of a red-ruffed badger digging deeper into her hole. She wasn't baring her fangs yet, but she was on the defensive, and her belly seemed to be her battleground.

Her wrist would linger over her midsection, or sometimes her forearm did the job. Twice she tried to hitch up the skirt, but it fell low on her hips as soon as she released it. She slumped and tugged on the edge of her shawl, but it would not cover that delicious little dimple of flesh.

What was it about her navel that had her feeling exposed? Was it only a cultural thing? Or was it the physical reminder that at one point in her life, she was connected to, and dependant on, another being? Whatever it was, the fact that she was so sensitive about it made him fixate on her smooth stomach and her lovely navel.

Soren shook his head and laughed at himself.

Now was not the time to be picking on her insecurities. He hated to see her uncomfortable, but he was intrigued that she could be so rattled. It made her seem less hard and much more real. He had seen her strong in the face of danger, but to see her try to face a different kind of adversity was enlightening.

He hoped she would let the subject of the wrecked ship drop. They were safe. The Makkolen were a generous and loving people who welcomed them into the family. If she could adapt to this place, if she would bond with him, perhaps their journey could end.

He watched as the queen led her toward the women's house. The large hall loomed over the small huts like a fat mother hen protecting her chicks.

Cyani looked beautiful with her pale creamy skin, lush green hair, and blue accents on her long arms and legs. She reminded him of a pool of fresh clear water on the burning savannah. The Makkolen clothing only accented her toned body and her hidden femininity.

"She is lovely," the prince said, as he approached Soren. Kaln had apologized for hitting him over the head on the savannah, and Soren had quickly befriended the man. "Some of our women choose to join the hunt, and they are always the most desirable."

Soren felt his blood heat with jealousy. "Kaln, I think it is best if we choose another subject to discuss."

"Why?" Kaln pressed with a subtle smile. "You claim she is not your woman."

"She would not choose to be my woman," Soren ground out between clenched teeth.

"I see. That is different then, isn't it?" Kaln laughed. "Would she choose to be my woman?"

Soren struck his hand out and grabbed Kaln by the front of his vest. Kaln wrapped his hands over Soren's and laughed harder. Soren's anger fought the influence, but Kaln's power overcame his instinct and Soren chuckled. The feeling shook his mind and body, but didn't lighten his dark heart. Kaln patted him on the back and released him from the thrall.

"I was only teasing you. Are all of your kind so possessive?" he asked.

"Yes," he laughed with a bit of honest humor instead of Kaln's influence. The rush to fight ebbed and he felt like himself again. "It's why our eyes change color. If we accidentally come in contact with another breeding male, we can see the other's aggression and put each other to sleep before we harm ourselves."

Kaln nodded appreciatively. "If our young men chose to influence each other with calm, instead of provocation, perhaps there would be less broken noses here as well. You come from a highly evolved people, Soren. Come, I hear that there's a boar roasting in the men's house. Your woman will be surrounded by other women, so you can rest easy for now. Eat with me. If the pig isn't done, we can comment on the quality of the fire, and make suggestions on how to tend it better."

Soren laughed openly. He felt warmth expanding his heart. It made him feel larger, whole.

He spared a glance at the women's house as he walked with

Kaln and wondered if Cyani would ever find humor in her situation. She just needed someone to help her sort through this new world. How long would it take before she let him help her?

AFTER FOUR GOURDS OF SOUR MELON WINE, SOREN FELT FAR HAPPIER THAN he could ever remember feeling in his life. Kaln joked with the other men as Soren drank. He laughed freely and with abandon, enjoying the feeling of his spirit growing strong again. He wished Lakal were there, drinking wine and sharing stories of hunting on the savannah and seducing bare-necked women. This was the experience that kept Lakal hopeful and strong, so Soren did his best to use it to honor his friend.

In the corner of his eye, Soren saw a man raise a gourd in salute. He turned, but no one was there.

He must be drunk. *Oh well.* It felt good. It felt free.

"Soren?" Kaln pulled a stool up opposite him. "I've been thinking about our conversation earlier. Do you know how our mating rituals work?"

He would have to bring that up. Without warning, the image of Cyani dancing with wild abandon on a sultry night with her back to a veil of flames flooded his mind. He had to force his reluctant attention back to the prince. The Lankana, Lakal had called it. What did he remember about the ritual?

"I know some. I know that you have fertility festivals four times a year. The women dance and the men give them necklaces signifying a bond. If the woman gets pregnant sometime before the next ritual, the pair remain bonded until the child is weaned."

"That's right," Kaln commented. "But if a woman does not get pregnant, in the infertile time before the festival, she is free to return her necklace and explore new relationships before dancing in the next ritual."

Soren was confused. What did this have to do with anything?

"In the next few days, that time of freedom is upon us. Those women not wearing a necklace can be pursued by those men with a necklace to give," Kaln explained.

Then it hit him.

Cyani.

She didn't have a necklace, and by the tribe's standards, she would be considered free to be pursued by any unbound male. They couldn't touch her. The deep red in his blood ignited once more. He would not let them touch her.

"I've heard things," Kaln whispered to him.

"What did you hear and who said them?" Soren roared as he rushed to his feet and spilled his wine on the sand.

The crowd of men in the large building stilled and stared at him. He could feel a hesitant collective push to calm down.

Kaln placed an arm over his shoulder and led him outside. "It doesn't matter what I heard or who said it," Kaln confided. "Those who speak aren't the same as those who act, but I'm concerned for Cyani. Stay close to your woman. In the next few days, keep her by your side."

Soren shook off Kaln's arm and marched across the village toward the women's house. He knew he should have been grateful for the warning—he was—but at the moment only one thing mattered. He had to find her. An irrational panic fueled by his possessive nature and the wine spurred him on. In the distance the last lingering glow of the setting sun faded on the horizon, throwing the village into a murky dusk as a pair of young men stoked the large fire in the center of the village. Thunder rolled from the dark clouds on the horizon.

"Where's Cyani?" Soren demanded of the young pregnant woman standing at the entrance of the women's house.

The queen emerged with an expression of cool concern. "She left here hours ago. She was exhausted and wanted to sleep. My daughter escorted her to the hut you share."

Soren stormed toward their hut. He had an ill feeling in the pit of his stomach. He threw back the cloth hanging over the door. Vicca stood on her cast and barked at him. The fox was alone.

"Blight, pestilence, and rot!"

He ran to the village gates. "Did the star flyer pass through here?" he asked the men guarding the entrance.

"No, we did not see her."

"She must have scaled the wall." Soren ran a hand over his face. *Of all the blighted things to do* . . . She went back to the ship.

Kaln ran up next to him. "What's going on?"

"Cyani wanted to return to the wrecked ship to send a signal to her people. She left alone. She's out there unprotected."

"Let's go. I'll get Lhiri. We'll find her."

HOW DID THEY EVER SURVIVE THIS?

Cyani dropped into the crushed cockpit and let her eyes adjust to the dimming light. Dried blood coated the walls, giving off the sickly sweet smell of death, while broken glass crackled beneath her sandals. Soren managed to free them both from their sideways harnesses and lift them out through the hole in the top of the wreckage.

She could barely turn without cutting herself on jagged metal and glass. The acrid scent of the charred ship burned her eyes and lungs. She had to be careful and get out of there quickly. She found her eyepiece under the overturned pilot seat. Where were the drugs?

Soren's seat hung in midair, as the cockpit came to rest on its side. Everything had fallen toward the pilot seat. She used a thick shard of broken glass to sift through the rubble.

Her heart leapt with hope as she uncovered the corner of the silver case that contained the drugs. She abandoned the shard and dug into the glass and debris, not caring about the scratches to her hands. Her flash of hope quickly faded to despair as she realized the body of the case had been crushed flat, pinned between two chunks of metal.

The drugs were gone.

There was only one way for Soren to survive. He had to find a mate. She had to get him home.

Taking her eyepiece in her hand, she carefully pulled herself out of the cockpit. Her skirt caught on a bit of ripped metal. She unhooked the fabric so it wouldn't tear then inspected the bent crescent of metal in her hand. It was all that remained of her com. Hopefully it would be able to upload the codes into a beacon. It was too damaged to wear.

A low howl haunted the open savannah as towering clouds rumbled in the distance. She scanned her surroundings from her perch on top of the cockpit. The last thing she needed was a hungry pack of wolves on her tail. She didn't have her scout, and her ear set could only enhance her hearing. Without the eyepiece, she couldn't see danger coming. She listened to the soft rushing of the grasses and the distant crackle of the burning fires. Hopefully the fires scared off most of the predators in the area.

Cyani pulled out her flick knife. It was her only means of protection. It was the only protection she needed as long as nothing surprised her.

She leapt down from the cockpit and hurried to the main body of the ship. The Garulen kept beacons on stingships. They used them to mark the locations of captured slaves for the transport ships. A beacon might have a strong enough signal to reach the Union base. If she could hack the signal with the com in her eyepiece, she could recode the message to a Union distress signal.

She stopped and listened. The hull of the ship provided shade from the scorching savannah. The damaged craft would be inhabited; any shelter on the open savannah would soon be inhabited by something. She had to get in and out as fast and carefully as she could. Ducking into the wreckage, she held her breath as she looked up at the side of the ship that became the ceiling above her.

"*Shakt*," she whispered under her breath. She paused to listen once more then climbed the support struts of the wall. Once she reached the ceiling, she swung hand over hand, gripping old piping until she reached the panel she needed. Hanging by one arm, she tugged on a panel door with the other.

It burst open. Using her well-trained reflexes, she snatched a beacon out of the air before it plummeted to the ground.

The rest of the beacons clattered against the broken ship, the sound echoing in the empty black cavern.

She winced in pain as the sound amplified in her ear. She swung her legs up and hooked her toes under a pair of support struts, then shimmied back to the wall and leapt to the ground.

"Gotcha." Cyani smiled, turning the beacon over in her hand. "And in a skirt, too."

She rushed outside and crouched in the shadow of the hull. Twin moons rose through the threatening clouds, lighting the savannah in a soft silvery light. Using her flick knife, she pried open the beacon and set to work connecting it to the com of her eyepiece. Once she had it synced up, it took a minute to hack into the programming before she could order the computer to relay the Union signal.

The top of the beacon glowed with a bright green light as it came to life.

"Yes," she whispered.

A slow tingle raced down her neck. She froze, listening. She heard a soft exhale.

Cyani grabbed her knife and whipped around, leaping in the air just as a dark leopard landed where she'd been kneeling.

The cat wheeled, the epitome of predatory grace and speed. Cyani watched its muscles, gleaning its next move as it lunged toward her with its razor claws unsheathed.

She ducked and rolled out of the way, the claws catching the edge of her skirt and ripping through the fabric. She spun to her feet and vaulted over the cat.

The great cat swiped, screaming at her with an alien howl,

then crouched back against the hull, its luminous eyes large, and its ears folded back.

Cyani gripped her knife tighter as she watched the beast, waiting for the next move.

"Aren't you going to run away, pretty kitty?" she asked it. Leopards were the same the universe over. If they didn't succeed in an ambush, they usually let their prey go and waited for an easier meal to stumble beneath them.

The cat hissed at her and bared her long fangs. Through her earpiece, Cyani heard two soft frightened calls inside the hull of the ship.

"Just my luck, you have babies."

The cat lunged again; this time Cyani threw herself on top of it and wrestled it to the ground. With her arm wrapped under the cat's foreleg, she reached up and grasped its lower jaw in an iron-tight grip, then tangled her arms and legs around the cat to immobilize it.

Now what was she going to do? She was stuck wrestling with an angry mother leopard in the open savannah of a backward planet, wearing a skirt that kept tangling around her legs.

"Cyani?" She heard the familiar voice, and her rush of relief almost made her grip on the cat's jaw slip.

"Soren, over here!" she shouted as loud as she could. The leopard tried to twist, but Cyani gripped her tighter, burying her face in the cat's red spotted fur.

She heard Soren's footsteps barreling toward her. He rounded the back end of the wrecked hull, and froze in his tracks.

She had to look ridiculous.

"Soren, can you put the cat to sleep?" she asked him, twisting her body in sync with the writhing animal.

Soren's eyes began to glow in the darkness. She shut her own and concentrated on holding the frightened cat. The leopard hissed and arched her neck, then suddenly went limp.

Cyani let go and scuttled backward. The mother cat lay still in the dirt.

She took a deep breath as her heart nearly pounded out of her chest. Soren stalked toward her, his eyes blazing with blue violet fury.

"What in blight infested rot do you think you're doing?" he demanded.

"I was subduing the cat, but then you came." It was a flippant answer, but she didn't feel like being dressed down by him. He held out his hand and pulled her to her feet.

Before she could stop her momentum, he pulled her into his body and wrapped her in his powerful arms.

He looked down at her, clasped her face in his hands, and kissed her. She tried to push against him, but gave up as the kiss stole her thoughts and will.

He mercilessly scorched her with his caress, nipping with his teeth, soothing with his tongue. He punished her with intimacy as he stole her breath, and gave her his.

Her senses heightened until the heat of his skin burned hers. She could smell him, she let his scent invade her, and she could smell another.

Cyani broke away from him and turned to the Makkolen man near them. He stalked toward the sleeping mother with a knife in his hand.

"Stop!" she shouted and threw herself toward the body of the sleeping cat. "Don't hurt her."

She stared up at the wild warrior as Soren's kiss made the world swirl in a new spectrum of iridescent light. She could see heat rising off the warrior's shoulders, and a strange firelike aura pulsing with the rhythm of his heart.

"Leave her alone," she demanded.

The Makkolen sheathed his knife.

"Kaln didn't mean any harm, Cyani. Get away from the cat before she wakes up." Soren offered her a hand, but she refused to take it.

Instead she stood on her own and heaved the large cat onto her shoulders. Cyani swayed under the beast's weight. The cat was as large as she was. With staggering steps, she carried the mother leopard into the hull of the ship. The soft fur of the cat's belly pressed in around Cyani's ears, enveloping her in the scent of sun-warmed dust and sweet milk. She couldn't leave the cat exposed on the savannah. She would be eaten. She had to return her to her cubs.

Cyani found them in the back, deep in the shadows. She gently placed their mother next to them, and rubbed their fluffy spotted heads before she turned and left the ship. She could hear the cubs purr as they snuggled in close to their brave mother.

She turned the volume on her ear set down. Now her ears could naturally hear things she hadn't heard before, and her nose alone could smell danger before it struck. She moved the beacon next to the cockpit, so if a landing party did arrive, they would stay clear of the hull of the ship. She gathered debris and made an arrow in the direction of the village then turned to face Soren.

He didn't say a thing.

Lightning flashed across the savannah, and reflected in his dark eyes.

"We must return to the village as fast as we can. Plains wolves come out at night." The Makkolen warrior placed his hand on the head of his large pet lioness, and began the journey back to the village.

Cyani followed him. She could feel Soren's gaze burning into the back of her head. What was he thinking? She knew he was angry, but his eyes had never flared so blue. Blue was the only color she couldn't read. It was the only color that frightened her.

11

"I DON'T UNDERSTAND YOU," SOREN GROWLED AS THEY ENTERED THEIR HUT. What was she thinking? Vicca snored in the corner with her feet dangling in the air and her tongue lolling out of her mouth. Cyani stroked her exposed belly, but the fox didn't stir.

"Sorry," Cyani offered with a casual shrug. "I planned to be back before you realized I left. But that doesn't give you the right to kiss me. I told you never to do that again."

A flash of light illuminated the interior of the hut, followed by a shattering crash of thunder. "You almost got yourself killed, and the only thing you can worry about is that I kissed you? Blight." Soren clenched his hands to try to hold back his fury. She didn't get it. She didn't get what would happen if she died. "You're still healing. And I'll never apologize for kissing you."

"It takes a lot to kill me, Soren. People have been trying to kill me for years. They haven't succeeded." Cyani turned and looked him in the eye. The light from a small fire burning in a hammered metal bowl flickered across her determined face.

"You were wrestling with a leopard!"

"And I was winning."

Soren kicked the stool and rubbed his face. What was he going to do with her? She thought she was invincible. Or maybe she just didn't care about her own death? "Could you at least bother telling me when you're about to run off on a suicide mission?"

She inspected the tear in the red layer of her skirt. "You're being dramatic. I was just trying to get us home."

"It's not worth your life."

"I know what my life is worth." Her voice dripped bitterness as she turned from him and lifted the edge of the cloth hanging over the window. The hushed roar of rain falling on parched clay encompassed them.

"You don't know what your life is worth to me."

Cyani stared at him, her hands trembling. She tried to still them by bunching the fabric in the window so the rain wouldn't seep in. He was too good at disarming her. She didn't want to have this argument. Not now, not ever. She knew what she was. A worthless mudbird. High-hawk fodder. She could be hunted for sport like an animal, raped, sold to a brothel, or killed. No one would care. If she defended herself, then she was a murderer. Her palms itched. She could still feel the sticky mud clinging to her skin, the filth pressing under her nails. She had defended herself.

"Why didn't you kill the leopard?" he asked. "You had your knife in your hand."

"I couldn't." She gathered up the skirt and rubbed the palms of her hands. They were dirty. Her skin looked clean, and felt raw, but she needed to scrub them harder. They still felt dirty.

"But you could, you're a warrior. You've taken more lives than you can count, both in and out of battle. What stopped you? You were under attack."

Damn him, why wouldn't he let this drop? She couldn't read his eyes, and didn't want to. She just wanted to be left alone.

"She was trying to protect her babies. It wouldn't have been right." She realized she was rubbing her hands again and forced them to her sides.

"So you kill according to a moral code?" Soren pushed her. Why was he doing this to her? Because he felt like he could touch her? Because they had nearly died together? It didn't matter that he was the only person she had really talked to in decades—that didn't give him the right to dig. He persisted, "Why are you on this path, Cyani?"

She glared at him. What was she supposed to say? That she had been attacked by a highborn man intent on raping her for sport? That in fear she struck out with her hands and stopped the man's heart? That she was guilty of murder and so deserved all of this? She had no choice. "I do what I'm ordered to do. I have orders to kill the Garulen, so I do. Don't try to tell me you think they don't deserve to be sent to judgment before the Creator. You've sent a few there yourself. You know better than anyone what those depraved leeches deserve."

"You didn't answer my question. Why are you on this path? You aren't a killer." Soren slowly stripped off his vest and let it fall onto his bed as he took a step toward her. Her eyes flickered over his chest as she retreated to the far side of the room. He looked too good. Her heart fluttered with nerves, anger, and the memory of waking inhaling the scent of his smooth, warm skin.

"I don't want to talk about this anymore." She'd tried to sound forceful, but she sounded as lost and alone as she felt. Another flash of lightning struck overhead as the angry rain continued to fall.

He took a step toward her, backing her against the wall. He had pinned her like this once before, and this time he had a look in his eyes that told her he wouldn't let her go, not until she gave him what he wanted.

He stroked his fingers down her cheek. "What happened to you?" The brief touch burned her skin. Her nerves set on edge, she glared at him. Why did he affect her? He was only a man. No, he was more than that, and she knew it.

Soren didn't back away; instead he waited for her answer with steeled patience in his expression. The light from the brazier flickered on the walls as the steady beat of the relentless storm surrounded their hut.

"I'm done talking about this," she protested.

"I'm not," he insisted, pressing even closer.

"You want to know why I'm on this path?" Cyani snapped, shoving him hard and slipping out to adjust the blanket covering the door. Rain had started to pool in the sand. She kicked the dry dirt over it. "They'll kill me if I fail. They'll carry out my death sentence, and I will fall to my death."

Soren didn't seem fazed. "Who will kill you?"

"The Elite."

"I don't understand; aren't you training to become one of them?"

"Ironic, isn't it?" Cyani cast her eyes back to the ground as she used the side of her foot to shove more dry sand toward the door. She couldn't let the rain in.

"What happened, Cyani?" Soren stroked the back of her hair. She stilled, her toes curling in the cool sand. She had forgotten just how alone she felt, how heavy her burden was.

"I really don't need this right now. It's over. End of discussion."

"It isn't over," he stated. "If it was, it wouldn't affect you. Talk to me."

Damn him.

"You want to know what happened? Fine." She kicked the dirt toward the door and turned on him. "I was checking bird traps with my brother and our friend when I ran into a high-hawk out hunting mudbirds."

"What are *high-hawks* and *mudbirds*?" Soren asked. She couldn't bear to look up at him. She knew he wouldn't look at her with scorn the way the other Elite did. His eyes would be filled with understanding, and she couldn't bear the weight of it.

"Catching mudbirds is a lovely little euphemism for high-born men, high-hawks, descending into the ground cities with three or four mercenary bodyguards, finding very young, defenseless girls, and raping them. In fact, the practice is so popular, flesh traders make a business out of catching pretty mudbirds, keeping them in brothels, and selling them to the highest bidder." The words spilled out of her before she could stop them.

Soren ran his hand over her shoulder.

"Damn it, Soren, don't touch me," she warned.

"Did this happen to you, Cyani?"

Cyani locked gazes with him. He understood. Of all the people in the entire universe, he understood what it was like to feel powerless and in pain.

"I wasn't defenseless. My mother had been the best Elite warrior Azra had ever known before she was banished for getting pregnant. She taught me too well. I struck the high-hawk that attacked me, and he fell dead before I even knew what happened."

Soren leaned forward, reaching out to fold her in his arms. No, she couldn't. She felt the mud on her hands.

"Don't," she shouted and ducked under his arm. In a blind fury she ran out the door into the pouring rain. She had to escape. The memories twisted through her mind. They overwhelmed her until she couldn't tell what was real anymore.

She fought, ran, plunging herself deep into the shadows and filth, hoping he wouldn't follow her there. The high-hawks from the canopy didn't like to be dirty. This one didn't seem to care.

He didn't back away. He just laughed at her as he rolled up his sleeves.

Cyani couldn't see as the rain streaked over her face. Her foot slipped and she fell forward into the sticky mud. She looked down at the red clay coating her hands. It dripped over her pale skin like blood.

"Cyani," Soren called as he followed her into the pounding rain.

"Cyani, wait." The cold rain seeped through her hair and drenched her shoulders. His feet slapped through the puddles until he knelt next to her.

She held out her dripping red hands to him. "One blow. It only took one blow with these hands, and his heart stopped cold. His mercenaries didn't know what happened. He just fell backward. I did it. I killed him. I wanted to, and I did, so don't try to tell me I am not a killer. I'm not kind. I'm not compassionate. I'm a murderer."

"Cyani," Soren implored, inching toward her as the pounding rain dripped into her stinging eyes. She tried to wipe her eyes with the back of her hand, but she was covered with mud. She was filthy, dirty, worthless. He reached out for her hand and placed his over it. She tried to pull away from him, but he wouldn't let her. With gentle care and attention, he rubbed the mud away.

Too drained to do anything more than watch, she stared, transfixed by his fingers sliding over hers, taking the dirt with them and leaving her clean hands gleaming in the wild rain.

He pulled her closer and tilted her muddy face to the sky. She felt the cold rain flow over her face, purifying her as his hands gently smoothed her hair, wiped her hot cheeks.

"You can judge yourself, but I won't," Soren whispered, tucking his face close to her ear. "You're not a killer, Cyani. You're my savior."

Thunder roared overhead as Cyani let her head fall on his shoulder. Her tears fell on his warm skin as he continued to bathe her in the falling rain.

"You are my savior," he whispered again as he lifted her to her feet and pulled her into the familiar circle of his arms.

He smoothed his hands over her wet hair and kissed her forehead, her brow. He kissed the tears from her cheeks as he comforted her. Each kiss tingled on her cool skin, reminding her of the intensity and power of his touch.

But his touch was nothing compared to his words. They entrenched themselves deep in her battered heart.

She looked up into his glowing blue violet eyes.

Her fingers trembled as she reached up and touched the skin along the edge of his jaw. He understood her. She rose, snaking her arm around the back of his neck. His wet hair felt cool and silky on her arm.

He pulled her closer, pressing her body into his.

She felt naked, vulnerable as she reached up, finding his lips with hers.

She kissed him.

His hands fisted in her wet hair as her lips slid over his. He took what she offered him, gently, as if in awe of her touch. She wondered if her kiss did to him the things his did to her.

Even as she thought it, she nearly collapsed with the rush of his kiss. She felt the adrenaline flowing through her head as her muscles felt heavy and languid. And like a dream just stealing the mind in the depths of sleep, the slow, heavy pulse deep in her abdomen pushed her to new aching awareness of him.

She opened her eyes as she clung to his wet shoulders and his soft mouth trailed hungry kisses down her neck.

The pounding rain burst in glowing waves of magenta, gold, green, and blue as it fell around them.

She was addicted to him, and she didn't care.

Lightning scorched the sky. What was she doing? Cyani's nerves stood on end as the crackling touch of electricity sizzled around them.

Soren lifted his head.

They had to get inside before they both got killed. Soren wove his fingers between hers, and pulled her back toward the hut. They ran through the iridescent sheets of rain, before tumbling through the door.

"I'm sorry," she mumbled as they reached the safety of the hut. She shook—she couldn't help it. Her whole body trembled, but it wasn't from the cold. "I don't know what's wrong with me. I'm acting like a lunatic. I'm not usually so irrational."

"I like it when you're irrational," he teased, as if nothing had happened. "It's the only way I can win an argument, and if you weren't a lunatic, you would have given up on me a long time ago."

She smiled, grateful that he was directing the conversation away from what she had just done. *Glorious Creator in the great center of all things, what was I thinking?*

"Thanks," she offered, wringing out her hair and letting it fall over her soaked shoulder. Her hands still wouldn't stop shaking.

"For what?" He asked as he tied back his own hair.

"For being my friend. I don't have many," she said. Out of the forty Elite, and the fifteen or so in training, only one of the women had ever treated her fairly, but she couldn't call Yara her friend.

"Actually," he countered, pausing to rub Vicca's belly, "you only have one, and I have no idea why she puts up with you."

Cyani chuckled as Soren wrapped a blanket over her shoulder then began to unlace her bodice.

"What are you doing?" she asked, snatching his hand away from the laces.

"Getting you out of your clothes." He shrugged and continued his work.

"Just because I admit I like you doesn't mean I'm going to mate with you," she protested.

"That wasn't on my mind," he said, his voice dark and defensive.

"Purple-eyed liar," she jabbed. Why did the hut have to be so small? With the hammock and the bed on the floor, she had no place she could escape him.

"You need to get out of those wet clothes before you catch a virus that even the kiltii water can't fix. I wasn't going to touch you." To prove it, he turned his back to her so she could undress.

"I won't catch a virus," she grumbled. Cyani felt like a heel. She couldn't blame him for having purple eyes after she had just kissed him until she couldn't think. She stripped off her wet clothes and hung them from the end of the hammock. She wrapped a blanket around her breasts, but the thin fabric clung to her wet skin and turned transparent. She scrambled to grasp a couple more before Soren turned around.

She was completely out of control.

With one hand he unfastened the buckle at his hip and his clothing fell off, leaving her a glorious view of his backside.

Ona forgive me, but you can't see this. She had seen him naked, but not like this.

He wrapped a fur around his waist and reclined on his bed. Everything about him was a blatant invitation, from his long, powerful body to his burning eyes.

Cyani clung to the blankets wrapped around her as she sat on the very edge of the furs.

"Tell me what happened, Cyani," Soren stated. The light from the brazier washed over his bare skin in golden waves. She couldn't seem to pull her gaze away from the edge of the fur wrapped around his lean waist.

"Cyani?"

"I don't think . . ."

"Have you ever told anyone the whole story?" he asked.

No. Who could she tell? The Elite? Justice didn't matter to them, only the social order.

"Talk to me," Soren ordered. His request reminded her of that first night alone together on the asteroid. He dipped his hand in the kiltii water, then slid his damp palm down her shin to clean some of the mud off. "It will turn into a monster in your mind if you don't."

She sighed. It was already a monster. She watched, mesmerized as he continued to stroke the mud off her calf, until he lifted her ankle into his warm hands.

"You can't understand what the ground of my planet is like," she began. He didn't respond, just listened, continuing his gentle work. "We live on islands. On the ground, the center of the island is a cesspool, all the light blocked by the cities in the trees above. It's dark, and it's ugly. The people there are criminals."

"You weren't a criminal." As the last of the mud dripped from her foot, he massaged her arches. She felt dizzy with pleasure as she curled her long toes.

Cyani shook her head. "That doesn't matter. I grew up in a small fortified city that my mother founded. Only good people who obeyed the rules were allowed in. My mother and father defended it with their blood, and taught those who lived there how to fight. It was a little high city of our own. The only place on the ground with any rule of law. At least it was safer than the chaos beyond the barricades. But there's no food, no way to grow anything, and no animals to hunt. We had to risk going outside the barricades to hunt sarbas or trap birds, or we wouldn't have anything to eat but woodborers and millipedes."

"They sound delicious," Soren quipped, gently pulling on each of her toes before moving on to her other muddy foot.

Cyani glared at him.

He quirked the corner of his mouth in an amused grin.

What was she going to do with him?

"Do you want me to continue?"

He squeezed her ankle. "Please."

She studied his face for a moment, her eyes lingering on the dimpled scars from the blinders. He was so beautiful, wet from the rain. And he was so strong. She felt like a coward compared to him.

She felt her heart stumble as she continued. "We were out checking traps near the sea cliffs. There are poisonous plants, and the felam beasts are very dangerous, but the cliffs are the best place to trap seabirds. I got separated from my brother when I noticed I had caught a fat groslin in a snare. They are a delicacy in the high cities, to catch one on the ground . . . It would have been like bringing my parents a little piece of the canopy, of their old life. I didn't even think it might have been a trap for me. I was so stupid."

"Cyani, you can't do that," Soren cautioned. His hands stilled on her foot.

"Do what?" She looked at him. His black eyes stared back with an expression she couldn't read.

"You can't blame yourself," he stated with quiet authority.

"Trust me, I can," she huffed. "Groslin don't ever come near the ground. I don't know what I was thinking. It was so obvious."

"You can't question why you ignored every warning you sensed. Why you decided to try to find the rest of your family instead of hiding, the way you were supposed to. Trust me, you can't blame yourself. It will drive you mad."

Cyani swallowed a lump in her throat as she realized he wasn't talking about her. What had happened to him? And was it so different from her story?

"It's funny the things you remember," she mumbled, feeling suddenly connected to him somehow. Her words caught in her chest, words she had never spoken aloud, even to Vicca when they were alone in the dark. She looked down at her hands, the hands he had washed clean. "I fell in the mud, it was all over my hands." Her voice didn't sound like it was coming from her, but from somewhere far away. She pulled her leg back and tucked it close to her body.

"I was so scared," she continued, "and my head hurt from where the high-hawk hit me. He ripped off the rag I used as a dress then laughed as I struggled to get my feet under me. I didn't think—I don't really remember anything but the mud on my hands, and the dark mark it made on his chest when I lashed out and landed a heart-strike. I had never done one before. I don't think any of the other Elite can do it, kill with a single strike to the chest. How did I kill him? I don't ever remember learning how to do it." She looked at him. "How did I kill him?"

Soren reached out and took her hand in his.

"The bodyguards caught me. I was so shocked I couldn't run. They beat me until I was just at the edge of consciousness. They even denied me the escape of passing out. Then they dragged me up to the Halls of Honor to face my execution for murder."

"Did you have a trial?" Soren asked.

Cyani huffed under her breath. "People from the ground have no rights, least of all to a fair trial. No one cares—they don't even think we're human. It didn't matter that my mother and father were both highborn. On my planet, I am worth less than nothing because I was born on the ground. You should have heard them chanting for my death, like it was a sport or entertainment. I had no trial, only another vicious beating that left me unconscious for two days and an ultimatum."

"How old were you?" he asked.

"Thirteen," she admitted. "I was barely a woman."

"You were still a child," Soren argued. "What was the ultimatum?"

"The leader of the Elite saw me. She stopped the execution. I guess a thirteen-year-old landing a clean heart-strike impressed her. She started me on the path to become one of the Elite in spite of the others who wanted me dead. If I survived, if I obeyed every rule, every code, and I didn't disappoint her, she said she would find my brother and raise him up to the high cities. If I failed . . ."

"They'd finish what they started," Soren concluded. "I'm sorry, Cyani."

"For what?" She shrugged. It was her lot in life. That was all.

"I'm sorry I didn't realize you have been enslaved as much as I have."

Cyani felt like she had taken a force kick to the gut. "I'm not a slave." She'd fought against slavery for the last five years. The Garulen and Kronalen enslaved others for their own personal gain. She had been given a second chance and had taken it. She wasn't being manipulated.

Was she?

"Do you want to become one of these Elite?" Soren asked as he stretched his shoulders and placed his hands behind his head.

"Of course I do." Didn't she? She thought about the temple, the long years of silence awaiting her. *Shakt.*

"It sounds to me like you neither like nor respect them, yet you want to be one." His eyes flashed. He was gearing up to dig into her again. She didn't need this. She didn't want to talk anymore.

"I'll survive, Soren," she snapped as she pulled herself up in the hammock. She sank into its woven embrace, glad she could no longer see him. "It's what I do—I survive. I survived the ground cities. I have survived the attempts on my life from the other Elite during my training. I have survived the war. I'll survive this."

"But what do you want?" he asked as he smothered the brazier and threw them both into darkness. The rain pattered on the roof as the smell of wet grass and earth filled the humid air. The fury of the storm had passed, and the light of the twin moons seeped through the clouds and the wet cloth at the window enough to cast them both in shades of gray.

What did she want?

There was only one burning want in her heart, but it was the one thing she knew she could never have. It was as impossible as wishing to live forever. She dismissed the tugging ache as she thought about her family still struggling in the darkness. She wanted to know they were safe. She just wanted to keep those she loved safe. She would sacrifice *anything* to protect them.

"It doesn't matter what I want," she told him. "It only matters what I do. I know what I have to do, and I'm doing it."

"Then you will lead a very empty life."

Shakt, he sounded like her conscience.

She sat up in the hammock and glared at the two glowing slits in the darkness. "How about this, then? I want to sleep. Is that okay with you?"

"It would be fine with me," he offered, "if you could."

"What are you talking about?"

"Your nightmares. The way you wake up thinking you're under attack, but you aren't really awake. You avoid sleep altogether to try to stop them, but it doesn't work, does it? They stole that from you, too, sleep. And yet, you're not a slave to them?" His glowing eyes closed, leaving her alone in the dark.

"Damn it, Soren." She didn't care if he was her only real friend besides Vicca. She felt like jumping down and giving him a swift kick. She could fall asleep if she wanted.

She tossed on her side and tucked the blankets around her like a constricting cocoon. She closed her eyes and took a deep breath, determined to prove him wrong.

She didn't know when she dozed off. She heard a boom in the distance. Bombs, they were under attack. She tried to move, but couldn't. They hit her, she was down.

"Tola!" she screamed. "Get them out!"

She felt herself fall.

"Cyani." Her name reached through her panic. "Cyani, wake up."

Cyani shook herself awake and fought to stand up, but a strong arm wrapped around her bare back.

"Cyani, are you awake?"

"What?" It was still dark. She felt cloth, and *skin*. "What in the name of the Matriarchs are you doing?" she half shouted as she pushed herself up from Soren's bare chest. She was sprawled out naked over him like a wanton lover.

"What am *I* doing?" he protested. "You're the one who started shouting and fell out of the hammock."

Cyani rolled off him and curled into a ball on the furs. Mortified, she took a deep breath while the cool night air kissed her bare back. Soren shifted behind her, moving closer. She tensed, but he pulled her blanket up over her shoulder.

"Do you want me to say you were right?" she asked bitterly. Why did he have to be right?

"No," he whispered near her ear.

She rolled onto her back so she could get a good look at him. "Then what do you want, Soren?"

"I want to be an old man," he admitted.

She sighed and turned away from him. She felt his fingers brush over her hair. "What do *you* want, Cyani?" he murmured against the skin of her neck.

"I just want to know peace." She sighed as his warm skin pressed closer to hers. "I've never known peace."

"That's a good thing to want." He snaked his arm over her side and pulled her into the shelter of his body, his hand resting protectively over her navel. Only the soft blanket separated their naked flesh.

She could feel his warm breath curling over the skin behind her ear as she stared at the wall. Even wrapped up in the comfort of his scent, his touch, the nightmares would come again. She was tired of death. She wanted a new life.

"Soren?" she whispered.

"Hmmmm," he murmured into her hair.

"Do it."

He rose up on one elbow. "Do what?"

She took a deep breath and stared him in the eye. What could blue mean? His eyes were turning more and more blue each time she looked at them. They glowed with dark fire now. "You know what."

"I thought you told me never to do that again." He lifted an eyebrow and blinked his dark lashes very slowly as the black lock of hair that fell over his shoulder tickled her cheek.

"I know what I said. I know what I'm saying now." She shoved him on the shoulder. "Will you just get this over with, already?"

"You'll be helpless," he warned, his midnight eyes burning over her face. He leaned in closer, his presence completely surrounding her. She didn't flinch.

"I trust you," she whispered.

He closed his eyes and took a deep breath as he leaned in and pressed his warm lips to her forehead.

When he opened his eyes, they swirled and glowed. She didn't shrink away from him, but embraced the beauty of his power.

12

LEAVE IT TO CYANI TO FIND A WAY TO GET WHAT SHE WANTED. SOREN watched her from a distance, marveling at how she had adapted the Makkolen clothing to suit her own needs.

She had gotten her hands on two more head scarves, and with them, she had turned the sensual and revealing clothing of the Makkolen women into a mysterious, and strangely threatening, warrior getup. She had wrapped a bloodred scarf over her head and face so only her eyes could be seen through a narrow slit. It masked her humanity, her femininity, until he could only see the cold power of her training.

With a second scarf, she cloaked her delicious belly by wrapping her breasts tightly with it, and lacing the bodice on top, then tucking it into the waist of her skirt. Even though it covered her skin, the allure of how the silk moved as her torso twisted in one of her kicks made Soren's blood burn in his veins.

And finally she had taken a ginger cloth and managed to turn her skirt into a strangely tied pair of flowing pants, complete with "undergarments" of sorts. She looked like a warrior born out of restless flames, but he knew the woman she hid beneath her cloth, her weapons, her control.

Crack!

Cyani swung an arm-length stick over her head and brought it down hard on the toppled trunk of a dead tree.

She shook her head, took three strides back then ran at the tree with full force. With one hand she vaulted over the trunk, landed on the other side, and brought the stick down with another loud *whack*.

She fought so hard.

What was she really fighting against?

It had been four days since the storm. He was still feeling remarkably well, even though he could feel the drugs fading. He figured the kiltii water and sleeping so close to Cyani had helped keep his system balanced. Each day he regained more of his humor, his hope, but the days had tortured her.

She rarely spoke with other members of the tribe. He had taught her a few phrases, but she used them reluctantly. Each night she stared out at the far moon and watched the pinpoints of light flying to and from the Union base there. Every morning before dawn, she came to this shadowed place near the outer wall and practiced her training rituals. While she had grown closer to him, she didn't seem to be adapting to Makko itself.

Soren turned the small round bead in his hand. With the edge of his knife, he deepened a slice to emphasize the edge of the fox's face he had carved into it. He had made a whole sack of beads, but they sat in the dark, not woven into a necklace for the only woman who meant anything to him.

He knew she'd never willingly wear it.

He couldn't ask her to. She would be trading her chains of honor for chains of a different kind.

She launched into one of her Ahora routines, swinging the makeshift "blade" around with the ease of a master.

He wanted her so badly. He wanted her to smile, to enjoy life here and relax, learn the language, and fit in with the people. He wanted her to bond with him.

He could picture them living out their days in the village. They could watch the sun set over the savannah as wrinkled gray elders, while their children began families of spotted and striped, blue- and gold-skinned, green- and red-haired ferocious little mind-bending warrior hunters who could make things grow.

He laughed, wondering if the Gatherers Cyani had told him about ever planned on something like that.

It was only a fantasy. She couldn't survive here. He could see that now.

The Grand Sister of her planet was smart: She offered Cyani a choice. Cyani didn't even realize she had been enslaved.

He was not her choice.

He rolled the bead for her necklace between his fingers.

What was he going to do?

She landed another blow on the tree trunk, and the stick she wielded cracked in two.

"I don't understand the fascination men have with a woman who does not act like one," a cool voice commented near his ear.

He glanced over at one of the pretty young Makkolen women. She had twisted her hair up to display her long, golden, completely bare neck.

She smiled seductively at him. It seemed the Lorna, the time of exploration, was upon them.

He didn't need this, not now.

"Shouldn't you be looking for Kaln?" he asked.

"Why would I be looking for Kaln?" she responded. "He's nothing special." The young woman pressed closer, touching his shoulder. He tried to ignore the feel of her fingertip tracing the edge of one of his stripes. "You are special."

Soren pushed her hand away. "I am unavailable."

"Hmmm," the woman murmured. "She doesn't wear your necklace. Why not take advantage of that fact while you can?"

Soren glowered.

"Awww, don't do that, your eyes are so much prettier when they're blue," she commented.

Soren felt as if a Garulen guard had just thrust the butt of a shock thrower into his gut.

"What?" He could barely force out the question. He must have misheard her.

The girl took his moment of shock to press herself up against him and trace her finger over his eyebrow. "Your eyes are the most beautiful mix of blue and violet like a dark sky."

Gracious Grower, giver of life. He was bonding with Cyani.

His heart galloped in his chest as he took a step away from the girl and leaned up against a tree.

How could it be?

They hadn't mated. They had touched, they had kissed, but he hadn't willingly bonded to her. His body was responding to her anyway. He had thought her presence could slow his deterioration, but it seemed she could stimulate new hormones, natural ones.

Hope warred with horror in his mind.

As long as he stayed near her, he would survive.

I can survive.

Unless she chose to leave him. If she did, his body would deteriorate quickly. Without her near, the hormones would shut down completely and he'd be dead in a matter of hours, not weeks.

How could he give her that choice?

"Are you okay?" the girl asked. "You look a little ill. Maybe there is something I can do for you."

She wrapped her arm around him and smoothed his hair back. His stomach turned in revulsion.

"Go home," he ordered her. "I belong to one woman, and that woman is not you."

He needed Cyani, but when he turned to look at her, she wasn't there.

CYANI FUMED AS SHE STALKED TOWARD THE VEGETABLE GARDEN, THE THIN shells of the bark nuts crunching beneath her feet. She wrenched a branch from one of the overhanging trees and stripped the smaller twigs off it then tossed them into the sticky mud with angry flicks of her wrist. A swarm of mudbiters rose up into the air and buzzed around a rotting gourd.

With a furious yank, she pulled her mask off and let it fall around her neck.

She shouldn't be so angry, but she was.

When she turned and saw one of the Makkolen women snaked around Soren like a parasitic vine, she fought the urge to throw something at them.

What was wrong with her?

Was she addicted to him?

Or was it something worse?

She smacked the branch against a gnarled tree then launched it like a spear over the high wall. She felt so trapped. The wall loomed, casting her in its shadow. She couldn't find the words to speak her mind, couldn't keep herself from being exposed, and couldn't escape.

Betrayal burned in her gut. After the storm, she only had one piece of comfort to cling to. She could finally sleep—with Soren's help.

She needed him.

And he was turning to another.

Could she blame him? How often had she pushed him away? And for what? For all Azra knew, she was dead or a slave of the Garulen, and those who wanted to see her fail had their wish.

What if they never escaped?

What would she do if he bonded with another and she was left in this world alone?

She needed him. She trusted him.

She . . .

She couldn't think about it anymore.

Cyani leaned against a tree and scooped up a handful of

nuts. She threw one of the nuts at a bloated gourd reclining in the mud. The mudbiters took to the air again. She swatted at the irritating little flies, scattering them like her thoughts.

It shouldn't have shocked her that the native women found Soren attractive. And it shouldn't have surprised her that he would notice them either, with their long copper hair, sun-golden skin, and wanton display of their bellies.

She threw another nut at the gourd with enough force to dent the vegetable's skin.

If he bonded with one of them, it could save his life. He was happy here. She didn't need to see the green in his eyes. He radiated joy and life.

He exuded warmth and tenderness, caring, patience, humor, and strength. With him she could dream, free from her terrible nightmares. She didn't want him to bond with one of them, she wanted—

"What are you doing?" she muttered to herself. "You have a mission. If he finds a way to survive here, then you'll have done your duty."

But at what cost?

Why was she even asking herself these questions?

They stung her as badly as the bites of the flies. She could avoid the flies if she kept moving; her thoughts were another matter.

"Were you speaking to me?" a low male voice asked too near her.

Cyani wheeled around in shock. A young native man stepped out from behind the tree. He wore nothing but his leather nuta and an intricate beaded necklace.

"No," she began, searching for the words. "I leave now."

The Makkolen reached out and grasped her hand, but she pulled it away. She gasped in shock as he snaked his arm around her waist and pulled her against his body. "You don't want to leave yet. We hardly know each other."

Cyani felt the sluggishness invade her mind. He pulled the scarf from around her neck and let his fingers trace over her bare skin.

"No," she shouted, whipping her forearm across his face with a solid crack. He fell to the ground and she tried to run, but her mind clouded with sudden unnatural panic. She froze on the spot, not knowing where to turn. Each option seemed more terrifying than the next.

A second male laughed from behind a tree. She found herself laughing too in spite of her effort to fight it, trapped by the newcomer and a wave of confusion.

"What, did you think she had the mind of a cow?" the second male asked the first. Cyani laughed. No, she shouldn't laugh. She was in danger. Real danger. A heavy blanket of numbing calm shrouded her mind.

"She is a predator, you stump. You have to treat her like a lioness or she will rip you apart." He stalked toward her with a look of triumph in his red eyes. "Do you know how the sight of you arouses me?"

Cyani felt a swell of pride in her long hair and toned muscles. Muscles she had to use to stop him. Muscles she could use to fight.

She fisted her hand and swung at his face. He caught her fist.

"Ah, ah ah," he murmured. "You know how my skin feels against yours. You know you want the pleasure of my touch." He pulled her fist forward and kissed the back of her hand.

Her mind flooded with want. She could picture his hands sliding over her arms and down her sides. He pulled her closer, leaning in to kiss her bare neck. Before she could stop herself, she had pulled the scarf around her midsection out from beneath her bodice.

She needed that scarf. She didn't want to take it off. No, she had to get it off her skin. She wanted to touch him. She needed to feel his body against hers. Foreign lust simmered beneath her muddy confusion.

His lips brushed her shoulder as his hand pressed into her bare back.

It didn't feel right. It didn't feel the way it did with Soren.

She shoved him away with all of her strength.

"No," she roared as she pushed his influence from her mind. She stumbled backward then fell to her knees in the sticky mud of the garden. The flies rose like a stinging cloud around her. She swung at them, swung at her attackers. She had to clear her head. She had to find Soren. She had to fight. Her hands were covered in mud. Suddenly her mind couldn't escape the gripping panic she felt as she desperately tried to clean the dirt from her hands. They were coming toward her. Not again.

"Cyani!" Soren called as he charged into the garden.

Cyani's heart raced as she struggled to her feet and launched herself into his arms. He grasped at her back and hair, clinging to her. She needed to feel him, to know what was real.

"Soren, they—" Her words fell short as she watched the

blazing red fire erupt from his eyes. She backed away as a low growl rumbled from deep in his chest.

He's going to kill them.

The two young men had staggered into the mud. She could see the look of concentration on their faces and feel the wave of calm they were trying to use to subdue Soren. It wasn't working.

"Soren, stop. Stop now," she commanded.

She knew what the men had tried to do, but she couldn't let Soren kill them. She couldn't. She had sold a part of her honor to that darkness long ago. She couldn't let it happen again.

"Stop," she insisted, grasping his arm and pulling him back. "Soren, listen to me."

She pushed in front of him and braced her hands against his chest, but he continued to stalk toward the other two men with murder in his eyes.

There was only one thing she could do.

Cyani reached out, took his face in her hands and kissed him. With her passion and desperation, she commanded him to respond to her as she savored the contrast of his soft lips and hard jaw.

Her body exploded with a colorful burst of awareness as she kissed him. It felt real—it felt right.

She pulled back, and Soren looked down on her then grasped her tighter, holding the back of her head as she pressed her cheek against his warm shoulder.

"Cyani, are you okay?" he asked.

"They tried to control my mind."

"I know," he growled. "They'll pay."

"Soren, please don't."

Soren rushed toward the two young men. They shouted in panic as a bright flash of light blazed in the shadows. Suddenly both went limp in the mud.

Cyani breathed a deep sigh of relief. She grasped Soren's arm and pulled him away from the two men.

"Leave them." She dragged him back toward their hut. "Come on, Soren. They can't hurt me now." Her muddy hands left dark marks on his forearm. She fought a wave of panic at the sight of her handprints on him. She had to get out of there.

She spared them a glance as she pushed Soren toward the village. The mudbiters landed on the still bodies and began their work. They would wake up with angry stings all over their exposed skin. They deserved it, but she didn't have time to think about that now. She had to get Soren alone and back in control.

As soon as the cloth hanging over their door swung back into place, Soren ravaged her with desperate, furious kisses over her face, neck, shoulders. His hands clung to her as his kisses burned her skin with their intensity.

His eyes blazed bright, pure blue as he looked at her. "If they had touched you . . ."

"I'm fine," she reassured him, even as her own muddy hands left streaks on his sides and back as she tried to cling to the comfort and familiarity of his body. "I wouldn't let them touch me."

Her words didn't seem to comfort him as he held her and stroked her loose hair. They didn't comfort her either, because she knew they weren't the truth. They might have broken her, and she couldn't fight it. She furiously tried to wipe the mud from his skin.

Soren sighed. He reached for a bit of cloth, dipped it in the kiltii water, and smoothed it over her face, washing away the filth from the garden.

Her stomach crawled with the awareness of the dirt clinging to her. She needed to be clean. She itched all over as her insides churned with the creeping feeling.

As if sensing her sudden unease, Soren dipped the cloth in the water again, and gently cleansed her temple, then her neck.

The cool cloth slid over her. Soren leaned forward and kissed her damp skin, as her body hummed with tension.

He carefully bathed her hands, drawing the cloth over each sensitive finger. He lifted her hands, and took the tip of each finger into his mouth. The hot pull drove her mad. She could feel the soft stroke of his tongue pulling her toward something deeper, something greater, something she was forbidden to touch.

She moaned softly as he placed a kiss in the center of her palm, then a hot laving caress on the inside of her wrist. He gently kissed each blossom circling her wrist. She swore she could feel them turning to him, growing for him.

His warm hands cradled her arm as his hungry mouth trailed up her arm with sharp nips followed by his soothing tongue.

Cyani couldn't think. Her mind was on fire. She looked down at him, cradling his head with her free arm. His silky hair slid over her forearm as she watched his face. With his eyes closed, he placed each kiss on her arm with the reverence of someone in the middle of a deep and holy rite.

She couldn't stand it. She resisted the urge to pull the laces of her bodice and let him clean the mud from her shoulder, and her bare breast.

"Soren?" Kaln called from outside the door. "My father wishes to speak with you."

They both froze, and Cyani felt the stab of disappointment deep in her gut as Soren cursed and dropped the cloth into the kiltii water.

"What's going on?" she asked, not expecting an answer. She felt heavy, aching and bereft, while at the same time her mind felt like it had been yanked suddenly from a dream.

"I don't know," he answered, looking as disappointed and torn as she felt. "Stay here until I return."

He stormed out of the door.

"Kaln," he ordered. "Protect her."

"I will," the prince replied.

Cyani quickly wiped the mud off her legs. She wondered how much it had to disturb Soren to leave her with another man, but his trust in the prince comforted her. If Soren trusted him, she could trust him, too.

"Happening, what?" she asked him in her broken Makko.

Kaln continued to stare toward the center of town. "Two men have accused Soren of attacking them. My father is sorting it out."

"What?" Cyani's heart thundered in her ears. "They attacked me. They tried to influence my mind so they could seduce me," she protested in Union.

"I can't understand you, Cyani," the prince said, "but I think I know what you are saying. They tried to influence you, didn't they?" he asked.

"Yes!" she shouted in Makkolen.

The prince nodded. "My father will make things right, just stay here. Soren is barely controlling himself. Right now I'm helping him stay calm and in control so he can bear witness against the men who attacked you. If he saw you now, I would lose my hold on him, and that would be bad for you both."

Cyani paced behind the door, then called for Vicca, but her fox was nowhere to be found. She was probably off hunting toads.

She found her flick knife, and with her agitation roiling, she tried to work through her nerves by practicing throwing it into one of the walls. It gave her plenty of time to think about what she had done, how far she had let things go. She couldn't do this. She wouldn't be able to let him go to find his own love and be free.

Finally after what seemed like an eternity, Soren returned. He greeted Kaln, and the two men whispered something before he patted Kaln on the shoulder and the prince took his leave.

He entered the hut with a somber look on his face. "I will make you a bonding necklace and give it to you during the next Lankana," he announced.

"What?" she gasped. "We can't go through their mating ritual."

"I promised the king."

"How could you?" she demanded.

"Because by the law of these people, if another man tried to touch you in any way, I could defend you," he answered.

"You mean you could kill them."

Soren shrugged. "They all believe I would, so no one would dare touch you."

"This isn't right," she protested.

"The king had to banish two of his own for the span of a year. That isn't right either," Soren said. Cyani looked at him, shocked. Her attackers were banished? Soren continued, "If you hadn't stopped me, I would have done something terrible. If we're going to stay here, this is for the best."

"If we stay here?" Her voice hitched high in disbelief. "We are not staying. As soon as the Union hears my distress signal, they will come and rescue us."

"Cyani, it's been five days now."

"It has *only* been five days," she snapped. "We're not staying here."

"What if we don't have a choice?" He reached out and placed his hands on her shoulders, then let his warm palms slide down her bare arms.

What if he was right? What would she do if the Union never heard the distress signal? She didn't want to think about that.

"Why aren't you getting sick?" she asked. The question had been bothering her for a couple of days now, and she needed to change the subject. He still had violet in his eyes, which meant the drugs were still in his system, but he should've been getting fevers by now, shouldn't he? Maybe if he realized he'd die here, he'd feel more urgency to leave.

"Must be the kiltii water." He shrugged.

"Are you sure?" The knot of uncertainty tightened in her stomach.

Vicca trotted in the door with a large locust in her mouth. Cyani scooped her up, and pet her ears as she moved to the hammock to try to hold back the crushing claustrophobia that had suddenly gripped her.

"I can't do this, Soren. I can't bond with you."

"I didn't ask you to," he said. He touched the kiltii vine that now covered the walls of half the hut, had grown up into the grass thatching, and draped across the floor.

"That's what you said. You said I would be bound to you. What do you think this ceremony is?" she demanded.

"It isn't even marriage to the people here, Cyani. It is only a promise to remain together for a time and see what happens." He plucked a few spent blossoms and rubbed their petals between his fingers to release their cleansing scent. "Isn't that what we are doing now?"

"I don't know what we are doing now, but I know what it means to bond to you and I can't do it. I just can't. I can't bear that weight. We have to stop this, Soren. We are walking on the edge of a very thin blade."

Soren crossed his arms and exhaled as he dropped his gaze to his bed.

"If you bond to me, then what?" Cyani asked. "Then if something happens to me, you die. I can't live like that."

"Like what? Like you have something to live for? You are so quick to throw yourself toward death."

"I'm free to do what I need to do," she protested.

"You're not free." His voice boomed in their small home.

"If I'm forced to bond to you, I won't be."

An uneasy silence fell between them as Soren's eyes slowly turned black. What was she supposed to do? Finally she broke the silence because she couldn't bear the weight of it. "I'll be chained to you, and if we finally make it out of this lack-tech pit, then I'm the one who will bear the consequences. If you die, it will be my fault," she stated, her voice sounding hard, even to her ears. "My fault," she repeated in a softer tone.

Soren crossed the room and eased into the hammock next to her. She refused to look at him. He stroked Vicca's ears as the fox snuggled between them.

"You should go through this ceremony with one of these women," she mumbled. "They're clearly interested in you. They can bond with you. You'll be safe."

"I don't want them," he said, leaning in to her shoulder. "Makkolen women would not be able to accept my need for them. If one wanted to leave the bond, I couldn't let her go."

"What about me?" she said as she squeezed to the edge of the hammock. "Could you let me go?"

He didn't answer.

"So what do we do?" she asked.

"Dance for me, Cyani." Soren touched her chin with his fingertip and gently lifted her face to his. "It is the only way to keep you safe. After that, I will go out onto the savannah with you, and we'll try to make the beacon work."

"But what about the bond?"

He leaned forward and placed a tender kiss on her forehead then looked her directly in the eye.

"I swear to you. I won't chain you." He smoothed her hair again. It was a tender caress she found comforting. He paused. His voice sounded soft when he continued. "Whatever our future holds, you will have a choice. I will give you a choice."

He promised her freedom, a choice. A small ugly voice whispered in the back of her mind: *What price would they have to pay?*

13

THE DRUMS, THEY CALLED TO HER. SHE COULD FEEL THEIR PULSE DANCING with the beat of her heart. She could hear their rhythmic seduction. The Lankana was upon her.

The last few days had passed by too quickly. Soren hadn't left her side the entire time. He tried to make his presence seem less imposing, but while it comforted her to have him so near, it only reinforced her gut feeling. She was trapped.

She had to do what she had to do. She'd go out and dance, then take the necklace and retreat back to the hut and go to sleep like any other night. She had to get it over with as fast as possible.

Apparently, tradition dictated that she wear her hair up off her neck, twisted and pinned by two sticks with dangling beads attached. She didn't have a problem with that. She had a problem with the rest of the traditional garb. Her woven bodice had been bad enough. The bloodred leather one she now donned practically became her skin as it dipped so low she worried about falling out of it. And she had no chance of covering her belly with the low-slung fiery skirt. She'd be lucky if it stayed on her hips at all, and without a head scarf to tie up between her legs, she had a sinking feeling she'd end up flashing her most intimate places to the entire tribe. She felt the flush of embarrassment color her cheeks.

But the drums, she couldn't get the pulsing beat out of her mind. It enthralled her as she stared at the glittering blanket of stars above.

This night wasn't like any other night. She had to be strong, or she would succumb to it.

From the dark shadows of the women's house, she could smell the rich, spicy smoke of the great bonfires raging in the open area between the two halls. Focus, she needed to focus on the things she could control.

Tonight she'd be free.

Tonight I will be bound.

"Nervous?" Lai asked, placing her palm on Cyani's shoulder.

Cyani turned to look at the queen. "No."

"Your hands are shaking."

Cyani crossed her arms over the tight leather that bound her breasts, and tucked her fingers into the crooks of each elbow to still them.

"You have no reason to be anxious, Cyani. You dance beautifully." The queen turned to walk away as Cyani looked back out at the clearing. The shadows of men and women formed a circle around the altar. It had been dressed with fur and cloth.

Fire burned from the tops of phallic poles circling the shrine, while long flags of shimmering red cloth undulated in the hot breeze.

"Lai?" Cyani called. The queen looked back over her shoulder. "What is that for?" she asked, pointing at the altar.

One of the queen's elegant brows lowered in a puzzled expression.

"It would be best for you to put it out of your mind. Try to enjoy this night." The queen smiled a motherly smile and continued to the other side of the house.

Like the low rumble of thunder, deep chanting voices rose up in chorus with the pounding drums. The men called out to them, luring them from the safety of the women's house. Part of her wanted to rush out into the night and abandon herself to the wild call, but she couldn't. She wouldn't. She didn't know if the feeling was real, and she couldn't just let go even if it was.

Do what you have to do, that is all.

Cyani glanced over the fifteen other women who would be dancing that night. All the other women of the tribe remained safely tucked in the arms of the man whose necklace they wore, the arms of the man whose child they carried, or nursed. She would never know that unity.

Angry at herself and her rebellious longing to fit in with the tribe, she tugged at a lock of her twisted hair and let her hand linger on the exposed skin of her bare neck. In truth, the tribe had been far more welcoming than her own people. They had gone out of their way to make her feel like she was a part of them.

Tonight she *would* be a part of them. She'd wear a necklace, Soren's necklace, his mark. Part of him would touch her, wrapped around her vulnerable neck. She could feel her own racing pulse beneath her fingertips. What if he was right? What if the Union never heard her call?

This world, this bond, she'd have to live with it. She'd have to survive.

The drums picked up their rhythm, pounding as urgently as her conflicted heart.

The queen walked toward the simmering cauldron in the center of the room. With one hand, she dipped a small clay bowl in the hot liquid then plucked a delicate white blossom from the vines. She dropped it into the bowl and held it aloft. "To new life and our greatest power," she toasted, then took a deep drink and passed it on.

As the other young women drank, the queen began to sing, her husky voice filling the room with words Cyani's com could not translate. It didn't have to. Somehow Cyani knew what this song meant.

As each finished their draught, they joined in the song. The clear ringing voices of the women danced over the low and suggestive words of the men outside.

Cyani felt a shiver race up her spine as she took a drink, then handed the bowl back to the queen.

"It is time," Lai announced.

Cyani's heart dropped down into her toes, as the other young women rushed out of the room in a flurry of shimmering red skirts and warm dark skin.

She balked in the doorway, unable to take the next step forward, a step into an uncertain future.

Steeling her nerves and swallowing her terror, she stepped out into the burning night.

The fires blazed on either side of the altar, casting the dancing women in the hot glow of writhing flame.

Where was Soren?

Panic grasped her throat as she spun around, searching the faces of the seated men in the circle while the women twirled around her. Their skirts caught up in the motion and flared out, licking their legs like tongues of flame.

Where is he?

Cyani turned on her heel and caught sight of two glowing blue violet eyes on the far side of the circle.

Her head spinning with relief, she ran around the altar and faced Soren. He wore a bemused expression as he took a long drink from a deep bowl and stared at her without a word. A very intricate web of dark beads hung around his neck, tapering down to a single bead, carved to look like the flowers on her tattoo. It was beautiful.

Suddenly Cyani felt very conscious of the night air touching her exposed skin. A chill slithered down her back as she brought her hand over her navel and began to dance.

Foot down, clap, turn, hands up, meticulously she performed the motions Lai had taught her. She just needed to make it through the ceremony and all of this would be over. She could go to sleep, and in the morning, she'd redouble her efforts to contact the Union. Soren had promised.

I'll sleep in his arms, under his thrall, dreaming of his skin touching mine, his kiss lingering on the tender place beneath my ear.

Cyani shook her head and realized she had stopped moving. With a quick rush of motion, she finished the last steps of the dance and stood before Soren.

With her heart pounding, she waited.

He didn't move.

"Soren?" She took a step toward him, but he just cocked his head to the side and smiled at her. "Aren't you supposed to give me the necklace now?" she asked. Had she forgotten part of the ritual?

"I'll give you the necklace when I see you dance."

"You son of an ill-bred mud worm," she hissed at him.

He laughed and crossed his arms.

"Dance for me, Cyani," he challenged.

She burned. She could feel the rushing heat of her anger and her humiliation rising in her blood, even as the touch of the bonfire behind her seeped into her skin. He wanted her to dance?

She'd dance.

She stomped her foot into the sand and slowly lowered her center as her arms snaked out to her sides. It was the beginning of the Ahora malka, the seduction of the tiger.

She would make him writhe.

Her body entered into the training ritual with a will of its own, the motions meant to teach smooth death strikes with wrist blades. She turned it into something different, something alive, something as beautiful and treacherous as the tiger itself.

She spun and let her muscles flow, her body open. She could feel the night air kiss the inside of her thighs, cool her heated core.

She became the beast, the Xalen tiger he often reminded her of. No, she was the tigress, his mate.

She could feel the electric tingle in her skin as she swayed toward him. She remembered how shocking his touch had been when he first reached out to her. Now she needed it. Was she addicted to him?

Did it matter anymore?

She remembered the first time he had kissed her. She had been helpless, terrified as he healed her paralyzed body with his potent embrace.

Her body spun and leapt. It knew the motions; they had become instinct. What other instincts had she denied herself for so long? Her body radiated with a new sense of power, a feminine awareness of her ability to enthrall, to create new life and beauty.

She thought about how she felt during the storm, raw and exposed, unclean from the mud and her own guilt.

He had washed it away as completely as the drenching rain could, and she had kissed him for it. Now she felt the call, the seduction of her deepest, most secret strength. The strength of her love, the strength of her freedom.

She locked her gaze on his as she stalked toward him with fluid grace. His dark eyes blazed with the violet passion he tried to leash for her.

If only he knew how much she longed to free it, to free him completely. If only he knew how free she felt with him.

She spun and whipped the sticks out of her hair. She heard a collective gasp as her hair tumbled down over her back. She shook her wild mane free and smiled at Soren.

He stood.

With the mysterious blue burning bright in his eyes, he slowly stepped toward her, lifting the necklace over his head.

She felt drained all of a sudden, and her knees almost gave out as he placed the necklace around her neck. It nestled against her skin as if it knew where it belonged. She ran her fingers along its edge, and looked up at Soren.

"You dance beautifully," he whispered near her ear as he pulled her into his body.

She trailed a hand over his bare neck as he leaned in to kiss her.

The crowd around them erupted in cheers, and Cyani broke away in shock, suddenly aware of their situation.

Soren laughed as he escorted her out of the circle, and let her settle down in front of him. He wrapped his arms around her as she leaned back against his smooth chest.

A little part of her felt a stirring of pride as she watched the rest of the dancers sway in the flickering light of the fires.

"Drink this." Soren handed her the bowl he had been drinking from earlier.

She gratefully lifted it to her lips and took a deep drink. The cool, tangy-sweet liquid burned down her throat.

She felt her eyes water and coughed in shock.

"This is not kiltii water!"

Soren laughed again. "No, no it is not." He nudged the bowl, and with a smile, Cyani took another drink.

She wasn't supposed to partake in intoxicants of any kind, but as the rich and slightly spiced wine began to loosen her muscles, she acknowledged she'd been doing a lot of things she shouldn't lately. The blood of Cyrila the Rebel wouldn't be ignored. She rubbed the scars on the backs of her thighs.

Perhaps a little freedom was the sweetest revenge.

"So what happens now?" she asked Soren.

She thought once she was done dancing she could escape to their hut, but now she found she didn't want to leave. She had enjoyed herself, and she wanted more.

As if to answer her question, the queen appeared out of the women's house. A breeze picked up, ruffling her skirt around her ankles.

The crowd hushed in anticipation, and the last of the dancers took their places with the men whose necklaces they earned. The king stood and took two steps closer to the queen.

She smiled at him. The look of love shining on her face radiated brighter than the fires. Cyani inhaled and found herself holding her breath as the queen began to dance.

It was mesmerizing to watch. While the younger women clearly tried to seduce, the queen's dance said something more. It was about strength, honor, and love. It spoke of intimate knowledge of one other, and the sharing of that life through good, through bad, through joy and pain. Cyani had no doubt why the king still kept Lai as his queen, even though it seemed her childbearing years were waning.

"Is she the only one allowed to dance for him?" Cyani asked, fascinated by the playful smiles flitting between the two lovers.

"No, but the others don't dare. They know he will only give his necklace to her. They have been together for many years. They are considered an exclusive couple, for lack of a better word, truly married."

"So he is the only man she has ever loved?"

"No, her two oldest children have different fathers. She is the only woman he has ever given his necklace to. It took him a while to convince her to dance for him." Soren pressed his lips against Cyani's shoulder. She could feel his warm breath flow over her collarbone and she shivered with the unspoken promise of the caress.

She spared a glance for Kaln and his two oldest sisters, but they had all busied themselves with their newfound mates. It seemed they didn't want to look at their parents' affection. Cyani giggled. She knew that feeling. Even in the darkest of shadows, her parents sought out each other's touch.

She found the habit mortifying and comforting at the same time. She had only been a child. Now she knew the depth of the dedication her parents had for one another. She could understand it. She hadn't thought about it in years. It was as if the small bits of good in her dark childhood had been locked away in the back of her mind.

The king lifted a hand, and the queen placed her hand in his. She flowed into him with a kiss that seemed to consume them both. Cyani felt the crowd melt away. The whole world became nothing more than two people in the light of dancing flames.

It frightened her that she was beginning to understand what that felt like. Soren kissed her shoulder, and fire raced over her skin.

She focused on the king and queen. They broke their kiss but not their bond. The king took the queen's hand and led her to the altar. The flags rustled in the slight breeze as the fires cast their shadows on the rippling fabric.

Apprehension tickled through Cyani's mind.

"Soren, what are they doing?" she asked. Her heart pounded in her ears as the king leaned the queen back onto the furs, so her body flowed over the altar like a sacrifice.

"What does it look like they are doing?" he responded. His voice sounded darker, heated with the tension humming in the air.

The king slid his hands up the queen's legs, sliding her skirt up her dark skin. With each inch, he kissed her legs, his image blurred by the undulating cloth.

"You don't mean they are going to . . ." Cyani tried to look away, but couldn't. Her heart beat so loud, it drowned out the hushed drums.

"Mate?" Soren didn't seem in the least bit perplexed or disturbed by this part of the ritual. She could feel the energy in his skin, the anticipation and hunger. It burned her where they touched.

"Why? In front of everyone . . ." Cyani could hardly catch her breath. The tribe seemed hushed, their golden eyes fixed on their king and their queen.

"So there is no question of the paternity of the king's heirs. The Makkolen women are all at their most fertile this night." Soren's voice tickled the sensitive flesh behind her ear.

It was such a logical answer, so straightforward. Why did it have to make things so difficult? Drinking a swallow of wine was one thing; this was quite another. She couldn't do this.

She tried to look away, turning to a couple to their right. The woman's abdomen was swollen to the point of bursting. She could deliver her baby at any time. Her mate's hand slid over her protruding belly and snaked under her skirt. The woman arched her back and moaned.

Cyani whipped her eyes to the ground in front of her. She tried to focus on her bare toes. Wriggling them into the soft sand, she kept her eyes fixed on the dirt.

The queen gasped then let out a soft cry. Cyani looked up before she could help it.

The king's hips nested between the queen's legs. He rocked with her, pulsing with the rhythm of the drums and something deeper, more elemental. Cyani recognized power in many forms, but she had never seen power like this.

She couldn't breathe.

Soren's hand strayed down her arm.

The breeze picked up, seducing the fabrics hanging around the mating couple into a yearning dance of their own.

This was life, the very beginning of life. Across all the worlds and all the different races and species she had encountered, this was a glowing golden thread tying them all together.

Life, not death.

It was breathtaking.

She felt a wave of pleasure rush through her body. She felt swollen, and slick with her rush of shock and awareness. She couldn't take her eyes off them. She tried, but she couldn't. She wondered what it would feel like, to have Soren's lean hips, his body, joined with hers.

Her head swam with dizziness. If she didn't breathe, she was going to faint. Soren kissed the back of her neck the way he had when she suffered from the shock blast during their escape from the slave cells.

She moaned and tried to stop her body from shaking. She felt like she was dangling off the edge of a great branch, and she wanted to let go. She wanted to fall.

The king thrust harder into the queen's body, pulling her into him as she frantically clung to his shoulders. He pounded into her with desperate ferocity over and over, and she took him deep within herself.

A lion roared in the night.

The king answered.

The queen cried out and arched her back, before falling languid on the altar.

A cheer erupted from the crowd as the king collapsed onto the queen, the sheen on his back glowing in the heat of the fire.

Cyani watched the queen weave her fingers into the king's hair and laugh.

Now she knew why this was forbidden.

This was power—power at its most elemental.

Now she knew why so many of the Elite risked blackmail and banishment to touch it, even briefly.

Now she knew why her father chose to banish himself so he could be with her mother in the darkness.

This was power, and she wanted it.

14

"DON'T LOOK AT ME THAT WAY," SOREN SAID AS HE LEANED AGAINST THE WALL of their hut. Cyani had a strange, focused look in her eyes. Her movements were slow, smooth, deliberate, like a great cat on the hunt. The lingering drums still called from the center of the village, reminding him of the way she had moved when she danced for him. It nearly killed him.

She smiled as she lifted the bowl of wine to her full lips. "Look at you what way?" she asked, taking a long, slow drink. He couldn't tear his eyes from the smooth column of her neck. As she lowered the bowl, her tongue darted out and stole a drop from her shapely upper lip.

Great Grower of life, she *was* trying to seduce him. The Lankana had gone straight to her head.

"I need to know something." She stepped toward him, her

fingertips teasing the beads of her necklace. "When you bond, is it a choice?" she asked.

Soren's stomach rolled over. He needed to sit down. He lowered himself on the furs as he contemplated her question. Normally, it was a choice. Normally, he would have had to acknowledge her with his mind, his eternal spirit, and his body to truly bond with her. Unfortunately, it seemed at least two of the three had made a decision without him. He was already partially bonded to her, and he couldn't break it now.

"Normally it is a choice," he acknowledged. "Bonding is a long process." He was slipping off the edge of the blade. He couldn't help himself. He was a weak and selfish man, but he needed her so badly. He needed her to breathe, to think, for his heart to keep beating.

She took another drink of the wine. Her hands trembled as she pulled it away from her lips. "So, it is possible for your people to mate without bonding."

He crossed his arms as he stared up at her. The light from the brazier flickered over the pale skin of her stomach and made the waves of her hair glow with soft green lights. Great Grower, he wanted her.

She tried to set the bowl aside, but accidentally spilled some of the tangy wine down her wrist. It seemed she couldn't control her shaking hands. She lifted her hand to her mouth and suggestively suckled one of her own fingers. He felt his heart pounding in his chest, pushing toward her with every beat.

"What do you want?" He had asked her once before, and she had trouble answering. Could she answer him now?

"I want to . . ." Her voice trailed off.

"Tell me, Cyani." He pushed her, he couldn't help himself. His body thrummed with lust for her. If they were going to fall, they would fall together.

She looked down at the floor then slowly brought her bright blue gaze to his. "I don't know who I am anymore," she admitted. "I know who I used to be. That girl is a stranger, but what am I now? A set of rules, of orders that I don't even believe in?"

"Cyani . . ." Soren began, trying to caution her against rash decisions they couldn't back away from.

"I know what I want," she stated, her eyes unwavering.

"Cyani, it's the Lankana," he protested.

"I want you," she whispered, cutting him off. "I just want you."

He felt a sparkling deep in his chest, like a shower of falling stars burning through his blood. She wanted him. He rose to his feet, stepping into her body as he looked down on her.

"Then take me," he murmured. How far would she really go?

He wound his hand into her hair at the base of her skull and brushed his thumb over the sensitive spot behind her ear. If she chose to give herself to him tonight, or if she didn't, it wouldn't matter. He belonged to her. He would never survive without her. How did he resist it so long?

She pushed him back. "Lie down," she murmured. "Please, I have something I want to give you."

He reluctantly lowered himself onto the bed. The few feet that separated them seemed like a vast ocean. She would have to cross it. She had to willingly come to him. He had to give her that choice. Did she really have the guts?

He fought back the memory of hot metal on his back, and the straps holding his hips and arms. He didn't like being on his back. He was exposed, in the same position he had suffered in for so long.

Cyani reached up and slowly pulled the leather strap from the hooks of her bodice and peeled the clinging leather from her skin. Every thought faded from his mind.

It took all of his control to remain on the bed. He wanted to leap at her, rip her skirt from her hips, and bury himself in her until he drove the pain away.

Her dark hair fell over her creamy breasts as she unclasped her skirt and stepped out of it. He clenched the furs in his fists and struggled to keep his sanity.

He had never seen a woman like this. Not like *this*.

She took one slow step closer to him and let her dark hair fall around her face. He held his breath as he felt his body reaching, stretching. A sweet ache blossomed deep in his abdomen as he drank in the glorious sight of her.

He loved her.

Her enigmatic smile, the one that only turned one corner of her mouth, touched her full lips. It had been the first smile she had ever given him. He hadn't forgotten.

"Cyani," he murmured, not knowing what else to say, not knowing what else to do.

Save me. Purify me.

She knelt on top of him, letting her hands splay out over his chest. She unlatched the clasp at his hip and pulled the leather kilt away from him. Then, with deliberate grace, she leaned forward. Her long hair kissed his chest, his face, until her lips met his in a teasing caress.

"Cyani," he moaned. He couldn't think about anything else, his mind flooded with hot violet. It burned as her hand closed around his aching flesh.

He exhaled and clenched his teeth. His muscles tightened through his shoulders and back, his hips, his thighs. He reached up and clung to her waist as she lifted her hips and hovered over him.

I am going to die. He tried to fight back the memory of hot metal closing around his exposed flesh, pinning him down. He tore off his translator then reached up to touch her. He let his hands slide up her cool, soft skin, and stroked the tips of her hair as they whispered over her smooth back.

My Cyani, my beautiful savior.

There was no abuse, no corruption, here. This was pure.

Her hot entrance kissed his tingling body as she slowly engulfed him.

She let out a long low moan as she eased down, letting him slide into her until her hips nestled completely against his. He sank into her hot sweet fire, undone by the pure pleasure of it. He tried to breathe but couldn't. He looked up at her face, at the long dark lashes closed over her beautiful blue eyes.

"*Ahria, cell atah*," she gasped out as she looked down on him.

He reached up and touched her face, trailing his fingertips over her cheeks, her lips. She turned her face into his palm, as he pulled the translator from her ear and tossed it over by his.

He gently pulled her face to his as he whispered to her. "*Behra en lyah*, Cyani."

I love you.

She kissed him as her shaking hands touched his temples.

He burned. He burned for her as she deepened the kiss and lifted her hips at the same time, only to slide down once more.

He shook—he couldn't help it—and he couldn't keep the hot tears from flowing down the sides of his face as she kissed him. She kissed away the tears, and gently kissed his brow that bore the small puckered scars of the blinders he had worn.

"Easy," she whispered in Makkolen. He clung to her arms, grasping to hold on to her. He couldn't control himself, couldn't control the flood of pain suddenly pouring from him. All of the darkness, all of the torture came rushing toward him like a black wave. He needed her so badly.

"It is okay." She stroked his face as his body shook beneath her. "Take me."

Cyani watched him closely as he looked up at her with such pain and awe burning in his aqua eyes. He had looked at her that way before, on the night she had freed him.

He was embedded so deep in her, she could feel the sweet ache of it behind her navel. Her body throbbed around him, so stretched, so full.

He wrapped his strong arm around her waist and lifted his hips into her. She gasped in shock as he turned her over and pushed his hips deeper into hers as the soft fur of his bed kissed the sensitive skin of her back.

She let her body splay out on the fur as he began to move, surging into her. She couldn't keep her eyes open. The push of his body sliding into hers made the colors swirling around the room pulse with vibrant blue and violet. It was too much.

She reached up and clung to his shoulders then let her hands slide down to feel the lean muscles of his hips pumping into her.

She felt helpless and whole, wild and alive. She felt wanton, hot, powerful, and free.

Glorious Matriarchs, she could feel something powerful building within her. With each hungry push of Soren's hips, she felt a tightening, like a bowstring being pulled to its limit. She couldn't escape it, it ached, it begged her to make it stop, but she didn't want it to. She didn't want it to stop.

She desperately grasped at Soren's taut muscles, raking her hands over his lower back.

He clenched her thigh and pulled her up into him. She cried out, desperate for relief from the frantic need coursing through her.

She looked up at him, reached up for him. She was going to fall. His face was a hard mask of concentration, so visceral, so male. Under hooded lids, his eyes glowed for her. Only for her.

She felt a pulse, a deep throbbing as he stroked her harder.

I'm falling.

She gasped. She felt loose and free, and frightened at the same time. She clung to him, but she was still falling and the exquisite torture of it made her cry out for him.

He exhaled and shouted as his muscles tightened and his eyes flashed bright blue. She tried to breathe, but couldn't stop shaking as she felt a sudden flood of heat bathe her center.

Dizzy and overcome, she pulled his shaking body down on hers.

He gasped as he gently kissed her face, and stroked her

hair. His warm weight soothed her as she concentrated on the feeling of being joined. He was within her, so deep within her, she didn't know if she could ever get him out again.

IT WAS STILL DARK OUT AS CYANI SAT ON THE LOG SHE'D USED FOR HER TRAINing. She ran her finger along a groove she had beaten into the old trunk with her stick. Where had all that anger, all that frustration, gone?

She glanced back toward the village as she gently stroked the beads of her necklace. She felt languid, loose and calm, and for the first time she had slept through the night without Soren's help.

She smiled. He had helped.

She laughed out loud before she could stop herself.

What had gotten into her?

She stretched her arms over her head and her thighs throbbed. Perhaps she shouldn't answer that question. Her nervousness returned. It had been plaguing her all morning, this feeling of elation followed by uncertainty and confusion.

Her hands shook as she brought them back down and smoothed her skirt. She had dressed in her normal Makkolen clothing without the extra scarves. They seemed pointless.

The sky lightened, throwing the old tree into stark relief. A bird began to sing as one of the lions roared on the far side of the village.

She wanted to feel the new light of dawn and for the first time, feel the promise it kept for her.

The clouds flushed with bright rose and violet, and Cyani felt the beauty of it deep in her heart.

"It's an extraordinary dawn," Soren commented as he took a seat next to her.

She smiled at him. "Yes it is," she admitted as she fiddled with the bead at the end of her necklace, the one that looked like the flowers on her tattoos. Her uncertainty plagued her, even as she tried to reason through the next step. This was a new path, and for the first time she had chosen it. She didn't expect to feel so vulnerable.

Soren seemed relieved as he pulled her against him and wrapped his arms around her shoulders. He planted a soft kiss on her bare shoulder. "I promised you I would go with you to check the beacon."

"It can wait." She needed time. They needed time if there was any hope to make a new life on this wild planet together. "This is a beautiful necklace, Soren."

"Thank you." He held her tighter as if he were unwilling to ever let her go again. "I enjoyed carving the pakka blossom for you."

"The what?" she turned so she could see him. The rose, pale blue, and lavender of the new dawn reflected in his eyes.

"Pakka vines, like your tattoos," he explained.

She lifted her wrist. "These are ciera blossoms," she chuckled. Then she sobered as she thought about the meaning of her tattoos. "They start their lives on the ground of Azra. They grow for decades, reaching through the darkness until they finally climb into the canopy. When they see the light for the first time, they bloom."

Soren looked thoughtful. "That's lovely."

"What did you think they were?" she asked.

"Pakka vines," he admitted. "They are a stubborn weed

with nasty thorns that make you break out in an irritating rash. I planted them over the entrance to my home."

Cyani laughed. "Why would you want to plant them there?"

Soren caught her face in his hand and brushed a tender kiss over her lips. The intimate caress shocked her and turned her mind to the incredible things his body had done to hers the night before.

"Because," he murmured, "when they bloom, their beauty is beyond belief."

Cyani wrapped her arms around his neck as he lifted her onto his lap. She kissed him deeply, forcefully.

"We should return to the hut," she suggested.

"Why?" He kissed a hot trail down her neck to her exposed collarbone.

"Anyone can see us," she protested, leaning back from him.

He chuckled as his eyes began to glow violet again. "In case you didn't notice, the Makkolen aren't too shy about such things."

"Soren!" She smacked him playfully on the shoulder. "I don't care if they have absolutely no boundaries, I still do."

Soren buried his face in her cleavage and kissed her there. She moaned before she could stop herself. "We'll work on that," he suggested.

Suddenly Vicca leapt up on them. She barked urgently.

Cyani's heart began to pound as she got to the ground and picked up her fox.

"Easy girl," she soothed. "Easy, what is it?"

Vicca pushed against her chest as she reached her muzzle toward the sky.

A dark shadow loomed over a cloud bank.

Cyani's gut dropped as she nearly stumbled and fell. Soren stood and shielded his eyes against the sun as he watched the shadow creep closer.

A distant rumble thundered over the savannah. The animals of the village scrambled about as the Makkolen emerged from their huts to see what was going on.

The sky suddenly went dark as the enormous ship blotted out the new rising sun.

"No," Cyani whispered to herself. *No, no, no, no, no.*

Soren stepped in close to her side and took her hand, even as Cyani buried her face in Vicca's fur.

The familiar roar of transport engines drowned the village in sound as the ship made its landing just outside the gates.

15

"WHERE IS HE?" CYANI BACKED THE LIEUTENANT INTO THE CORNER. SHE WAS tempted to reach out and grab a fist of his shadowsuit and shake him. "Tell me where they took him right now. That's an order."

Everything that had happened from the moment the transport landed on Makko had been a rush. The Union heard the beacon and found them, but the unfamiliar soldiers had been shuffling them through protocol ever since. Cyani had had enough.

She'd tried to contact her men, but her team was already deployed on another assignment on Felli. She didn't know anyone on this base, and had no one she could trust but Soren. Now she didn't know where he was.

They'd each gone into the sterilizers alone. She'd assured Soren she'd meet him on the other side. She patiently changed clothes while the pure white room cleansed her, believing Soren was in the sterilizer next to her. But when she came out of the sterilizers, he was already gone, ferreted off somewhere. *Not for long.*

She'd get him back. The sight on her eyepiece focused an ominous red dot right between the poor soldier's eyes.

"They took the Byralen to Med for observation," he stammered. "My orders are to escort you to C.R. One Sixty-seven for a briefing with Commander Qin."

"Show me where Med is first," she demanded.

"I'm sorry, Captain, but I can't. My orders are clear. The commander needs to see you right away."

Cyani exhaled and ran a hand over her hair, smoothed-back and tied in a tight, uniform knot at her nape. Maybe it was best to get the commander off her back first, then she could be with Soren.

"Vicca," she snapped. Her fox turned in a quick circle and sat, awaiting her orders. "Find and guard Soren, com open."

Vicca barked then ran off through the corridor, her claws clicking on the polished black floors. Cyani could hear the clicking continue as Vicca rounded a corner. Her ear set had linked to the microphone in Vicca's collar successfully. At least she'd be able to hear Soren, and communicate with him if she had to.

She turned on her heel and stormed down the corridor. The lieutenant stumbled to catch up with her then led the way to the conference chamber where she could meet with the commander. She didn't want to deal with bureaucratic myhrat dung, but such was the life of an officer. *Get this over with, and get out.*

She entered the bleak meeting room, nothing more than a gray square box with a steel table and neat rows of black chairs on the polished floor. Far-flung moon bases didn't receive a budget for anything less austere. Cyani stood with her hands clasped behind her back at attention, waiting for acknowledgment from the base commander.

He seemed deep in conversation with another man by the large shield-screen overlooking the docking bays. The commander's face pinched in displeasure as the other man mumbled something to him.

Who is he?

He looked familiar to her, but she had met few people during her assignments for the Union, and he wore no rank or planetary insignia on his shadowsuit. That meant he was a hired hand, a liaison. Cyani knew better than to trust him. Liaisons usually had their own agendas, and more often than not, they involved brokering money, power, information, or all three at once.

The liaison looked up at her with very dark eyes. Was he part Hannolen? He had cropped pitch-black hair and an athletic frame she expected to see on a command trooper, not a bureaucrat. He gave her a quick perusal, a curious observation of her, nothing more.

"Ah, Captain," the Fellilen commander greeted. The tattoos masking his face pulled upward into a fearsome grimace as he smiled. "So good of you to join us. This is Cyrus Smith, one of the Union's finest cultural liaisons and a very talented linguist."

She *had* seen him before; she was certain of it. She nodded her head and waited for the commander to continue. If he was a mere linguist, she was a squira monger. There was something calculating and precise about his blank expression, almost sinister.

"He is going to be in charge of gathering information for us about the Byralen you brought into custody," the commander mentioned.

"I didn't bring him into custody, I freed him from enslavement. According to the Union Code of Rights and Ethics, he is to be returned to his native planet immediately. I would like to volunteer myself for that mission."

The liaison's eyebrows rose very slightly.

"I am sorry, Captain, but the raid on Hanno was your final mission. The Grand Sister of Azra has been contacted about your survival. She insists you return to your home planet immediately for decommissioning, and she can be a very persistent woman." The commander lifted a glass of an amber liquid to his lips without seeming concerned in the least, but Cyani felt as if her heart had been ripped out and tossed on the shining black floor.

"Before you go, I am putting you under the command of Mr. Smith. You are to do as he requests regarding the Byralen male so he may complete his task of gathering information. The Union is very interested in discovering the location of Byra. I expect you to aid in that endeavor."

"Are those your official orders, sir?" Smith asked with a clear Earthlen accent.

"Yes. Com, log orders." The commander set his glass down and walked toward the door. "Thank you for your service, Captain."

He walked out of the room, leaving her with the liaison. As

soon as the door hissed shut, Smith pulled a small disc from his belt and tossed it into the air. It hovered as an aura of pink and green shifting light radiated out from its edge, turning it into a glowing orb of color. A round black sphere appeared from the top of the disc as the machine dipped down and seemed to be looking around the room with its small black eye.

Smith pointed to his eyes, then his ears, and swept his hand out over the room. The disc dipped in a strange little nod then zipped around the room, flashing a bright green light.

Shock whipped through Cyani's mind. Outrageously expensive and borderline illegal A.I., not standard tech for a linguist.

Who is he?

The disc flashed, leaving a faint glowing green light hidden along the seam of the shield-screen, then it flew back to Smith and beeped.

"Are you sure that's the only one?" he asked it.

"*Chirp*," it answered.

"And it's been disabled?"

"*Chirp*." It nodded again.

"Look, Bug, I love you, but if we have a repeat of the incident on Ubora, I'm going to use you as a coaster from now on." The liaison crossed his arms and glared at the disc.

"*Werp. Buzzzzz.*"

"Don't get smart with me. You're supposed to be artificially intelligent, not artificially petulant. Now go back to sleep until we're safe on the ship."

The disc made an irritated grinding noise as it settled back into his hand and turned off. He stashed it back in his belt.

"We don't have much time; Bug can only block the signal

on listening devices for a few minutes," Smith said, as if he hadn't carried on a conversation with a machine.

"Where's the Byralen?" he asked.

A chill raced up Cyani's spine. She couldn't trust the man anywhere near Soren.

"Cyani," he softened his low voice, and for a moment his accent melted away. "*Help me help him.*"

Cyani's heart sped up and stuttered in her chest. He had spoken Azralen, and not schooled Azralen, ground-shadow Azralen.

"Med." It was all she could say in her shock.

"We have to go," he ordered. "Now."

Just then she heard the clicking from Vicca's claws stop. It had been a constant static in her ear. Cyani turned her attention to the sounds coming through her ear set. Vicca barked once, and a door hissed open.

"I'm not going in there," a disembodied voice proclaimed. "Nrea hasn't woken up yet."

"What did he do?" another asked.

"I don't know."

"We should prepare the sedatives."

"If you try to gas him, we're all going to be on the floor."

Vicca barked again.

Cyani moved to the door and broke into a run. Smith followed her. She continued to listen to the disaster unfolding in Med.

"What is that scout doing in here?"

Something crashed.

"Keep her away from the door, she's going to let him out," the second voice shouted.

"This way," Smith pointed, turning down another corridor. They rushed down it at full speed.

Cyani heard clanging, a victorious bark, and the hiss of a door, and suddenly everything went silent.

Something thumped against the floor. It sounded like a body. Was it Soren? What had they done to him?

Her heart raced with stark terror.

By everything that is powerful and holy in the universe, please let him be okay.

Smith grabbed her arm and pulled her down another corridor.

Finally they turned the corner to Med. The large white doors hissed open.

Cyani stopped in her tracks.

The bodies of four medical officers lay on the floor, passed out. Soren bent over one of them, inspecting the officer's head while Vicca perched on the man's thigh.

Soren looked up.

The yellow red in his eyes blazed blue violet as he rushed to her. He caught her face in his hands before he kissed her with desperate hunger. She wrapped her arms around him, feeling his clean ponytail slide beneath the fabric of her gloves. She ripped them off and wound her fingers in his hair, as he continued to take her breath as if he hadn't been able to breathe without it.

Finally he broke the kiss and buried his face in the top of her hair. He inhaled deeply as he held her. The skin of his neck felt hot on her palm.

"Soren, are you running a fever?" She felt his forehead.

"I'm going to be okay." He took her hand, kissed it, then pulled her toward him again.

Cyani heard a soft snort, and realized that Smith was standing in the doorway. She jumped back as if Soren had turned into high-voltage current while a hot flush rushed through her face.

The liaison seemed highly amused. He had the Rebel's own smile plastered all over his face.

"What's your brother doing here?" Soren asked.

Cyani felt like someone had just knocked her over the head with a short staff. She turned to Smith in disbelief. He looked as shocked as she felt, shocked—and guilty.

"What?" she stammered.

"Your scents—they share the same family base scent. That only happens with siblings."

Cyani grabbed the liaison's arm and yanked his sleeve. A red and black snake coiled around his blue-tinged wrist.

"Cyn," she gasped.

He put a finger to his lips. "We don't know who's listening," he whispered. He pulled out Bug and let him fly. The A.I. returned quickly without marking anything in the room green. Cyn sighed, stashed his pet, then his eyes hardened.

Cyn had green eyes, not black? What was going on?

"Byralen, we don't have much time," Cyn said. "We have to get you out of here and on my ship before anyone notices this mess. There should be a spare Med coat in that closet. Throw it on. Hopefully no one will question your hair. Cyani, stand guard, and send your scout out to patrol the hall."

Cyani moved to a defensive posture at the door.

My brother? He was her brother.

Soren stepped up, dressed like one of the Med unit.

"Let's go." Cyn motioned to the door and led the way.

They hurried through the corridors toward the docking bay without saying another word. Cyani stepped out into the docking bay as one of the Union ships sank through the force-shield that floated like a thick bubble over the docking platforms.

The roar of its engines filled the docks as Cyani carefully followed the pulsing orange trail winding through the docking stations.

Vicca had jumped off the gravity generators and was taking enormous four-meter leaps through the air and landing again with her pink tongue dangling out of her mouth.

"Vicca," she scolded as Cyn led them to a modest Earthlen I.S. Cruiser with a black snake painted near the cockpit.

She ducked under the belly of the ship and climbed up the rung ladder into the cargo hold.

Cyn helped pull her up then took Vicca as Soren handed her through the hatch.

Soren climbed through and paused before swinging the hatch door shut.

"Welcome to the Black Serpent," Cyn announced. "We can speak openly here. The ship is free of transmitters, Roglen tele-amplifiers, and hull rats, for the most part."

Just at that moment, Vicca jumped behind a crate and pulled out a spindly legged rodent with wiry hair and began chomping on its head.

Cyn scowled then shook his head. "Clever scout you have there." He let Bug loose. The disc tipped down toward Vicca. She put a paw on her prey and growled while her tail swished back and forth.

"I thought I told you to get rid of the rats," Cyn scolded.

The disc turned pink for a moment and tipped in a way that seemed to shrug. Cyn shook his head then looked back at them. "Come into the bunk hull; I'll explain everything."

Cyani felt dizzy from shock and the millions of unanswered questions floating around in her head. Cyn suddenly bent over, then looked straight up, blinking rapidly.

"Son of a bitch," he grumbled. He stopped at a basin near the door to the bunk hull. He bent over, and it looked like he swiped something from his eye.

He looked over at her. One eye was pitch black, and the other bright green.

"Contacts, ancient Earthlen technology," he explained as he dropped some liquid from a vial onto a small dark object on his finger. Cyani watched in horror as he touched it directly to his eye. He blinked a couple of times then stretched his neck as if he hadn't stuck a foreign object directly on his cornea. "The Earthlen go to great lengths to manipulate their appearances. Sometimes it comes in handy. I wasn't willing to have permanent color injected. That's just creepy, and much less versatile."

He was definitely her brother. The world could be crashing down around them, and he'd talk about something completely trivial. Cyani felt her patience running out as she slipped into the bunk hull. Four beds covered with exotic woven blankets jutted out on platforms, and a small galley filled one corner. Trinkets from far-flung reaches of the galaxy floated in antigravity cases strapped at the ends of each bunk. Was her brother a shadow trader?

Bug floated into the room and rested on a quilted pillow on the edge of an antigravity case.

"Cyn, if I don't get some answers right now—" Cyani didn't have time to finish her sentence because Cyn wrapped her in a huge hug. He squeezed her tight, so tight she could barely breathe. She wrapped her arms around him and took a moment to just feel safe. He was her brother. He was alive. She held on to him tighter as she struggled with a surge of overwhelming emotion.

"God, I missed you. I thought I lost you," he said. "I thought you died on that damn asteroid. I've been watching every assignment you've had for the last four years, but you've been too deep in the war zone for me to contact. When I intercepted word that you were alive, I pulled some strings and nearly busted my ass to get here in time."

Suddenly all the questions didn't matter. He was safe, alive, and out of the shadows. It was all she had ever wanted. She missed him so badly. She felt a hot stinging in her eyes and pressed them into her brother's shoulder before she let any tears fall.

She had to get control of herself. She took a deep breath and let her brother go. Soren leaned up against the archway leading to the cockpit and crossed his arms. He eyed Bug with a suspicious scowl. Her head was still swimming. She had to focus.

"Do you really work for the Union? Why are you pretending to be from Earth? What happened to Mom and Dad? Damn it, Cyn, you have to tell me everything, and you'd better not start talking about the weather on Cirat's fourth moon." She sat down on one of the bunks while Cyn picked up a dented cup and filled it with something from a tall, narrow flask. He lifted the flask toward Soren, but Soren waved it off.

"I'm pretending to be from Earth because I am from Earth," he said. "No one knows my real identity, and I prefer to keep it that way. The Grand Sister has no idea we are out of the shadows. I want her to think we are rotting down in the ground cities for as long as possible."

"We?" Cyani could barely push the word out of her constricting throat.

"Mom, Dad, and I escaped Azra and fled to Earth two years after you were taken. We thought you were dead. We were certain they killed you. It wasn't until the Union hired me as a linguist that I learned you were still alive."

One thing at a time, she could only process one thing at a time. Her mother and father were alive, too, and safe. Her whole family was safe. Suddenly she felt like the last dozen years struggling to become one of the Elite meant nothing. She had been fighting to find a way to save her brother, and the whole time he had been safe.

"So you're a linguist for the Union, then?" Soren asked.

"I offered my services as a cultural liaison when I caught wind that Cyani had survived so I'd have an excuse to come here, but I've discovered some very disturbing information. The Union is far too interested in where Byra is, and not interested enough in making sure you reach home," Cyn confided. "The ongoing innuendo I've had to suffer through is that I should glean as much information from you as I can before you die and call it a day. Your people are priceless in the shadow trade, and the Union considers you primitive. That's a bad combination. Corruption can run deep, even in societies with noble intentions."

"That's comforting," Soren huffed.

"How do you know all this?" Cyani asked.

He chuckled. "C'mon, sis, you know me. Let's just say I'm involved in some crap I'd rather not speak about, and I've come across some information through my—how should I put this?—shadier business partners that directly concerns you." Cyn tipped his cup to Soren, but Soren didn't say a thing. The only sound in the ship was the sickening crunch of Vicca's unfortunate snack.

"What are you involved in?" Cyani crossed her arms.

Cyn scowled at her. "I trade valuable information, that's all. The point is, I intercepted a transmission from one of the nastier shadow market dealers. The guy is pure scum, but he is very rich scum. He's expecting something worth over seven hundred and fifty thousand bars of conductive trillide to come into his stock within the next twenty hours, from this base. If you sold everything on this base and all the people in it, it wouldn't be worth that much, and only small transports are due into the base tonight. There is only one thing on this base worth that much money."

"Me," Soren supplied.

Cyani's heart raced as she turned to look at Soren. "Who's behind this?"

"Probably a Med officer. I know someone purchased a karnul extract on this base, and a medic would be able to hide it and handle it." Cyn swallowed the contents of his cup, and winced.

"What is karnul?" Soren asked.

"A poison. Sneaky stuff," Cyani explained. "It is very difficult to detect, so it's a favorite of assassins."

"If you also have the antidote, it's handy for faking someone's death, especially someone whose race has a reputation for dying suddenly anyway." Cyn tossed his cup in a sanitizer. "I have to go pull a few more favors to get the flight permissions to leave. I'll be back as soon as I can, and we'll talk in macrospace."

"Where are we going?" Cyani asked.

"Where do you want to go?" Cyn cocked his head as he looked at her. Her brother was fond of word games. She had a feeling this was a test.

Damn him. Cyani felt the endless weight of the universe closing in on her like a heavy dark net she couldn't escape. Soren's eyes burned as she looked at him, then her brother. The Grand Sister knew she was alive and expected her to return immediately. If she didn't return, the Grand Sister would know she'd openly defied her.

She couldn't risk the Grand Sister ordering a bloodhunt on her family. If they were on Earth, it wouldn't take much to track them down. The Earthlen were practically drunk on sharing information. The only reason they hadn't been found already is because no one was looking. Now that she knew her family was safe, the thought of an Elite bloodhunter capturing one of them sickened her. She couldn't stand it.

The Grand Sister would send Yara. The Elite warrior was smart and relentless. Yara took great pride in her bloodline. She was a true daughter of Yarini the Just. The rule of law was black-and-white for the exceptionally talented but untested warrior. It didn't matter what disguise Cyn wore, she'd find him. She'd find him, and if the Grand Sister ordered it, she'd kill him. Yara never questioned her orders. Cyani couldn't contain her rising panic. Her family had to stay safe. She had to protect them. It was all she had thought about for over a decade. She had no choice.

"I have to return to Azra."

Soren dropped his dark gaze to the floor. She couldn't read Cyn as he turned away from her and entered the cargo hold.

"You don't have to return," Soren said as soon as they were alone. "Your brother could help us escape."

"I can't escape now," Cyani admitted. "Soren, if I tried to run now, the Grand Sister would send a bloodhunter after us, after my family. It was one thing on Makko when no one knew I was alive, but now that I know Cyn is safe, he has a life to lose, too, and I can't be responsible for that. You haven't bonded to me." A chill ran down her neck. "Have you?"

He didn't answer.

"Soren, did you bond with me last night?" she asked again.

He took a step forward and reached out for her, but she backed away. "Tell me the truth."

"No," he said as he retreated back into the opening to the cockpit.

She didn't know what she would do if he had bonded with her. She couldn't pretend that there were no consequences anymore.

She sighed. She had to take him for his word, and no matter what, from this point on out, she had to resist him.

How could she resist him when her body knew what he could do to her?

"Then you'll be safe, and you can find a mate to heal you once we get you home." She tried to hold back the bitterness that edged into her voice. A flash of what he had looked like stretched out beneath her with the firelight playing in his hair and over his golden skin taunted her from her memory. They had shared something holy. No other woman could give him that.

She had to stop. Her thoughts would only hurt them both. "I promise you, even if I can't go with you, Cyn will help you. I'm not going to let you die." It would rip her heart out, but she would not let him die. She felt torn between saving him and protecting her family.

Soren lightly touched her face, drawing her toward him. She couldn't help herself. She leaned forward as he whispered near her temple. "Is this really what you want, Cyani? A life without being touched, a life without passion or love?"

He brushed his lips over hers, so soft, so full of promise. Her body hummed with tension as she felt herself come alive with feeling. In her mind she could see the colors swirling together. She needed him so badly.

"No," she whispered against his lips. "It's not what I want, but I have no choice."

"There's always a choice," Soren murmured, then kissed her.

16

THE GLOWING, FLYING, MECHANICAL CREATURE LET OUT A PIP, THEN A DRAWN out whistle that sounded remarkably like "*woo-hoo.*"

Soren cursed as they broke the kiss. Cyani pulled away from him.

"Soren," she murmured. "I can't do this anymore. I can't." She paced between the beds like a trapped animal.

She had to. His life depended on it. He wasn't satisfied with reaching his home so he could die anymore. He wanted her. He wanted a long, peaceful life with her by his side, and in his bed. He had to convince her to take the risk. They could find a place to hide and live in peace. The universe was large enough to conceal them.

He pressed a hand to the center of her chest, stopping her restless motion. His thumb feathered over her collar. The beads of the necklace he had given her pressed into her flesh from their hiding place beneath her uniform. She knew what the necklace meant to them both, and she hadn't taken it off. She wanted this bond, and he knew it.

"Why are you still wearing this?"

She touched her hand to his and slowly pulled it away.

"Defy her," Soren said, his anger and frustration putting an edge to his voice. "She has you trapped, she has you chained, and for what? You're stronger than she is, Cyani. You fear her assassins, but you have much more talent than they do. I know you do. Her assassins have been trying to kill you your whole life, remember? They haven't succeeded, and you've been right under their noses."

Cyani stepped away from him, but didn't say anything. She seemed deep in thought. She retreated into the cockpit. Bug followed her and hovered near her shoulder.

She sat down in the copilot's seat and ran her finger along the edge of a slightly worn control screen.

"It's not me I'm worried about," she admitted without looking at him.

Her brother opened the door to the cargo hold and entered the living quarters. Bug zipped over, did a quick loop, and tapped the top of his head to greet him. Cyn caught the edge of the glowing disc and spun it with a quick flick. It let out a high-pitched "*Weeeee*" as it spun around the room. Cyn's wry smile betrayed his amusement as he crossed the room and walked into the cockpit.

"I've got clearance for a macrospace leap to Azra. We'll be there in a gnat's nut. Whoever's after Soren is either still asleep, or not on the base, because so far, no one's trying to stop us." He tapped commands into one of the overhead panels, then jabbed a lever with the heel of his palm. "Let's not press our luck." Cyn threw himself in the pilot's seat.

"So, is that our destination, sis?" He leaned back in the pilot's seat and crossed his arms, then kicked his heels up onto the edge of Cyani's chair, as if her choice didn't matter to him, but the steely gaze he leveled on her said far more than her brother wanted to reveal. Soren was far too adept at reading expressions for him to hide his intentions. He was testing her, and so far, she was failing. What was driving him? Her brother seemed to change faces, even personalities, as quickly as Soren's eyes changed color. He was a man of deception, and Soren wasn't entirely sure he could trust him or his motives.

Soren turned his attention to Cyani as anger and frustration tore at his gut. She taunted him with her indecision. It gave him hope. He watched carefully as she lifted a hand to her neck and traced the edge of his necklace beneath her uniform. "I have to return to Azra," she said, but her voice told a different story.

Cyn cast a dark glance back toward him. "Fine. Better have a seat, Soren."

Soren eased onto one of the bunks, leaning his back up against the wall where he could still see into the cockpit. Cyani's brother was a mystery to him, but perhaps he had an ally.

The ship lifted into the air and pushed forward through the docking shield into the open expanse of empty space. The glowing orb of Makko fell away into the black abyss. He nodded a good-bye to Lakal, and in his heart he wished his friend's spirit peace and happiness in his afterlife.

The ship surged forward, and with a lurch, settled into the peaceful stillness of macrospace.

The last time he and Cyani had made the leap, he wasn't sure if they'd live or die. The same sense of dread fell over him. He didn't know what his fate would be as soon as the ship dropped out of macrospace.

Cyani sat in the copilot seat, staring at the blank screen. She looked as lost as he felt.

He pulled Vicca up into his lap and closed his eyes. His mind was filled with Cyani. He remembered the first time he saw her face after an endless stretch of nothing but darkness. It was beautiful then; she was ethereal now. He'd never forget the way the light played on her naked skin as she straddled him. She was the only woman he'd loved, the only woman he would *ever* love. He tried to convince himself that it was enough, that it was more than he thought he would ever have in his life through his long years of torture, but it wasn't enough.

How could he finally break through to her?

She glanced back at him, a stolen look in the dim silence. She was reaching for him, too. He had to convince her to hold on, in spite of the consequences.

"We're about to drop out of macrospace," Cyn announced. His little machine whirred around the cockpit then landed on the worn patchwork pillow tied to the edge of one of the cases bolted to the wall. Six tiny metal claws emerged from the underside of the disc and hugged the pillow tight.

The ship dropped, and the screen in the cockpit came to life. An enormous turquoise planet loomed before them. Soren watched in fascination as they tore through the fiery atmosphere and flew over a churning ocean. On the horizon, a land mass arose. High dark cliffs dropped straight down into frothing waves. At the top of the cliffs, a mass of tangled jungle clung to the rock.

Soren could see other islands in the distance. The planet was littered with them, jutting up out of the violent sea. The ship rose to nearly the top of the tree line, flushing thousands of birds from their perches, and landed on one of six white platforms floating near the canopy of trees.

Cyani didn't move as she stared at the swaying leaves, but her face paled. Cyn rose first and pulled the sleeves of his shadowsuit down then adjusted his glove to carefully hide his tattoo. What lengths would the man go through to hide who he really was?

With a quick bark, Vicca leapt off Soren's lap. She whined and put her paws on his knee. He stroked her head. The fox blinked up at him, then snuck over to Cyani with her tail dragging on the ground. Without a word Cyani led the way into the hold and descended the ladder. Soren followed her, tempted to reach out and pull her back into the ship, but Cyn was at his back, waiting to descend onto the platform.

Soren had to shield his eyes from the light glaring off the pristine platform. A small open ship hovered at the far end.

Two warriors stood with emotionless faces at the transport. Their pure white clothing clung to their bodies while the sun glinted off the knives strapped to their bare forearms.

Had Cyani ever been so hard? So cold?

She tried to form her face into an emotionless mask, but she couldn't hide the sadness in her eyes. He would always be able to read her.

"Stay safe," she said to him. Her voice sounded rough. She paused as if she wanted to say something else, but she dropped her head and joined the other two warriors. Vicca trotted obediently at her heel but looked back over her shoulder at him, holding her ears low against her head.

Soren felt his heart rip as if she were pulling part of it with her. He tried to steel himself, but couldn't. She was killing him.

She stepped into the ship, squared her shoulders, and held her head high. She became the warrior, strong, noble. Her eyes—only her eyes—turned back to him as the ship took off into the trees.

He felt Cyn's reassuring hand on his shoulder, a solid weight of a common bond.

"Don't worry. We haven't lost her yet." Cyn gave his shoulder a quick thump then strode back to the hatch. "Come on, we don't have much time. I could use your help."

Soren watched the trees for a moment, unwilling to let go of the image of Cyani standing on the platform. When the heat radiating off the platform became too much, he reluctantly followed Cyn into the ship. The man sat in the pilot's seat, quickly stabbing at the various panels and watching a line of gibberish flash across the main screen too quickly for any normal person to possibly read.

"They're getting tricky," he mumbled to himself. He typed almost as quickly as the figures scrolling across the display. "Not tricky enough. Got 'em."

The screen went black, and Cyn smiled. He rose from his chair and stood near one of the beds. He immediately stripped and donned a pair of black pants then threw a loose black shirt with slit sleeves over his head.

"How did you knock out the people in Med?" He pulled a pile of clothing out of a storage locker and tossed it on the bed followed by two dagger harnesses. "Are you going to change?" he asked. Soren looked at him like the man had just sprouted a third arm.

"Why do you care what I did to the people in Med?" he asked, his words tinged with caution. The hair on the back of his neck rose as he took one of the knives. "What's going on?"

"Just curious," Cyn responded. "Your talent for making people keel over might come in handy where we're heading." He buckled leather cuffs over his forearms, carefully hiding his Azralen coloring and his tattoos.

"I'm not going anywhere with you."

"Don't you trust me?" He flashed his sardonic smile as he tied a sash over his head. The back draped down, giving him the impression of long dark hair. He looked like a criminal.

"If you think you're going to sell me, I'll show you exactly what I did to the people in Med, only you won't wake up," Soren challenged.

Cyn turned to him as if Soren had just gut punched him. The irreverent smile disappeared like a fleeting illusion. His face turned hard with sudden anger. In a moment he looked like he had aged about ten years. He pulled the collar of his shirt aside, revealing a slashing scar over his chest. "I received this from a flesh trader when I stole his *meat*. I free people. I don't sell them."

Soren grabbed him by the shirt, bunching the material in

his fists as he thrust his damaged wrists up so Cyn could see them. "These scars say one thing. I'm worth seven hundred fifty thousand of your bars of rat shit. And until you tell me exactly what's going on, I have no reason to trust you. For all I know *you* are the one who wanted to sell me to *your* seedy contact and that is why you were in such a rush to get off the base and come here."

He shoved Cyn back and widened his stance. He could feel his eyes flashing, and he didn't care.

"I think I like you," Cyn said. "Get dressed. What I'm doing is right up your alley. It's your chance for a little revenge against those scars. I'm wrapped up in some complicated business on this planet. But before I leave, I'm going down to the ground cities and smuggling out a couple of kids from under the nose of a flesh trader who sells them as whores," Cyn confided, his tone turning serious. "That's the truth."

"What will you do with them?" Soren asked, still suspicious, but the threat he had felt had left. The man completely baffled him, but perhaps he could trust him.

"I take them to a planet whose people accidentally sterilized themselves trying to vaccinate against a plague. They need children to adopt so their culture doesn't die. I give them the kids they desperately want, but the fun part is stealing those kids from the mudrats on the ground below us." He strapped a knife to his thigh then seemed thoughtful. "Well, it's rewarding so long as you don't die or end up with large scars across your chest. That's why I need your help. You in?" Cyn asked him.

Soren reluctantly stripped off his shirt and changed into the one Cyn had tossed on the bed. He couldn't stand back while Cyani's brother went on a potential suicide run to save a bunch of abused babies. The man was insane, but if he was anything like his sister, at heart he was noble. Soren chose to trust him, for now.

"I'm in," he growled. "If only to keep an eye on you."

"Good," Cyn said with a smile. "Let's see what else I have stashed in here."

He sorted through a small arsenal of weaponry, and they both strapped enough knives to their various limbs to take out half the Garulen army.

"Only knives?" Soren asked.

"Fire off anything interesting in the ground cities and you'll be mobbed for it. Knives aren't in such high demand down there. You ready?" Cyn asked as he pushed into the cockpit and tapped quickly at the control panel. "Once we leave the ship, call me Cobra. If the Grand Sister decides to get her panties all bunched up again, I don't want her or one of her bloodhunters to find me."

"Understood." Soren switched his translator to project Azralen. "I'm starting to think you're a good man, Cyn."

"Don't spread it around, or I'll lose my reputation." Cyn slapped him on the back.

"Don't make me change my mind." Soren tied his hair back and pulled on a pair of thick boots.

The ship hummed and trembled, as if it was storing energy but couldn't hold on to it. Suddenly a sharp crack sounded through the hull, like electricity discharging.

"We don't have much time. The pulse will only disrupt the Elite monitoring systems for an hour."

He dropped down the hatch and Soren joined him. In the

shadows near a tangle of swaying vines, a dark-haired woman dressed all in black stood with her arms crossed. A scar puckered her pale skin on her lower cheek and chin.

"Asara, my pleasure," Cyn greeted.

"I'm sure it is," she grumbled. "You had to land on an Elite platform, didn't you? Is landing in the mid-cities not enough of a thrill anymore? Who's this?"

"He's trustworthy. He's here to help. Any news on hacking the array?" Cyn strode over to another small ship like the one Cyani had left in. Soren stepped up onto the hovering deck of the black vessel.

"It's going to be impossible. We'd need tech we don't have, or we'll never be able to communicate with the mining bases. Uyl would need a com blocker that is already coded to the Azralen array at the very least," she responded, her suspicious eyes never leaving Soren.

"I'll work on that. How many this time?" Cyn asked.

"Three: one boy, two girls. The eldest carries," the woman answered. "Be quick—I don't know how long I can distract the Elite."

"Just drop us down and lift us back up. That's all I ask."

"Yeah, right," she huffed. "Hold on."

The ship hovered over the edge of the white landing platform then plummeted straight down without warning at a gut-churning speed. Soren held on to the seat as they plunged into the darkness through whipping branches. The thick, humid air choked him with the smell of rotting vegetation and mold, but soon turned to a strangling odor of sewage and death.

The branches fell away until all that was left were ghostly

pale trunks of enormous trees rising over stifled fires below. It was unlike any forest he had ever seen. The forests of his home world were open and full of life from the treetops to the rich soil below. On this world, the cities in the canopy choked out all life and light below.

The ship slowed, and Soren had a fleeting memory of the failing gravity generators on the stingship. He couldn't lift his hands off the seat as the weight of the stop forced him into a stoop. The pressure let up as the ship landed delicately on a platform slapped together from the hull of a rusted-out transport.

"Be careful, Cobra. They're waiting for you at Cular." With a nod, the woman took off again, shooting straight up out of the oppressive shadows. If the people here mobbed for a sono, Soren didn't want to think of what they would do to get their hands on a ship.

"Welcome to the real Azra," Cyn ground out. "Keep your eyes open as soon as they stop watering, and stay wary."

Soren wiped his eyes as he adjusted to the rank smell. A city, if you could call it that, rose up out of the sticky black mud like rotting teeth in a rabid wolf's mouth. Buildings had been slapped together from garbage, the castoffs of wealth from above, to form ramshackle huts and alcoves of jagged metal. Rotting tree trunks thrust up out of the ground at odd angles, while bits of threadbare fabric hung over makeshift doorways.

A corpse rotted in the mud to their left. Soren stared, horrified as a red and black snake peered out of the gaping eye socket. The corpse's pale lips had rotted back to reveal a cruel welcoming grimace.

Cyani had grown up here?

The stillness unnerved him as he jogged next to Cyn. He could feel desperate eyes, dangerous eyes, watching him from the concealing darkness.

Fires burned in upturned cans or in any large bit of metal with a basin. His foot sank into a deep bit of mud, and he could see living things churning just beneath the surface, bugs feeding off the wretched decay.

Cyn gave him a hand and pulled him out. This was far worse than the slave cells of the Garulen. At least they hauled out the dead. How could anyone live here?

They turned a corner into a sloppy street of sorts. "Soren," Cyn whispered. "I've counted five armed men following us. Looks like an ambush. How do you knock people out?"

"They have to come close and face me," he mumbled back. Awareness trickled down his spine as he pieced out the five moving shadows as well. "It is better if I can hit them all at once. We need our backs to a wall."

"This way," Cyn grabbed his forearm and turned them into a dead end.

They heard a chuckle, then an answering laugh. Like blood ravens circling wounded prey, the five men slowly emerged from the shadows.

"Stay behind me and close your eyes, just in case," Soren warned. The dark shadows stalked forward. Firelight glinted off a jagged blade. He gathered his strength, waiting for the right moment. They had to come closer. He could see their eyes shining with cruel hunger.

"Uh, Soren, now would be good," Cyn prompted as he reached for his daggers.

Soren pushed out with all of his strength. The flash of light illuminated the dark alley like a strike of lightning. One by one the men swayed and flopped into the squirming mud with a satisfying *splat*.

Cyn chuckled. "I wish I could take you along every time I did this," he commented.

"I think I'll pass on the smell, the rotting corpses, and the murderous gangs of thugs, thanks. The only reason I'm here is the children," Soren responded as they ran out of the alley and down another shadowy street.

"Unfortunately it's part and parcel, my friend." Cyn ducked down, and motioned to Soren to stay put as he peered around a corner. He climbed up the rusted plate behind them and onto a thin metal beam with silent precision. He crept across it until Soren lost sight of him. Soren pulled his knife. He heard a thump, a surprised grunt, and a body fall into the mud.

Soren turned the corner to see Cyn crouching over the body of a big beast of a man guarding the bottom of a staircase.

Cyn didn't seem fazed by the body at his feet. "No matter what, don't let yourself get wounded. The mud is toxic."

Soren nodded, but didn't say a word.

They climbed up the spiral staircase cut into the trunk of a long dead and decaying tree. The stairs felt spongy beneath his feet, and several had rotted toward the trunk until they were nothing more than a crumbling nub of soft wood, or a platform of springy fungus. Soren tried not to think about one giving way beneath him and throwing him down to his death. At the top perched a building, the only sign of any money in the area.

Its red brown walls looked like they had been painted with

dried blood and sagged at odd angles, giving the building an uncanny resemblance to a lopsided, bleeding fungus on a rotting log. A relatively solid-looking landing pad seemed out of place as it hovered at the front of the building, while dim blue lights flickered inside.

"I need you to care for the children and get them down the staircase and to the ground. I'll handle the guards. One of the kids is probably around thirteen—she'll be able to help you, but I have no idea how young the other two are. They may be beaters."

"Beaters?"

"Offspring of the whores," Cyn growled. "They beat, cut, starve or brand the babies if one of the mothers steps out of line. That is, until the babies are old enough to start earning money themselves."

"I'll get them out," Soren promised. He would protect them with his life and the fury born of knowing their darkness and pain.

"Good man." Cyn swung one-handed beneath the support beams. He hooked a leg up and gave Soren his hand as he hung upside down by the crook of his knee. He punched through a trapdoor in the floor of the building and they struggled up through the hole, careful not to make any noise.

They crept down a narrow hall. Loose slats of boards let light through thin slits in the rotting wood. They reached a ladder and climbed up a level. A girl in her twenties met them. Her wide eyes betrayed her fear. Like an abused animal chained to its suffering, she moved with jerky, nervous steps. "Come with me," she whispered, her pale face ghostly in the dim light.

She led them to a tiny room at the end of another long hallway. Cyn slowly opened the door. Three children huddled in a corner in the dark, their spindly limbs wrapped around one another. The eldest couldn't have been more than fourteen, and yet her stomach was swollen with new life. She stroked the filthy hair of an eight-year-old girl with dark, haunted eyes, while a toddler boy with branding scars on his chest cuddled in her lap.

"Are you the Cobra?" the young girl asked.

"Yes," Cyn answered. His voice sounded soft and almost melodic. He knelt down and smoothed a bit of hair from the girl's forehead. "Do you know what I do?"

"Master says you steal children to eat them," she said, lifting her small chin in defiance.

"Do you believe it?" Cyn asked.

"No," she said. "He lies."

"What do you believe, little one?"

"I believe you're magic, and you will take us someplace pretty and safe. Is that true?" she challenged.

"It is," he answered with his characteristic smile. "Every word. Are you ready to go?"

She placed her tiny hand in his. The pregnant girl nodded with tears in her eyes.

The woman who had led them cradled the boy's face in her hands and desperately kissed him. "Go with the Cobra, my dear little one," she whispered. "He will keep you safe." The baby reached up and fisted his small hands in her hair.

"Mama go?" his weak little voice asked.

The house shuddered as the whine of ship engines filled the small room. Lights from one of the flying vessels shone through the slatted planks of the outer wall, casting the room in a frenzied light.

"The master's back early," the woman said as she spun in a frantic circle. She wiped the tears from her wild eyes and handed the baby to Soren. The little boy reached out for his mother.

"Mama!" he cried as he struggled. Soren snuggled him close to his body and stroked his greasy hair. The poor baby weighed nothing. "Mama, you go?" Soren couldn't stand it anymore. He turned the boy's face to his and sent him to sleep.

"We're getting you out, too," Cyn told the mother as she touched her baby's face to make sure he was okay. Cyn grabbed her hand and placed a knife in it. "Ask for Ceer at the tavern in Ahul. Tell her I sent you. She'll help you escape to the refugee colonies. If you want, I can leave your boy."

The woman shook her head and clenched the knife. "No, get him out of this place. Please, I want him safe, to have a real mother."

Cyn placed his hand on her cheek. "You are a real mother. When I can, I'll try to get a com image of him back to Ceer. He'll be happy."

"I know," she whispered. The thunk of men's footsteps rattled through the timbers from the floor above. "Get them out."

Without another word, Soren stepped forward and took the hand of the little girl. She looked at him with faith and trust he didn't deserve. If fate never allowed him to be a father, he'd make up for it now.

He had to get them out.

He led the children down the hall while Cyn branched off down a second passageway.

With great care, he helped the children and the mother down through the support beams and onto the staircase. He pressed his back against the trunk to let the pregnant girl slide past him so she could be in front. She shook so badly as she passed him he was afraid she would collapse.

He heard the sounds of shouting, of metal striking metal from the hall above.

The mother paused, and almost turned back like an animal running into a burning thicket. Soren took her arm and forced her down the stairs.

"Go," he commanded her, knowing she didn't understand his words. "Go."

She flew down the staircase while he raced down with her. The rotting wood crumbled and compressed under his heavy steps, but he didn't have time for caution. He'd have to cling to faith. A man charged up the stairs from the ground, brandishing a sharpened stake of metal. The pregnant girl screamed and fell down on the stairs, sliding toward the attacker. The step in front of them crumbled and Soren pushed forward, catching the pregnant girl as the child behind him clung to his thigh. The attacker lunged forward, his eyes wide with depraved victory as he rushed toward them.

Soren let his eyes flash, and the man stumbled and fell off the stairs to the ground below. The pregnant child screeched and jumped back toward Soren. He pushed her ahead of him and forced them to keep moving until they reached the ground.

The mother turned back to him. She took the boy into her

arms. With a desperate hug and a kiss to his sleeping head she whispered to him. "I love you, baby. Know always I love you."

"I won't let him forget," the pregnant girl assured in a shaking voice. "He *will* know who you are, and what you did for him."

Tears streaming down her face, she pushed the baby back into Soren's arms. She gave the others a quick hug and slipped into the dark shadows.

Soren led the two girls into a shadowed alcove. The pregnant girl looked fearfully up at him while her hand splayed protectively over her belly. The little girl curled into his side. Her trust in him unnerved him.

"It's going to be okay," he whispered to them as he placed the sleeping baby in the shaking arms of the oldest girl. It seemed like such an inadequate thing to say. They couldn't understand him anyway. He unsheathed two of his knives. The younger girl flinched and cringed away from him. What had they suffered?

He knew. That was what killed him—at the heart of it, he knew.

He took up a protective stance at the mouth of their small metal cave. They had to wait for Cyn before they could return to the platform. He would return. He was Cyani's twin.

Just then Cyn leapt off the last few stairs and landed on a thick pipe with the grace of a cat. A streak of blood splattered over one side of his face. He wiped his red hands on his shirt. "Don't worry, it's not mine," he mentioned as if he wasn't wearing the brutal evidence of his deadly nature on his face. He really was Cyani's twin. "Time to go," he added. Soren took the baby back to save the girl's strength. She would need it.

They raced through the shadows until they reached the platform. Asara waved a frantic hand to hurry them as she reached down to hoist the children onto the landing pad. The girls stumbled as she helped them into the pod. Soren lifted them onto the seats as he fell down, still clinging to the baby asleep on his shoulder. The rush of adrenaline made his muscles feel rubbery and weak. He could only imagine how the girls felt as they clung to one another.

"You're a mess," Asara commented to Cyn as she landed in the seat in front of the controls.

"It could be worse—you should see the other guy." He shrugged.

"One less rat to worry about. Stash the children, and anything else you have that's interesting in your ship. The Elite have ordered a search."

The children clung to Soren as the ship shot straight up out of the darkness into the twilight of the branches. He stared in wonder at the floating cities built into the trunks and out on the limbs of the great trees. Above them light streamed through the green leaves of the canopy.

They came to a stomach-lurching halt at the glittering white platform where Cyn's dark ship perched. The children couldn't open their eyes in the glaring light. Soren had to squint himself as he helped lead the blinded children into the Serpent. Muddy tears streamed down their gaunt faces. Soren felt helpless to comfort them. They had probably never seen the light before. Some of the most glorious things in life could be painful. He had learned that lesson as well.

As soon as they were inside the hull, Cyn went to work on the shocked children.

"Here," he said as he offered them a small round ball. "Lick it. It's sweet. And drink this." He gave them vessels of water. "What are your names?"

"Essa," the pregnant one responded in a small lost voice. "She is Calya, and the little one is Sene."

"Nice to meet you," he said. "Soren, take the baby into the cleanser. I have clothes and a diaper for him here on the bed."

A pirate with diapers. Cyn was nothing if not prepared.

Soren stepped into the cleanser. He had to fight back his own fear as he held the baby in the cramped silver tube. Reluctantly he shut the door, and pressed his hand to the activator. The walls glowed with pearl-like waves of light. The baby stirred in his arms as warm air swirled around them. The terrible smell of the ground cities dissipated as Soren watched the grime melt away from the baby's skin. His curly hair fluffed up, revealing iridescent flashes in the dark locks, like the wing of a blackbird.

As soon as they were clean, Soren gratefully stepped back out of the cleanser. For claustrophobic technology, it wasn't that bad. Cyn crouched in front of the girls, keeping his posture low and unthreatening.

"But that was the only way the monkey could escape," he said, caught in the middle of a story. Bug flew around them doing loops and shining with different colors.

Cyn stood. He handed the girls neatly folded dresses. "Time to clean you up. Don't worry. It's magic. It won't hurt. The baby didn't even wake up."

He shuffled them both into the cleanser as Soren tried to figure out which way the diaper fit on the baby. He brushed his fingertips over the scars on the child's chest. He was too young to know such pain.

"I'm sorry, little one," he whispered as he glanced at the scars around his wrists. "I'm sorry for both of us. It'll be better. I promise."

The girls came out of the cleanser wearing the clean white dresses. Calya giggled, smiling for the very first time. "You really are magic," she laughed.

Essa smiled, too, as if she couldn't quite believe the ship was real. She kept running a hand through her clean hair.

"I need you to hide in here," Cyn explained to Essa. He opened a hatch in the hull, and inside was a small chamber with pillows, blankets, and a couple of toys. "Keep them quiet. We will leave soon for your new home."

"Thank you, Cobra," she whispered. "I'll protect them."

In that moment, Soren saw Cyani as a child. Now he knew the extent of the darkness that had haunted her childhood and the depravity that honed her into a determined warrior. He had witnessed firsthand one of her nightmares. He couldn't shake the sick feeling in his heart as he thought about the children. He and Cyn had ripped them from everything they had known, including the toddler's mother. Yet they faced the challenge with guts he couldn't help but admire, just as Cyani had done.

Cyn closed the safe cocoon around the children and jumped into the cleanser. He came out as if he'd never been touched by the shadows of the ground cities. He was dressed in his shadowsuit.

He transformed from ground city outlaw and smuggler to

a respectable Union officer right before Soren's eyes. He punched more codes into the control panel. Suddenly, the antigravity cases and parts of the hold pushed back into the walls of the ship as if they never existed.

Bug flew up and buzzed with irritation as his pillow disappeared into the wall.

"You're coming with me, Bug," Cyn said in a commanding voice. Bug sank down a few feet in the air and then reluctantly landed on Cyn's hand. He promptly tucked him into his belt.

"Where are you going?" Soren asked.

"I'm going to get my sister back," he answered. "I'm not through with her yet."

17

TOWERING STATUES OF THE GREAT MATRIARCHS LEERED DOWN ON CYANI AS she passed through the Halls of Honor. They loomed at least ten meters tall, carved out of the pure white branches of the canopy. Leaves rustled, casting a dappled soft green light through the open archways onto the polished alabaster floor.

Through her training, she had remained in the lower levels of the Elite complex. She had not walked beneath the eyes of the Matriarchs since the first day they dragged her beaten and broken into the high cities.

Execute her.

The memory echoed through the archways as if the Matriarchs whispered it themselves.

Cyani felt the weight of her necklace press against the center of her chest, the dark beads a stark contrast to the austere white canvas of her training robes.

Cyani peered up at the last Matriarch standing guard over the traditions of Azra. Cyrila the Rebel seemed to smile at her.

She passed through the cavernous throne room. The empty seat of authority floated above the floor, suspended by a spiraling branch carved with ornate steps. The first time she had seen the Grand Sister, her holiness sat upon that throne, untouched by the chaos and rage seething in the crowd below.

A whip snapped, echoing through the empty chamber.

Cyani steeled herself and entered the Grand Sister's personal quarters.

Purified rainwater trickled through intricate channels in the walls and fell over tiny bells that lit as they chimed. Leaves rustled, crowded under the bleached awnings stretching overhead.

The whip cracked again. Cyani stiffened, unable to control the reflex that had been beaten into her.

"Cyani, my dear child, come in." The Grand Sister had removed her embroidered mantle, exposing bony shoulders as they flexed beneath pale skin. The Grand Sister's short hair had faded to nearly white as if her whole body had been leeched of color. She let the braided whip slither over the floor as she ended one of the Ahora routines. Her bony hands slid suggestively over the thick shaft of the whip.

"I've read the reports from your service in the Union. You performed admirably. I'm surprisingly pleased with your ingenuity. I didn't expect that from you." She turned. Her eyes shone vibrant blue. They were the only thing keeping her from looking like one of the statues of the matriarchs come to life.

Cyani knew to remain silent. The Grand Sister had a way of twisting words. The less she said the better.

"I am disappointed in the performance of the scout V-166A, though. Refusal to obey simple commands, independent behavior. Clearly poorly bred, it has far too much white in its coat for a respectable scout. I'm surprised the breeder didn't crack its neck when it was a pup. It will be sold to a trade transport as a ratter. It was never fit for more than that. My scout recently had a litter of kittens. I'll have the one with the most potential reserved for you."

Cyani blinked repeatedly, the only outward sign of her inner shock and fury. How many times had Vicca's independent spirit saved her life? And if she ever disobeyed, it was for good reason. She couldn't lose her scout.

The Grand Sister slowly coiled the whip, keeping hold of the handle, then lifted a clear goblet with an opalescent liquid to her lips.

Cyani couldn't protest. If she showed undue affection for Vicca, the Grand Sister would kill her scout to make a point about remaining unattached to anything.

After her shock began to wane, she realized the second part of what the Grand Sister had said. She wanted to give Cyani one of the offspring of her scout? *Why?*

"That would be an honor." She managed to force the lie out of her constricting throat. "But why would I need such a well-bred scout? Won't I be assigned to the temple?"

As soon as she took her vows, she assumed she would be one of the low-level orderlies of the religious rites. Even though Cyani was clearly the most talented warrior, not a single member of the Elite placed her dagger with Cyani's during religious ceremonies. The placement of daggers signified support and loyalty. No one stood with her. The sisters with several daggers behind them could initiate changes to law or policy. The ones with no backing faded into the temple and remained silent.

The Grand Sister chuckled as she swirled the contents of the goblet, her laugh hard and dry, like the sound of a cracking limb. "I have much *grander* plans for you, my niece."

Niece?

Cyani struggled to contain her shock.

What? How could that be?

Her father. He had been a highborn man. He couldn't possibly be the brother of the Grand Sister. Could he? Cyani locked her gaze to the Grand Sister's identical blue one.

By the mercy of the Matriarchs.

"I see by the look on your face, your father never told you about your heritage, my child," she slurred, her eyes looking glassy. A wild desperation hid deep within them. If Cyani hadn't grown accustomed to watching Soren's eyes so closely, she never would have seen it.

"How unfortunate. I thought perhaps your drive to excel in the trials was due to your desire to make me proud, but I see now perhaps it was only the lingering death sentence. What a pity." The Grand Sister circled, looking her up and down with an appraising nod as if she were inspecting the stature of a well-bred scout.

She was the Grand Sister's niece.

Merciful Creator, she was the living blood of the Grand Sister.

A new dawning shock rushed through her. If she was the

niece of the Grand Sister, then she was a descendent of Fima the Merciless. The living blood of the greatest warrior Azra had ever known ran in her veins. She held the living blood of not one but two of the Matriarchs. It was unheard of. The thought fogged her mind, crowded out any others, until she felt numb and slack. She couldn't focus on anything. She had to concentrate. She needed her wits. She reached up and touched her necklace without thinking.

The Grand Sister's cold gaze locked on her fingertips. She drew her hand back down to her side, but there was no covering her blunder.

"Unfortunately your mother gave you a name from her own line. But make no mistake, Cyani, you and your brother are the last of the line of Fima, and *you* will be the next Grand Sister."

Cyani felt like she was falling. The Grand Sister was going to name her heir? Everyone assumed Yara would be heir to the throne. *By all that is right and holy, this is insane.* She thought she knew the course of her life, and now this? It wasn't her. This wasn't her life. She scraped, and fought, and struggled. She did not sit on high thrones, honored by throngs of people fearful of her power. And what would she have to do to protect it from Yara and those that supported her?

"I will see my legacy continued," the Grand Sister interjected into her thoughts. "And our great bloodline grow in power."

The Grand Sister slid the whip down Cyani's back, then, as she turned, brought the whip under her chin. "There is only one thing that concerns me."

With a flick of her hand, she brought up a holo-screen out

of midair. "Ah, here it is. Remaining in the presence of an aroused Byralen of the opposite sex can cause altered states of consciousness. How very fascinating." She touched the butt of the whip to Cyani's necklace. "Has your conscience been altered, I wonder?"

Cyani's heart pounded as she forced herself to find the strength to remain standing. With every microgram of her will, she kept her body still and her face impassive. She had to regain control.

The Grand Sister lifted the goblet once again to her lips, and a nearly imperceptible shudder trembled in the old woman's shoulders.

"That is a lovely necklace," the Grand Sister commented. Her voice sounded slow and complimentary, but there was no hiding the steely rage burning in her aging eyes, eyes that should have reflected nothing at all. "Was it a gift? Or have you simply forgotten you should not be adorned?"

The Grand Sister tangled the necklace in her bony fingers, and with a quick jerk, she snapped it off Cyani's neck.

Cyani couldn't breathe. She forced air through her nostrils as she stared the Grand Sister down. The Grand Sister uncoiled the whip and calmly walked to the edge of an archway. With casual disregard, she tossed the necklace into the canopy.

Cyani's heart fell as she watched it disappear into a cluster of ciera blossoms.

The Grand Sister swung the whip, slicing one of the blossoms off the vine and sending it plummeting into the shadows.

"I have single-handedly ruled this planet for nearly thirty

years," she said as she sent the whip blazing into the flowers once more. Her shoulders moved with a fluidity that shouldn't have been possible with her arthritis. None of the Elite were supposed to know about her suffering, but her knobby joints betrayed her. She wouldn't remain in power much longer. Whatever was in the goblet was killing her pain and dropping the hard wall of control she used to protect herself.

"Thirty years of my life I have guided our people, maintained our traditions in the face of growing diplomatic pressure to change from the people who call themselves our allies. They know nothing of Azra." The whip sliced through the vines once more with a hissing snap, the sound it made when kissing skin. The Grand Sister's jaw set with the unforgiving look she used to wear as she beat Cyani for any sign of weakness.

"I am all that stands between order and chaos. Without my guidance, our traditions, our culture, our very covenant with the Creator, it would all be destroyed and we would be no different from the rest of those uncultured heathens that claim to be civilized members of the Union."

She swung around on her heel, letting the whip slide over the smooth floor. Her eyes darted back and forth. She took another draw from the goblet then sent it crashing to the floor.

"I will not let that happen, Cyani." Her voice hissed and snapped with the same cutting bite of the whip. "You understand. You grew up on the ground. You know how depraved those ill-bred animals are. You know that filth can never be allowed to touch our pure world. Treaty for the common rights of all humanoids. Bah, some are no better than apes.

"And men, if they ever had a voice in our government, they'd only try to dominate the women the way they do on countless other planets. It's hypocrisy at its most disgusting. Men cannot be trusted—just look at your father. The pitiful fool followed your mother into banishment, for what? Love? I commanded my brother. I *commanded* him to raise you and your twin *here*, under my supervision. He betrayed me, betrayed our bloodline, and nearly ruined you," she shouted, lifting the whip and sending it flying toward Cyani.

Cyani leapt in a flash of pure reflex and brought her bare fist around to connect with the Grand Sister's swinging arm. The old woman blocked the strike with her forearm. "I have to admit," the Grand Sister cackled, "being raised with the beasts has given you a bold ruthlessness I rather admire."

Even if Cyani could find words, she would never have been able to string them together. She pushed away from the Grand Sister. Cyani had never seen her like this. She seemed frantic and desperate, grasping for something that was sliding through her stiffening grip. Was it the influence of the drug in the goblet, or the slow, dawning realization that Cyani was far more than the unquestioning, unfeeling drone she'd been trained to be?

"The first time I saw you, you had already shown the power of your blood." The Grand Sister smiled. It was little more than a stiff grimace as she rolled the whip shaft in her palm. "I recognized you immediately, Fima reborn, a tested and accomplished warrior and still only a child. You may have your mother's skill, but not her weak will." The Grand Sister coiled the whip again. "She wanted to turn the Elite into figureheads and have a representative government. She was willing to cower to pressure from the Union. You understand I couldn't allow it."

Cyani always suspected the Grand Sister had something to do with her mother's banishment. The confirmation of it just churned in her gut like burning acid.

"You manipulated her," Cyani stated, baiting her. The Grand Sister shook her head with a low chuckle.

"I only trifled in the obvious. Her attraction to my brother was blatant. It didn't take much to put them over the edge and make her break her vow of chastity." The Grand Sister widened her stance and placed her hands behind her back in a sparring posture. It was an invitation, one Cyani couldn't pass up.

"What did it take, drugs?"

The old woman struck, and it was Cyani's turn to block. The sharp jolt of cleansing pain to her forearm helped focus her rage.

The Grand Sister huffed. "Your mother may have given birth to you, but I was the one who conceived you. I couldn't allow my brother to sire my only heirs, the last of the line of Fima, with some ill-bred bitch who had failed the trials. He deserved better. You would have been tainted with weakness.

"No." The old woman stepped back, her weight balanced over her haunches as she remained on her toes. Cyani watched her gathering her center for the next strike. "Only the most talented warrior was fitting for our bloodline, and your mother had true talent. Talent you possess, which is why of all the Elite, you are the only one fit to rule, Cyani. You are perfect." She struck again. Cyani blocked and seamlessly threw a counterstrike. In the time of her training, she had spent countless hours sparring under the Grand Sister's scornful eye. In those years, the Grand Sister had seemed untouchable, unbeatable, but no more. She was no different than any of the others.

"You are ruthless." The Grand Sister tried to kick, but Cyani leapt over her foot and landed a blow on the older woman hard enough to force her back a step. She would show the old woman *ruthless*. She wanted to show her just how much merciless blood ran in her veins.

"You are cunning." The Grand Sister swung the whip again, but Cyani spun and slid toward the Grand Sister's desk. The old woman held back the lash as the delicate communications lattice threatened to crash to the floor.

She chuckled as she coiled the whip again. "You are also intelligent, and by my teaching, obedient. All that I did, I did out of dedication to what you could become."

Dedication to sculpting a perfect puppet. That is all she wanted. She didn't know Cyani at all, or did she? When she left for her Union assignment, she never questioned anything. She had blindly obeyed orders. She led her men into battle, and she won, but she never let herself question any of it.

Not until now.

"You've manipulated my entire life. You turned a blind eye to the others' attempts to kill me." Cyani's seething hate boiled in her throat as she tried to force words out.

The Grand Sister let out a dismissive huff. "I made you stronger than any other warrior the Elite have ever known. I needed to know you could best any of them, and survive any attempt on your life." She placed the whip on her desk, but kept her palm on the handle. "I'm dying, Cyani. All I have is my legacy. That legacy is you. Think of what you could do for Azra. Think of the power."

So that was it. All the power in the world couldn't save her aunt from death. Only an heir in her likeness could maintain her rigid control on Azra and make her mark on their world last.

She had her puppet. She made sure Cyani's strings pulled tight. For more than half her life, Cyani had never fought them. No wonder the old woman thought she could still pull them now. The Grand Sister had no idea who she was dealing with.

Not everyone craved power. Cyani didn't want the throne. She wanted peace and safety. But like a snake, the call to duty crawled into her heart. She could dispense justice. She could bring light and order to the underbelly of their world and lift the innocents back into the fold of their society. She could instill the representative government her mother had been ruined for and revolutionize Azralen culture.

She alone could save her planet.

And due to the conniving of her aunt, she had the strength to fight off any assassins that tried to stop her. Once the others knew she was the true blood of Fima and Cyrila, they would fall in line. She would have justice for her people.

But she would never know peace.

She felt the chains that had tied her to the Elite constricting even tighter around her heart. She would have the power to change her world. She had to return.

She couldn't leave her people in the darkness, not even for the promise of love.

Her fate was sealed.

She felt the Grand Sister's bony grip close around her arm. "You are Fima reborn. My blood, my daughter. Cyani the Ruthless, the next and greatest Grand Sister."

A ringing chime echoed through the room.

"What is it?" the Grand Sister asked without bothering to hide the aggravation in her voice.

"There is a Union representative here demanding that Captain Cyani depart with him," a disembodied voice announced.

With a grumble, the Grand Sister slowly lowered the mantle over her shoulders and marched out into the throne room with a slight shuffle in her deliberate steps.

Cyani continued after her with a new wave of panic. What was Cyn doing? He was going to be recognized.

The Grand Sister stopped just short of him and looked up into his disguised black eyes. He smiled at her.

"Cyani has been relieved of her duties and belongs to me," the Grand Sister announced.

Cyani watched Cyn carefully. She could barely recognize him. Even his expressions seemed different as he calmly addressed her as a Union diplomat.

"I apologize for the misunderstanding, but Captain Cyani has not been cleared of her final mission. She is to aid me in my current assignment as is clearly stated in the log orders filed U.C.O.-55467.82 section L. Until I sign her clear, she is under the jurisdiction of the Union Treaty of Common Arms and is subject to criminal prosecution under military tribunal if she rejects this assignment. Surely you don't want to break the Treaty of Common Arms, your holiness. The Union and

Azra have a long-standing alliance in good faith. It would be unfortunate to have Union rights enforcers rethink your exemptions from the T.C.R." Cyn prattled in the flawless Earthlen accent he had undoubtedly picked up during his leisurely youth on Earth, while Cyani suffered through the trials for his freedom.

The Grand Sister flushed, though her face remained as stony as ever. She brought up the holo-screen and scrolled through the standing orders. As she read, her lips pressed into an even harder, thinner line.

"Earthlen," she grumbled. "We had an incident on the landing platform where your ship is docked. It seems a trans-shift energy pulse went off. You wouldn't know anything about that, would you? Because deliberate interference with our communications systems could be viewed as an act of aggression on Azra." The Grand Sister carefully studied him, but Cyn didn't even blink.

"I apologize. My discharger must have been damaged during my last assignment. No offense was meant. As you can see, my ship never left the landing platform." He bowed to her.

"Indeed."

"And after your very thorough search of my ship, I trust that you are satisfied with the confirmation of your security measures." Cyn smiled his most charming smile.

The Grand Sister drew a long slow breath before turning her back to Cyn and addressing Cyani. "I expect your return," she stated. "You know what's at stake. If you fail me, I will send Yara to the ground cities for your brother. Are we clear?"

Cyani fought the urge to look at Cyn. In the corner of her eye she could see him absentmindedly study the carvings on the Azralen throne as if he had not just heard orders for his own execution.

Yara was the best, the only member of the Elite capable of beating her during a sparring match, though their record was about sixty–forty in Cyani's favor. Yara was relentless, driven, efficient, loyal, and very, very good at striking when least expected. If she had a weakness, it was her adherence to her training instead of instinct. Yara had never been in a fight for her life, but Cyani had no doubt the woman would be deadly if unleashed. Cyn wouldn't be able to hide from her, even with his Earthlen disguise. She would find him. She was the Grand Sister's true puppet. Yara would obey orders, even if those orders were to kill.

"I see we have an understanding. Good. We have much to discuss when you return."

The Grand Sister gathered the edge of the mantle and, with a flourish, disappeared back into her chambers.

Cyani felt dizzy and sick as she drew her gaze to her brother. He had no idea what she had just been through. From the revelations of her family ties, to the heavy weight of her future on Azra, she needed time to adjust to her new future.

And then there was Soren.

She would honor her promise and see him reach home, but how would she find the strength to walk away?

Cyn offered her an understanding smile. "Get your things, Captain. It's time to leave this place."

18

IF THE GRAND SISTER DIDN'T MURDER CYN, CYANI WAS READY TO DO IT HERself. What was he thinking walking directly into the snake pit? Cyani had just discovered her brother was safe. Safe from himself? That was another matter. She was grateful she'd be able to see Soren safely home, but it wouldn't change anything.

She had to return.

She held the future of Azra in her hands.

She lifted Vicca into the ship, thankful that the Grand Sister hadn't been able to take her away without giving Cyani another scout to replace her. For the moment, Vicca was safe.

The thought of returning to the halls sent a cold chill down her spine. She couldn't dwell on it. Like learning nerve strikes, it was best to take the pain quickly and be done with it. She had to get Soren home as fast as possible and say goodbye, before her heart could betray her head.

She glanced up and locked gazes with Soren. He reclined in the corner of a bunk, holding a sleeping toddler with the tell-tale dark hair of a ground dweller. Soren's eyes faded from their clear violet blue to a deep blood black.

"Where is your necklace?" he asked as his brow lowered over his dark eyes.

Cyani felt sickening unease crawl through her gut. *Shakt*, she didn't want to hurt him, but what did he expect? She wanted to tell him what had happened, that the necklace had been ripped from her. She had not given it up. That part of her wanted to collapse into his arms and just cry for the loss of it, but she couldn't. She had to sever her connection to him, even though it would be like slicing out a part of her. Perhaps it was best that the necklace was gone. Now she couldn't cling to it, and it couldn't tie her.

"What are you doing with a ground baby?" she asked instead, keeping the conversation from her necklace. How did he get a ground baby? Gracious Esana the Noble, they had gone to the ground. His eyes darkened even more as a muscle twitched in his clenched jaw.

"You didn't answer my question."

"And you didn't answer mine." What had they done?

Vicca leapt up on the bed and licked the baby's elbow.

"I'm helping smuggle them out of this blighted place," he snapped.

"They aren't properly smuggled until we get them off the planet," Cyn interjected as he passed between them into the cockpit. He released Bug, who went to work touching off launch codes on the copilot side. "We've got to move, now. You two can fight later."

"Girls, are you strapped in?" he shouted.

Cyani spun as a young girl streaked through the hold and launched herself onto the bed with Soren. She giggled as Vicca licked her face. What was going on? How many kids were on the blasted ship?

She felt the presence of another. Her heart sank as she turned to a young girl, no more than thirteen, her abdomen swollen with pregnancy. Her long dark hair rested on her shoulder in a neat braid, but her haunted eyes studied Cyani with a wary resentment.

"You are one of the Elite," the girl commented.

Cyani felt like she was staring into her past, a past that hadn't been, but could have been. This is the girl she would have been if she hadn't fought, if she hadn't killed.

"I am," Cyani whispered. She didn't like the accusation in the girl's eyes.

Why didn't you save me?

The girl's hands strayed over her distended belly as she lowered her head in reluctant submission and passed Cyani on her way to the bunks.

Cyani braced herself in the doorway. She didn't want to look Soren in the eye. He rested his cheek against the curls of the baby boy as the little girl pressed into his side, snuggling Vicca.

Cyn had taken him into the ground cities. She could see a new understanding in his eyes. He had empathized with her before based on his own darkness, but now he knew the truth. Cyani felt ripped open and exposed as the thread of a new intimacy wove between them. He knew her.

The Elite never braved the shadows, but he had. He knew.

Her hand strayed to her necklace, only to touch her bare collarbone. She clenched her fist and slammed it against the wall. Every foul curse any of her men had ever uttered in the thick of battle raced through her mind.

"Hold on," Cyn announced as the ship wobbled as it rose off the landing pad then streaked out over the swaying green tops of the high canopy. The ground plummeted out from beneath them as they flew over the savage ocean. Then the nose of the ship lifted, and with a sudden push of acceleration they launched out of Azra's atmosphere into the black emptiness of space.

Cyn punched commands into the controls and the ship surged forward into macrospace. Cyn stretched his shoulders and entered the now crowded quarters. "We have to make a stop near Fagawi to meet with a friend of mine. He'll take the children the rest of the way before we continue on to Byra. Soren, what are the coordinates?"

"What coordinates?" he asked.

"For Byra," Cyn prodded.

"How in this blighted pile of rot would I know?" he snapped.

"Easy, tiger. I was just asking. Cyani, do you know?"

"The Union doesn't have a clue where Byra is. That's why they're paying you, remember?"

"So you're telling me, none of us knows where we're going?" Cyn growled. Bug zoomed around, either confused or amused by Cyn's irritation.

Cyn vigorously rubbed his shorn hair and ran his hand

over his face. "Fine. I'll ask Xan when we meet him. If that old space rat doesn't know where it is, then we'll have to get creative."

Soren didn't like the sound of that. At the same time, any delay in reaching his home world was a blessing. All that waited for him there was the grave. As long as he remained with Cyani, he had hope.

But she had taken that hope and left it behind. It was nice to know that it only took an hour or two for everything they had shared, everything they had survived together to mean nothing to her. She looked hard and regal in the white clothing of her planet.

He had offered her a way to escape, and time and time again, she returned to her duty.

He loved her so terribly it was going to kill him, and yet he came second to her orders.

And even with all of that, he could see the price she paid for her duty. It was killing her, too. The way her hand had strayed to her neck hadn't escaped him. She wanted the necklace. Her face seemed shadowed and hidden, as if she were trying to hold back from him.

She should have known she couldn't do that.

"What duty did the Grand Sister lay on your shoulders?" he asked. At the very least she could tell him why she chose her path instead of his.

Her eyes slowly pulled up as her full lips pressed into a stiff line. "It's nothing," she mumbled.

"No, it's not," he countered. He was losing her, and with her, his life.

The gut-dropping surge from the drop out of macrospace caught Soren off guard. He cradled the baby closer, protecting his little head with his palm.

"Right on target," Cyn commented as Soren caught a glimpse of a large, tattered ship orbiting a deep blue and gold moon.

"Damn it, Cobra, do you have to jump down so close?" a very deep voice boomed through the popping static of the communication channel.

"I've got three for you, Xan. Keep it down, the baby's asleep," Cyn answered. He carefully maneuvered the ship above the much larger one, and with a shuddering clunk, they docked. "Are you ready to go, little ones?" Cyn asked the young girl.

She clung to his hand. "I don't want to go. I want to stay with you."

Essa put her hands on Calya's shoulders as Soren stood up from the bunk, still carrying the baby. He understood. He didn't want to let go either.

Cyn knelt down. "I'm sorry, princess. I can't go with you. You can trust Xan. He will take you to your new home."

"I'm scared," she admitted.

Just then the hatch opened and a hard-looking man with shoulder-length barley gold hair entered the hold. He had the confident swagger of a man who started fights—and won them. Even though he wore dark eyeshades, he lifted his hand to shield his eyes from the dim light.

"For the love of a fat woman, Cobra, are you trying to blind me?" he grumbled. "Again."

The pirate crossed his thick arms and squared his heavy shoulders over his somewhat stocky build. He cocked his head to the side.

He gave Cyn a quick appraising look. "You look too damn respectable. Who do you have for me?" he asked before glancing at Soren. "A Byralen? Where'd you find him?"

Soren felt his eyes flash in warning. Calya tucked herself behind his thigh.

Cyani crossed the quarters to stand at his side. "Don't worry, Soren, he's Hannolen."

"He's scary," Calya commented.

The pirate laughed, then knelt down and motioned for Calya to come closer. She peeked from behind Soren's thigh, but wouldn't budge.

"It's okay, duckling. I'm going to help you." Like magic, with a flick of his wrist, he pulled a scarlet flower out of thin air. The little girl reluctantly came forward only a centimeter.

"You look like a very bad man," she scolded.

He smiled. "It's a disguise," he admitted in a conspiratorial whisper.

"That's true," Cyn added. "He's really a prince."

Calya looked up at Cyn, then back at the pirate, who managed to glare through his dark shades.

Essa took Calya's hand as Soren reluctantly handed the baby to her. "Don't worry, Calya, I'll protect you," she stated, though her voice wavered. "Thank you, both of you. I will keep them safe." She nodded a quick good-bye and joined a sweet-faced female crew member of Xan's ship who helped them through the hatch.

Soren's arms felt very empty and cold. He took a step closer to Cyani, but she closed herself off from him. Vicca wound around his legs, but it was little comfort.

Cyn and Xan clasped hands like old friends.

"I wouldn't ask this of you, unless I had to," Cyn began. "We need to know the coordinates for Byra. The Garulen know where it is."

"I haven't come across it, or heard of anyone who has. If the location of Byra became common knowledge . . ." The Hannolen tipped his head to the side.

If the location of Byra were known, Soren's home would be overrun the way Hanno was.

"You could ask your people," Cyn suggested. "The ones still held by the Garulen might have heard something."

The pirate stiffened. "I'm going to forget you just said that, and don't ever ask again." He turned back to the hatch. "I'm sorry I couldn't help." He glanced up at Soren, "Good luck finding your way home." And with that, he disappeared.

"Now what?" Cyani asked, collapsing into the copilot's seat.

Cyn shrugged and stalked over to the cramped galley. "I say we get drunk." He poured a glass of amber liquid from a silver cylinder, and tipped it toward Soren. Soren flicked his wrist to take him up on the offer. He could use a drink.

Cyani shook her head at them, but Cyn just smiled at her. His face fell when the ship detached and shook with the force of Xan's ship departing.

"Godspeed, little ones," he muttered and lifted his glass. Soren solemnly took a sip and nearly choked. The liquid burned like fire down his throat and left his mouth filled with the taste of smoke.

"Well," Cyn mentioned, cracking his knuckles. "I guess we'd better do this the hard way. Tell me everything you know about Byra. Start with your star system. Do you have any moons?"

"One, it's small but close. And there is another world in close orbit with ours."

Cyn motioned toward the two cases in the hold where they could sit, talk, and drink. Soren took another swallow of the liquid fire, enjoying the sensation of being warmed from the inside out.

"The Pyri come in ships to trade with us every other month." Soren sat across from Cyn and rested his elbows on his knees, rolling the glass between his palms. "I'm not sure what they look like. They have to wear masks when they come because they are sensitive to something in our atmosphere, and our climate is too warm for them. Without protective suits they overheat and become very ill. They are about the same height as we are, but tend to be heavyset. They have white hair and colorless eyes. We trade fresh food, textiles, handcrafts, woodworks, and sometimes plant specimens for metalworks, plows, tools, technology, cold storage boxes, and ice." Soren stole a glance at Cyani. She seemed lost in thought. It looked as if she had tuned them out completely.

"And do they wear translators?" Cyn asked, drawing Soren back into the conversation.

"No, they speak strangely, but we can understand each other." Soren felt like he was spinning for a moment as realization dawned on him. "When I taught the translator Byra, it learned very fast. It made mistakes that sounded like the sorts of errors the Pyri make."

Cyn pulled off his translator and placed it next to him on the crate. "Talk to me."

He glanced at Cyani, still lost in her own world.

Soren started to speak then paused. The bitterness of her rejection of him still burned in his heart. Even angry with her, he could only think of one thing to say.

"I love her," he admitted softly in Byralen. "I don't know when it happened, but I bonded to her completely. If she leaves me, I won't survive. And she is turning away from me."

Cyn intertwined his fingers and pressed his lips to them.

"Cyani," Cyn called. "I know where we're going, but you're not going to like it."

He replaced his translator as she entered the hold. "How did you figure it out?" she asked.

"I'm a linguist, remember?" he admonished. "The language Soren is speaking is actually a dialect of Yeshulen. That is why the com learned the language so quickly. As soon as it recognized the bridge to the language it knew, it adjusted for pronunciation and idiosyncrasies in the grammar."

Cyani paled. "That is why the Garulen rarely raid the planet. I'd wondered why they didn't just invade in force."

"What are you talking about?" Soren asked.

"The Yeshulen are a violent, paranoid, and extremely technologically advanced race. There is an old saying on Earth, shoot first and ask questions later. Well, they don't bother with the questions, they just shoot to kill." Cyn smiled, a look that reminded Soren of a fox trying to sneak into the fowl nests.

"The Pyri aren't violent," Soren protested.

"Not to you. You have something they want," Cyn chuckled.

"If they are so technologically advanced, why do they squabble with us over the price of vegetables?" Soren insisted.

"Because their planet is almost entirely covered in ice. I'm sure the tundra sage is delicious. Your vegetables are probably rare and expensive delicacies. You should hold out for more money."

"They aren't going to look kindly on a Union ship near their borders. They detest the Union. They think the Union only wants their trillide," Cyani interjected.

"There's a lot of truth to that," Cyn commented.

"Do you think we can sneak past them?" Cyani asked.

"Absolutely not," Soren protested. "I won't risk having them fire on this ship and kill us."

"We're in trouble if they recognize this ship," Cyn stated. "That's the bottom line."

"Cyn, where did you learn Yeshulen?" Cyani asked, suspicion darkening her voice.

Soren decided to put a stop to the haphazard conversation.

"We will approach the Pyri cautiously, with a great deal of respect, and deal with them openly. If they are suspicious, we will not add to their paranoia with our actions." Soren swallowed the rest of the fire and brought his glass down on the crate with a heavy thud.

"You don't understand these people, Soren," Cyani began.

"No, you don't understand them. I understand them far better than either of you," Soren admonished. Cyn looked down and away as if he were embarrassed by something. Soren continued, "The Pyri are friends of my people. I will talk with them. They can be fair and friendly when treated with proper respect." He glanced at Cyn's shadowsuit. "But first, you should change into something less militaristic. Now set our destination for their borders. We'll skirt the edge until they notice us, and open communications when they approach. I'll do the talking."

"Yes, sir." Cyn tossed Soren a stiff salute as he eased into the pilot's seat and sent the ship into the dimensional fold once again.

19

"IT'S LATE," SOREN SAID AS HE STRETCHED HIS SHOULDERS IN THE COPILOT'S seat and watched the chunks of shadowed rock slowly drift past the screen. "Perhaps you should get some rest, too," he offered.

Cyn rubbed his eyes. "I can't."

They'd been sitting in the midst of the asteroid field for the last five hours, waiting. Two ships lurked on the other side and a third had just joined them. All three were armed to the teeth.

"If they respond, I'll handle it," Soren stated.

Cyani had curled up in one of the bunks three hours earlier, but her rest was fitful, if she actually slept at all. Soren longed to crawl into the small bed with her and pull her into his body. He wanted to bury his face in her soft hair and drown in the smell of her. He was still mad at her, but he couldn't help it. He was addicted.

Bug decided to entertain himself by "singing" a soothing melody of trilled beeps and low bell-like tones.

Cyn reached into the riveted pocket of the faded blue canvaslike Earthlen pants he was wearing. He pulled out Cyani's necklace and placed it on the panel. Each soft click-click of beads coming to rest on the metal jolted in Soren's ears. Soren stared at it, unable to tear his eyes away from it. His chest felt suddenly tight, like a great squeezing snake had coiled around his heart. The muscle fluttered like the wings of a dying bird in the grip of the serpent. The snake coiled through his insides, turning his stomach until he felt sick with it.

"A peace offering." Cyn eyed him like a man who knew a thing or two about making peace with women. "You shouldn't be fighting."

Soren reached out and took the necklace. He rubbed the edges of the carved blossom with sad reverence.

"It won't do any good. She took it off." He could almost taste the bitterness in his voice.

"Bug," Cyn commanded. "Show him."

Bug stopped his singing and floated in front of Soren. A small square of light appeared above him like the one that would float in front of Cyani's eye machine. It filled with color, and Soren could see leaves and a gleaming white flower that looked like Cyani's tattoo. The leaves dropped down, and through a small gap in the foliage, he could see Cyani and an older woman with a white whip.

The older woman spoke. Soren barely processed the conversation. He couldn't take his eyes off of Cyani.

The view on the small screen zoomed in until Soren could only see the still expression on Cyani's face. She was holding back. In the depths of her eyes, he could see her fear and her rage.

"That is a lovely necklace," the old woman said. "Was it a gift? Or have you simply forgotten you should not be adorned?"

She reached up and snapped it off Cyani's neck.

"Hold there, Bug," Cyn ordered. The screen filled with the unmistakable look of horror on Cyani's face as the necklace was torn from her.

Perhaps the expression had only lasted a moment, but Bug had caught it. There was no mistaking her anguish. She looked as if someone had just plunged a knife into her heart.

"Bug caught the necklace when the Grand Sister threw it off the balcony," Cyn mentioned.

Soren let himself fall back in the chair, numb with shock.

Cyani loves me.

She really loved him. She couldn't hide it. It was there in her clear blue eyes.

He clenched the necklace, squeezing the beads until they dug into his palm. He pressed his lips to the necklace and tucked it away in his pocket.

"Soren, listen to me, Cyani can't . . ."

Soren didn't listen to him. Instead he launched himself into the living quarters.

Cyani woke with a start, drawing her flick knife across her chest in defense.

"Soren, what is . . ."

He took her face in his palms and kissed her hard. Her soft

sweet lips parted beneath his as he poured all his love into the intimate kiss.

Her shock waned, and she relaxed into his caress for only a moment before she stiffened and pulled away.

"What in the name of Isa the Bold do you think you are doing?" she asked him. Bug floated near his head and made a low clucking sound that sounded distinctly like a metallic chuckle.

Suddenly a female voice crackled through the flight controls.

"Tell me why I shouldn't kill you now, Cyrus Smith, an alleged Earthlen, shadow trader, Union linguist, rogue smuggler, ralok champion, and Falc blade expert. Am I missing anything?" The voice sounded cold, skeptical, and far too knowledgeable about Cyn.

"How completely unflattering, Nu. I believe you forgot Hunmalen Ale master craft brewer, Lavarilen temple apprentice of the art of Tanro, and most importantly, humble servant to the glorious and beautiful people of Yeshu," Cyn responded in flawless Pyri. Soren raised his eyebrows at Cyn's tone. He sounded as if he were talking himself back into the graces of a scorned lover.

A square on the screen flashed with the picture of a stern woman with stark white hair, icelike silver eyes, and very pale skin. "Humble? You are as humble as a rutting yak, and if you dare bring up Tanro again, I'll skin you alive. What do you want, Smith?" she asked. "I'm not going to fall for your crap a second time." Her eyes flickered toward Soren as he climbed back into the cockpit, and her attention caught immediately.

"I greet you with generosity and honor," Soren offered.

She looked shocked then a smile broke over her face. "I am

Commander Nualsha of Hel. What is the name of your family honored Byri?"

"I am Soren of Eln, Nualsha of Hel. Yours is a strong and noble family. We have had many honorable and fair trades between your blood and mine," he responded, careful to keep to the formal trade language between their people.

Murmurings rumbled in the background as the Yeshu ship came to life with voices shouting and cheering.

"Ranock's feet! I don't believe it. Soren, son of Councilhead Rosson?" she asked. She seemed to have forgotten Cyn's presence completely.

"Councilhead? My father is councilhead?" he responded with a swell of pride. His father had been barely past the waning. Now he oversaw the council of elders? Soren wondered if his mother was still alive, if his younger brother prospered and had attracted a bride. And his sister.

Suddenly the rushing surge of joy ebbed as he thought about Rensa. He didn't have time to think. He didn't want to think. He only wanted to enjoy this moment.

"Your family has been looking for you a long time, Soren of Eln." Nu waved to her jubilant crew. "Don't mind them. You just won us forty casks of vintage Eln blackwine and some rich trading rights courtesy of your fruitful family."

"I'm sure your crew will enjoy them with Eln's blessing," Soren offered, amused. The Pyri never changed, and neither did their taste for blackwine, it seemed.

"We will return you to your home with joyous hearts, Soren. Wait while we initiate the docking sequence."

Cyani entered the cockpit. The Pyri glanced up at her. "An Azralen Elite?"

"She is the one who freed me, and I would ask that she be allowed to accompany me to my home," he insisted.

The woman's brow furrowed. "For what purpose?"

"Byhirn," he stated, knowing the translators couldn't understand the word for Byra's mating ritual. He had no garden to invite her to, but she didn't need one. She loved him. If they couldn't survive in his overgrown mess of a garden, they would find a way. They had always found a way together.

The Pyri looked shocked. "Really? How exceptionally interesting. Very well, she can accompany you so long as Smith remains on my ship as my"—she paused, and a wicked smile crossed her face—"guest. We have some unfinished business to attend to. When you send us word, we will release him back here with his ship."

Cyn shot a glance at Soren.

"What's going on?" Cyani asked.

"Cyn?" Soren didn't want to throw him into the fire, but if he wanted to jump . . .

"I'll be okay. You worry about you," he responded. The fox-like smile slowly spread over his face.

Soren placed a hand on Cyn's shoulder as the docking commands entered into the ship's controls, and the ship began moving out of the asteroid field automatically.

Cyn managed to hack into the computer enough to signal the ship to go into lockdown. Once again, the cases disappeared into the walls, and even Bug reluctantly worked himself into a small slit beneath one of the bunks.

Cyani clutched Vicca as the ship docked. She looked lost, tired. She took an automatic step closer to him but then caught herself and tried to take a step back. What was wrong with her? Why was she being so distant?

Arctic air poured up through the hatch, biting at Soren's face and neck as Nu climbed into the ship. She shared the classic greeting with Soren then gave the hull a quick once-over before turning and giving Cyn a heated glare.

"Leave all com units and your scout's collar. We will provide translators if you need them." She handed them long silver overcoats. She shoved Cyn's coat hard into his chest, but he caught it and held her hand to his heart for only a moment.

Soren slipped on the overcoat, which instantly warmed, taking the chill out of the air. He watched Cyani as she pulled her com off and slowly removed Vicca's collar. Vicca's fur retained the imprint of the collar as she looked up at Cyani with her big blue eyes. Cyani stroked her ears, as her face radiated her longing and sadness. Something wasn't right. What had the Grand Sister said to her? Suddenly he wished he had paid closer attention to the old woman's words on Bug's projection.

The sinking feeling that something was terribly wrong melted into his growing sense of elation as he climbed down the hatch. The shield surrounding the ladder was transparent, and the feeling of dropping out into open space thrilled him. He could see his sun, and in the distance, his home like a swirling blue gem.

Soren dropped into a brightly lit hold. The white walls glittered with what appeared to be a thin sheet of ice. Soren let his curiosity get the better of him as he greeted the crew. The Pyri never let any of the Byralen onto their ships. It was a fascinating glimpse into their world. Several little discs zoomed around, exact copies of Cyn's mechanical pet.

Had he stolen Yeshulen technology? Or had he seduced it out of the commander of the ship? The man knew no boundaries.

Commander Nu approached Cyani with a small silver sphere in her hand. She placed it near Cyani's ear, and it hovered there without touching her.

"Our translators can broadcast as well, so you can speak freely, Azralen," she explained.

"Thank you," Cyani replied. To Soren's surprise and delight, her words broadcast almost immediately in Cyani's voice.

"Commander, a Garulen transport has tried to hide in the far void. They have released a raid ship," one of the crew stated.

Nu's eyes turned as cold and hard as the ice they resembled. "Hija, pursue and destroy the scout; Fuj, disable the transport and search for prisoners."

"Come." She motioned to Soren and Cyn. "Let the others go hunting. We must contact Byra with the good news of Soren's return."

Nu led them to an area with shaggy fur cushions low to the ground and hovering tables. Delicate music that reminded Soren of the sound of dripping water filled the air as Nu offered them steaming cups of thick sweet cream.

"Don't worry about the Garulen," Nu said to Soren. "Not a single ship has made it through to Byra since you were taken. I'm surprised they keep trying. Your father started a campaign to cut off all trade unless we agreed to protect Byra from the

Garu. It was our pleasure. We have no love for those mammoth mounds. If we had known sooner that the Garulen were stealing our honored kin, they would have paid dearly."

"So, Rensa?" Soren's voice cracked. Unbidden flashes of memory invaded his mind. Her scream seemed to echo from a distant corridor. His skin tingled. He rubbed it to brush out the cold, but the numbness began to spread through his body.

He was having another memory attack. He could feel the shock blast, feel the hair of the Garulen's arms as he ripped the beast from his sister and shoved her down the slope and into the brambles. He couldn't move.

"Soren, are you okay?" Cyani asked as she nudged him.

He snapped out of it with a shudder. He struggled to recapture the sense of ease and happiness he had only moments before, but couldn't quite grasp it. Cyani took his hand. The simple touch was all it took.

"They didn't take your sister," Nu stated, drawing Soren back into the present. "Her account of what happened that night is legendary, a call to arms for both our peoples. Without her as a witness, we wouldn't have known to look for the Garulen. You are a hero, Soren. You should hear the songs recounting your sacrifice." Nu dropped her gaze, a gesture not common for the Pyri.

Cyani looked shocked. "You were captured because you saved your sister?"

Soren scowled. "It isn't what you think. How long have I been gone?"

The question seemed to take Nu aback. "It's been fourteen years. Frankly, I'm shocked you're still alive."

"I'm thirty-two," Soren muttered. "I don't feel thirty-two."

He felt much older, and at the same time, a part of him seemed frozen in time.

The ship surged and then slowed. In a matter of minutes, they landed. Nu left to change into her gear.

Soren stiffened. He clenched his jaw until it ached as he tried not to drown in his shifting thoughts. His home rested beneath the hull of the ship. His people waited beyond its walls. He closed his eyes. He could feel his thoughts like living things churning within him and it made it hard to focus. His unbound joy and relief danced in his heart, but to a song tempered with uncertainty and sadness.

He would have given anything to wake and see the sun rise over the sweeping grasses of Makko again with Cyani warm and welcoming in his arms. Perhaps his home could be another haven for them. He hoped so. It was that emotion he clung to.

"Soren, I think you're in shock," Cyani whispered.

Soren tried to shake out of his turbulent thoughts. "I'll be fine." He offered his hand to Cyn. Cyn took it before pulling him into a half hug and patting him on the back. Cyn gave Soren a lopsided smile. "Take care, brother."

"You take care," he cautioned. "You need to."

Cyn chuckled. Soren patted him on the back, but his hand started shaking. He fisted it and sank it into his pocket.

Nu entered, wearing her mask and suit, then led them to a gleaming staircase descending through a swirling shield. With each step down, Soren's stomach seemed to knot tighter. Jittery anticipation rushed through his veins as he clung to Cyani's hand.

A roar of cheers reverberated through the ship and shook

the steps beneath their feet as they stepped through the shield. The red sunset painted the towering clouds in vibrant shades of violet, pink, and flaming orange. Soren shielded his eyes from the light. The cool breeze kissed his face, carrying the heady fragrance of a million flowers.

A tearful throng had gathered in the circular plaza of the Eln market. Their stamping feet thundered on the worn white stone, flushing a flock of long-winged doves from beneath the thatched roof of one of the small trading houses. The crowd sang with throaty voices as their long pellays caught and rose in the joyful wind. Colorful strips of feather-adorned fabric fluttered like dancing birds from the ends of the long bowing reeds the crowd waved above their heads.

Soren froze. His whole body shook. He felt drugged. His urge to throw himself into the throng in joy fought his overwhelming desire to retreat back into the ship. Cyani squeezed his hand tighter as the crowd parted and his father strode toward them.

His father opened his arms wide, tears in his glowing blue green eyes. The years had been hard on him. Lines of worry and sadness had etched into his face, but there was no mistaking the unbound joy in his eyes.

Soren couldn't move. He recognized his father, but he felt disconnected somehow from the man before him. What did he expect?

Cyani gave Soren a nudge and he stepped down into his father's arms. His father crushed him, and he welcomed it as the second level began. They communicated not with words, but by scent, touch, and the shifting meaning in their eyes. He could feel the sparkling energy of his father's relief and joy radiate from his body. His eyes burned so bright green, Soren could barely see his pupils. Soren tried to take it in, but in the second level, he couldn't hold anything back, and his memories felt too raw to share.

He had tried to speak this way to Cyani. Sometimes he thought she understood, but to be free to speak on the second level again was both a relief and a burden. Soren smiled, trying to tell his father he was happy to be home, but he had to force back the dark thoughts.

His father returned his smile, but Soren could nearly taste his uncertainty. In his mind he could feel the unspoken questions. Questions his father did not really want answers to. They were answers he didn't think he could give. Only Cyani knew the truth of his darkness. In the end, all he could give his father was his love. He hoped it was enough.

He caught the scent of his mother. She ran toward them, her silver white-streaked hair flowing like her regal dress. She pulled Soren from his father, studied his eyes, and touched the scars at his wrists.

In the second level, her emotions suffocated him. Soren pulled his wrists away from her. She smacked the back of his hand, then touched each scar before smoothing her hands over his hair the way she had done a thousand times when he was a little boy. He felt her pain at each hurt she knew he suffered. It took all his strength to keep the other hurts from her. She didn't deserve his suffering.

His mother looked in his eyes once more then turned to Cyani. Her hope and surprise floated between them like the scent of fresh sweetbread. Soren smiled with relief. He could give her this.

Cyani lifted Vicca to her face and rubbed her eyes against the back of Vicca's neck. Soren heard a sniffle.

"Damn pollen filters," Nu grumbled from behind her mask.

Cyani laughed, drawing the back of her hand under her own nose.

Soren smiled and offered her his hand.

She descended and took her place at his side.

"Mami, I'd like you to meet Cyani," he forced out of his tight throat.

"Welcome, my child," his mother offered.

She took Cyani's hand, folded it in hers, and pressed it to her heart, then patted Vicca on the head.

"Soren?" Cyani turned. The cheering crowd pushed around them.

Just then, Soren caught sight of a beautiful young woman standing near a team of fine silkas hitched to a wagon.

The pain sliced through him in one terrible cleansing stroke.

"Rensa," he whispered.

She rushed forward and hugged him. He let the tears finally fall as he held his baby sister. He thanked the Grower, she was safe. All he had ever done, he had done to protect her.

Rensa shook as he hugged her, but she pulled back. She wiped her own eyes then looked up. Her brow furrowed then shot straight up in shock as she noticed Cyani for the first time. She looked back at Soren, puzzled, then she smiled. Soren smiled back.

"Welcome, sister," she greeted, then looked like she didn't know what to do with herself. Finally she motioned toward the road. "Come. I have the wagon waiting for us. Let's get out of here while father makes his speech."

Soren took a moment to greet the silkas. He never thought he'd see one again. He ran a hand down each long velvety nose. They watched him with deep dark eyes beneath their long sweeping lashes.

"What beauties," he whispered to them. "You have the look of my old Mum-mum." One shook its head, its long white hair floating around its elegant long neck. Soren ran a hand over the braids in their smooth coats. They had been tied with blue and green ribbons that bobbed over their shoulders and around their graceful legs.

With a sigh, he checked their harness, patted the nearest one on the rump, and climbed into the wagon.

Rensa wouldn't stop staring at Soren's wrists. He didn't bother to cover his scars.

"Rens, listen to me. I'm glad it was me. It's okay," he said.

"No, it is not," she countered. "I'm sorry."

Soren took her hand. "I don't ever want to hear that again. Do you understand? It was my fault, not yours."

She nodded, though the motion was shaky.

"Rensa, I'm home."

She smiled then, her eyes sparkling. She turned her attention to the silkas as she expertly drove them with soft taps of the lead-rod to their flanks. A flood of news poured out of her mouth, as if she had been saving every missed conversation from the last fourteen years.

She told them about the new relationship with the Pyri, and their willingness to share more of their technology, their father's rise in power to become councilhead, the twisting political battle that ensued when a man took over the traditionally female position, and their brother's struggle to keep the pandas from eating his reed thicket.

"I swear, the things breed like rats," Rensa commented.

"Where is Nens?" Soren asked, wondering which garden his younger brother tended.

"You'll see him soon. He's harvesting for the feast." She smiled.

"So his garden is ripe then?" Soren asked. He leaned toward Cyani.

"As ripe as his bride's belly," Rensa chuckled. "It smells like she carries a boy. They were going to name him for you."

"And what about you? You've grown so lovely from the gangly girl I knew. I'm surprised your mate's not here to guard you."

Her face fell. "I haven't chosen."

"Why not?" Soren sat up.

"I've been busy."

Soren glanced outside, and his face blanched. They had turned down the road that led to his lifegarden. "Why are we going this way? Rensa, I don't want to go back there yet."

"Relax, brother. It has been taken care of," Rensa mentioned as she flicked a long pole along the flank of one of the silkas.

They passed along an impenetrable thicket until they came to a huge open archway. Luminous pale cream pakkas bloomed like trumpeting stars over the entrance, their fragrance spicy, heavy and seductive. Tiny blue birds hung upside down from their petals as they licked the fluffy pollen off the burst of tendrils dangling from the mouth of each blossom.

The birds trilled in greeting, fluttering blue and gold wings in the light of the setting sun. So the pakkas had survived. That didn't surprise Soren. He brushed his thumb over the tattoo on Cyani's wrist. They could survive anything.

Soren reluctantly let his eyes drift upward, and the vision that greeted him stole the breath from his lungs.

Cascades of blossoms rolled in thick waves, their colors and intoxicating scents surrounding the wagon. Enormous orange and violet broadwings danced over the draping blooms, fluttering over an endless carpet of awe-striking beauty.

Beyond the initial gardens he had carefully planned and planted, fertile slopes of deep green grass fed fat silkas and round-bellied goats with long spiral horns.

His vineyard and orchard crowned the rolling hills by the creek. Beyond that, the towering forest sheltered several buildings alive with the dancing light of fires within.

Soren leapt from the moving wagon and collapsed on the ground.

Cyani flung herself over the edge of the cart and placed her hand on his shoulder.

He buried his hands deep in the soft black soil at the side of the road. He couldn't seem to get them deep enough.

Cyani let her hand wander over his back in an attempt to comfort him as his tears watered the ground. Before his eyes, new budding leaves unfurled in welcome as the faces of the endless blossoms turned to him in greeting.

20

IT LIVED. HE GRIPPED THE MOIST SOIL IN HIS FISTS. HE COULD FEEL ITS HEALTH, smell its rich fertility. How had it lived? The countless plants stretched before him in the greeting gardens. He knew each of them by name, by feel, by scent and sight. He had started their life with the skill of his hands, nurtured and protected them.

"How can this be?" he asked.

"Nens and I have worked hard," Rensa said as she stepped down off the wagon. "Father helped, too, though I always thought for him it was a memorial."

"What was it for you?" Soren asked as he rose to his feet.

"I knew you'd come home." She smiled. "I had to believe it."

Soren hugged his sister once again, "Thank you," he murmured to her.

"You thought it was dead?" Cyani placed Vicca on the

ground as she took an angry step toward him. Soren released his sister.

"Rensa, you'd better take the silkas back to the field. I'll meet you at the house." He held his hand out to Cyani, but she brushed it aside.

"Cyani," he began. Rensa hopped into the wagon and started the silkas in a brisk trot.

"The entire time we've been together, you believed all this was dead," she repeated.

"Yes," he confessed.

"So that entire time I was fighting to get you back home so you could find a mate to save your life, that whole time, you believed you were going to die anyway." She slapped her hands down to her sides and began walking after the wagon. Soren jogged to catch up to her and caught her hand. She yanked it away.

"Rot, Cyani. Listen to me," he demanded, taking her hand again. "Yes, I thought I was going to die. If I did, I wanted to die here. In my home." He gently pulled her toward him. He needed her to understand. "You gave me hope. You saved my life. I don't want to fight. I want to see my home—see what you've given me."

"Soren, I—" she stammered.

"Stay." He put pressure on her hand, nothing more than a gentle hint to come to him.

Indecision flashed through her wide blue eyes. He didn't need them to change color; he could read them anyway. She pulled her hand away.

"Will you join me tonight?" he asked, keeping his hand

open to her. It was a loaded question, one with too many meanings. Soren hoped that she wouldn't pay too much attention and assume his invitation was only for the evening. He wanted much more than that.

All she had to do was take his hand. If she did, it would seal his fate. By asking her to stay, he had committed to her with mind, body, and spirit. He had twisted his words so that they didn't sound permanent, but what he felt for her was forever.

She stared at it. Her eyes flickered over his scars. Her mouth pinched into a contemplative line before she looked out over the greeting garden. Soren plucked a velvety purple blossom from one of the bushes and offered it to her.

With a sigh, she took it and placed her hand in his.

Soren felt the tingling thrill as she took his hand. The bond spread through his body, pushing all his power in a sudden rush through his blood. He could feel his hormones like fire under his skin. He was bonded to her, completely, in every way. If she left him now, death would be swift and merciless. All of the chemical pathways had opened completely to her. Without her presence, they would shut down just as quickly.

He just needed to convince her to stay. She loved him. Azra couldn't offer her all of this. He only had one evening to do it.

They walked in silence down the path. Cyani pushed back the feeling that she was being foolish. *So what?* Now was not the time to worry about Azra. She didn't have long before she'd have to return. If this was the only bit of peace and beauty she'd have in her life, she wanted to cling to it, even if it was only for a few hours.

This world entranced her. Her visions of the glorious afterlife couldn't compare. She'd been mistaken about her impressions of what a lifegarden was. She'd thought of it like a farm, or a tended plot of land, but instead, it was an intricate and perfectly balanced ecosystem. It was hard to imagine Soren as a young boy struggling to create such a pristine wonder on his own.

He pointed out the different species of butterflies floating over the blankets of flowers adorning the path. For the first time since she freed him, he truly seemed at ease.

Yes, she could believe he created this. It was his nature to find beauty and watch it grow.

They walked down the path to the fields of spongy grass where a small flock of white beasts grazed. They reminded Cyani of camels with more elegant features, draping hair, long floppy ears, and only a slight hump. She had never seen anything like them on any other planet. One of the foals cavorted toward her.

Cyani laughed and ran as the little thing galloped around on unsteady legs. Soren caught her and held her in his arms as he chuckled at her. Vicca chased after the foal in a futile attempt to herd it back toward its sleepy-eyed mother.

"Come on," Soren whispered in her ear. "I've got something to show you."

The sun faded fast as they crossed the field and made their way over a series of large flat stones embedded in the cool creek. They followed the creek bank up into the edge of the forest. The ground sloped down into a shady grotto. A chorus of chirping insects hummed in the trees. Curling ferns lingered beneath the sweet-smelling needles of the conifers. A trickling waterfall played over moss-covered rocks. The soft flowing plants were the same color as her hair.

"One of the very first thoughts I had when you freed me, was that you reminded me of this place," Soren admitted.

"You thought I had mossy hair?" she teased.

"You reminded me of my home," he answered. "Look."

Cyani turned her attention to the place he was pointing and gasped. Amidst the ferns tiny pinpoints of light swelled and faded as they floated like magic over the fronds. They lit in bright shades of green, yellow, violet, and blue as they drifted about, lighting and disappearing again.

"What are they?" Cyani whispered in awe.

"Light bugs," Soren answered. "They're hoping to find a mate."

"Creative name." She smiled at him. He shrugged as he sat in a patch of cool, sweet-smelling flowers.

Vicca leapt at one of the bugs and took a swipe at it with her paw. She twisted in the air and landed with a loud splash in the creek.

With a squawk, she threw herself back out of the water and scurried under a stand of ferns.

Laughter bubbled up out of Cyani before she could help it. Her amusement was carefree and spontaneous. It came from her alone, unlike her feelings on Makko. Soren's deep chuckle melded with hers until she had to cling to her side to ease the pinch there. The moment was bittersweet. She would miss her scout.

Cyani gathered her legs in her arms and buried her toes beneath the round velvety leaves at her feet.

"Cyani, what's wrong?" Soren asked.

"It's nothing."

He touched her chin. The pad of his thumb traced the edge of her jaw. "Talk to me."

She bit her lower lip.

"Are you thinking about Azra?" he asked.

She nodded without looking at him.

"Are you thinking about this?" He pulled her necklace from his pocket.

A chill rushed over her shoulders and down her arms as she stared at it in shock.

"How did you?" she gasped.

"Cyn."

She reached out and took the necklace. The beads felt secure and heavy in her hands as she pressed them to her chest. She felt the stinging behind her eyes as she clung to it.

"Stay here with me, Cyani," Soren whispered, nuzzling close to her ear. "We were free on Makko. We can be free here, too. Azra will never find you."

Before she could draw in a breath, his mouth met hers in a tender kiss.

It had been only hours since he had last kissed her, and yet her body screamed for him. She felt as if she had been lost in the desert, and he had just offered her the coolest water.

He broke the kiss but lingered only a breath away from her lips.

She surged forward and wrapped him in her arms. She couldn't press herself close enough to him as she scorched him with her kiss. She wanted this. *Shakt*, she wanted him. The grotto swirled in a magical display as the light bugs danced through the rainbow of colors painting their small haven.

"I can't do this," she gasped against his neck. The spicy scent of him nearly drove her crazy as she tasted his warm skin. She couldn't help herself.

"I know," he whispered, as his hot hands undid the magnetic clasps of her ceremonial robes. The cool air kissed her bare neck and chest as a mist began to fall.

His hair brushed over her face as he pulled her clothes from her and eased her back onto the bed of flowers. His hot mouth kissed a trail of exquisite torture from her neck to her navel.

She sat up as he pulled her robes out from under her hips and slipped off her shoes.

He lifted one of her feet and kissed the center of the arch. A shot of pleasure careened up her spine as she fisted her hands in the soft foliage beneath her.

With agonizing deliberation, he nibbled up her calf, to the inside of her knee, and to tease the exposed flesh of her inner thigh.

She felt so naked, so exposed to him. The universe closed in until nothing existed but the small grotto by the creek. Even the flowers crowded in the edges of her vision, as if sheltering her from all the ugliness of her world. She wanted to stay here forever, bare, natural, wild, free.

She shouldn't be doing this.

The damp mist cooled her heated skin as her fingers wound into the long silky strands of Soren's hair. His mouth edged lower, ever closer.

Great Mercy of the Matriarchs.

"Soren," she gasped.

His hot mouth closed on her flesh, and the sensation of his intimate kiss ricocheted through her nerves. She had never felt anything like it as his soft tongue teased her. She felt helpless and cherished, as if this was their altar, and the fires of Makko surrounded them once more.

His hands smoothed up her bare thighs. The rush of pleasure was so intense, so drugging, she closed her eyes and clung to his hair. She tried to escape the waves of color washing through the grotto, but they had invaded her mind until she could see nothing but scalding violet and the soothing love of pure clear blue.

She couldn't think.

"Soren, please." She pulled at him, desperate for a reprieve from the addictive torture he was putting her through. He slid up her side with a seductive grin on his face.

"Will you stay, Cyani?" he asked.

She fought hard for her thoughts, for control, but they had slipped through her hands long ago. She was falling now, and nothing could stop it.

"I can't," she confessed.

He closed his eyes for a lingering second then opened them again.

Cyani's heart thrummed in her chest faster than the wings of a hoverbird.

He leaned forward and kissed her. Hard and tender at the same time, the kiss flooded her with sad longing and sweet possession.

She gently pushed him back.

With soft nibbling bites to her lips, he let her pull away.

"The Grand Sister named me as heir. I will rule Azra," she whispered. She said the words, but they didn't feel right; they only felt bitter.

"What?" He stiffened, his hands clenching her robes beneath her, as his eyes searched hers with heartbreaking disbelief.

"I will be the Grand Sister," she said. She felt like she had her hand on the hilt of a knife, driving it deeper.

He let out a slow breath he had been holding as his eyes faded to black. She couldn't bear the sight of it, so she pushed away from him and gathered her knees to her bare chest.

He covered her shoulders with her training robes. Their slight weight oppressed her as she slid her arms into the garment and began fastening the clasps.

"I'm sorry, Soren," she said. "I have to go back."

Thunder rumbled in the distance. The heavy clouds that had lingered on the horizon at dusk marched toward them. Soren blinked up as he tried to fight back the angry surge of emotion rushing through him. It was all for nothing.

"Soren?"

He stood. He couldn't speak. He paced to the far end of the grotto and stalked back and forth near an overhanging bank.

"Soren, say something," she begged.

What could he say? *If you leave, it'll kill me before daybreak?* How could he shackle her with that guilt when he knew what she could do for her people?

Essa, Calya, and little Sene needed her. All the other children that had grown in the darkness needed her. She could save them.

"Blight, pestilence, and rot!" he shouted as he threw his fist into the muddy bank.

"Soren, please."

"You need to go," he said. His was one life. Theirs were many. She had to go.

A heavy crash of thunder rumbled through the grotto. The light bugs took shelter under the ferns.

She took a step toward him and held out the necklace. He reached for the necklace, and placed it back around her neck where it belonged. "Keep it."

She looked up at him with tears shining in her eyes.

"Protect it," he murmured through his tightening throat. "Don't ever let anyone take it from you again."

"I won't," she promised as she stepped into the circle of his arms. "If I had a choice—"

"Don't." He smoothed his hands over her hair. The mist had dampened it and the dark locks clung to the sides of her face. He pressed his lips to her forehead.

"I want you to keep Vicca," Cyani mumbled as she kept her eyes down. "The Grand Sister wants to sell her off as a transport ratter. I know she'll be happier here."

Soren nodded.

At least he wouldn't be alone in the end. He felt crushed. A feverish chill bloomed across his skin. He was too bonded to her. He wouldn't survive the night. He prayed it would be swift. He didn't want to live a night without her. He was afraid his heart would stop beating that second, the ripping pain was so fierce.

"I hope your mate is happy here. It's beautiful, Soren," Cyani mentioned as she pulled out of his arms.

"Go," he ordered, before he changed his mind and locked her in his garden forever. "Your people need you."

She jogged across the grotto. At the edge she turned back to him. She couldn't hide the love in her eyes.

Then she was gone.

21

CYANI'S FEET POUNDED THE HARD DIRT ROAD AS SHE RAN. THE TWISTED brambles of dense thickets rose on either side of the road. On occasion she'd pass an archway and catch a glimpse of flowers beyond, but the road stretched on before her like the entrance to an enormous labyrinth.

She stopped running and stood in the middle of the road. The storms closed in. Their booming voices rumbled as they rolled forward. The sky darkened above her, blocking out the view of the stars.

Cyani crouched, resting her forehead on her arms as her terrible pain overwhelmed her.

What have I done?

Loneliness gripped her, and her tears splashed against her arms. She made no attempt to stop them.

She cried until her lungs burned, her eyes swelled, and her

skin felt raw. The soft tapping rain fell into her hair, prodding her to stand, to pull herself together.

She tried to remember the Codes of Honor that she had studied for nearly half her life.

"Emotion leads to . . ." she choked out. "*Shakt!*"

She couldn't remember a damn thing. It all sounded like empty words. Thrusting her palms on her knees she propelled herself up and forward. She jogged on, letting the rhythmic motion push everything else from her mind.

She kicked a rock. It skittered across the road. She remembered waking up next to Soren as his eyes shone green for the first time. He was throwing a rock for Vicca as she scurried around in their small shelter.

She tried to take a deep breath, but ended up gulping a hasty mouthful of air. The rain fell on her shoulders, dripping through her loose hair the way it had that stormy night on Makko. She felt her heart stutter in her chest as her body remembered what it felt like to reach out, throw her traditions and shame into the mud and kiss him until she couldn't breathe.

She slowed to a stop.

The cold rain fell, turning the once clear path to sludge. She turned and stared back up the road.

"I'm sorry," she whispered.

She reached for her collarbone, and the soothing feel of her necklace gave her the strength to move forward.

She had to do the right thing.

Why does it feel so wrong?

Pushing herself at an agonizing pace, she wound through

the maze of lifegardens until the road curved and opened into the empty market square.

A couple of old men drew down a heavy tarp over the front of one of the small buildings at the periphery of the market.

They looked at her with a mix of curiosity and concern. She turned away from them and darted up the stairs and through the shield to the Yeshulen ship. She needed to find Nu and convince her to launch the ship. The quicker she left, the less time she'd have to feel the ripping pain coursing through her.

Unless I feel it the rest of my life.

Two guards gave her a double take.

"What are you doing?" The Yeshu immediately widened their stances. Cyani braced herself for attack. Why did the Yeshu all have to be so defensive?

"Where's Nu?" she asked. The chill of the ship seeped into her wet clothing. Suddenly the icy air seemed to stab deep into her bones.

A group of crew members came running.

"Azralen, what are you doing here?" the leader asked. He hastily grabbed one of the silver overcoats and offered it to her.

It warmed her skin, but did little to ease the sickening chill in her heart.

"I must return with Smith to his ship. Where is he?" she demanded.

An orange glowing A.I. disc let out an encouraging *pip* and a *whirr*, then flew off through one of the corridors. Cyani followed it, leaving the protesting crew members at the mouth of the ship. If the little thing was anything like Bug, it would lead her to Nu just to stir things up.

After winding through a maze of halls with simple silver doors, they came to a large door at the end of a corridor. Cyani looked closer in amazement as orbs of light drifted slowly within the metal of the door. The A.I. darted around the door, touching the drifting lights in a specific order. The door dissolved before Cyani's eyes to reveal the commander's personal quarters. Ice sculptures of giant fanged cats stood to either side of the doorway, guarding the entrance to a room with plush furs and colorful woven tapestries filled with flower and vine motifs that had to have come from Byra.

Cyani stepped into the room, turning a corner. She stopped in her tracks.

Cyn had Nu backed up against a wall, her hands pinned behind her back as he kissed her. She flowed into his body as she hungrily kissed him back.

Cyani shook off her shock. So much for wanting to kill him. She didn't have time for this.

"What are you doing?" Cyani thrust her hands on her hips.

Cyn managed an awkward jump back that looked like he had been jabbed in the ass with a Romlen ox prod. Nu flushed as she shoved him to the side.

"What am I doing? What are you doing?" he countered as his expression shifted from shock to anger. "Where's Soren?"

"He's home," she answered. *In his beautiful garden full of warmth and life.* She had to stop thinking like this. She steeled herself. "I did what I had to do. I got him here. We need to leave for Azra." And the sooner they left the better. She had to purge herself of all this emotion. Taking the mantle would be a trickier and deadlier task than crossing a pit of cobras. She needed her strength and her wits.

"Cyani, you don't belong on Azra," Cyn stated.

Nu took a step to the door. "I have work to do," she mumbled. She shoved the small troop of Yeshulen guards back out the door just as they skidded to a stop in her room. The doors reappeared behind Nu, leaving Cyani to face her twin alone.

"You don't understand." She crossed her arms, but it didn't help warm her.

"You love him."

No. Cyani stumbled backward. Slowly she sank onto a red woven cushion on the floor next to an ice fountain. Warm water cut through the channels of ice, melting the hard crystals into tiny flowing rivers while vapor danced in seductive curls toward the ceiling.

Great merciful Creator.

How could she deny it? She did love him.

"Damn it, Cyani. Stop being such a stubborn ass. This is where you belong." Cyn knelt in front of her and placed his hand on her shoulder.

"I can't do this," she murmured as she watched the water flow. Before her eyes a cold shard of ice slowly melted. "I can't let myself love him."

"But you do," Cyn prodded. "Why are you wearing this?" He flicked his finger under the center bead of the necklace.

"Cyn, there are things going on that you don't know about," she protested.

"What, that the Grand Sister made you her heir? Oh, I

know. That manipulative old bitch is playing you. Again. And you're walking right into her claws without a fight." He shoved her shoulder in disgust.

"Were you spying on me?"

Cyn snorted. "I deal in information, remember? Bug caught an earful during that conversation. Luckily it wasn't the only thing he caught."

Cyani placed her hand over her necklace.

"So you know I have to go back. I'm the only one who can change things on Azra." She felt like she was in a fog. Her misting breath curled around her face as her frozen tears stung her cheeks.

"There's the arrogance of a true Elite. And here I thought they hadn't brainwashed you," Cyn grumbled.

Cyani's anger flared. "If I don't go back and take the mantle, what then? Who will fight for the children of the ground cities?"

"It's not your fight, Cyani."

"Whose is it, yours?" she shouted at him.

His eyes hardened. Slowly a smile crept over his face, but his eyes remained as dark and hard as the shadows they grew up in.

"Damn you, Cyn." It was her turn to pound him with her fists. He caught them and held them. "What are you involved in now?"

"I live my life my way. It's time for you to let me live my life and learn to live your own. I'm a man, Cyani. No matter what the Elite told you, I'm not helpless. I'm certainly not stupid. My worth and my strength as a man have nothing to do with you. And I don't need your protection." He brought her fists together and pressed them to the center of his chest. The irritation and bitterness in his voice was tempered by the understanding in his eyes. They were so much alike. Why didn't she see it before? She would have never allowed him to sacrifice his happiness for her.

"Listen to me," he continued in a softer tone. "A revolution is brewing, and I don't want you caught up in it. You can't lead the Elite against the attack, Cyani. They'll turn on you in the midst of battle and they *will* kill you. To them you are no different than the mudbirds rising against them."

"I can fight them," she protested.

"You can't fight them and all of Azra! To the Elite, you are the enemy. Don't feed me any bullshit about how they'll learn to respect you. You know it's not true. Forget about mercy from the ground-dwellers. If you become Grand Sister, you will be their enemy, too. Whose side does that leave you on?" His jaw set as his brow furrowed, but there was no mistaking the subtle desperation in his eyes. "You can't win." He was trying to protect her.

"Shit," he continued. "For once in your life, will you listen to me?" He stood and stalked over to the other side of the room. He lifted a vessel made of ice and downed the liquid inside.

She wanted to. Great Matriarchs, she wanted to. Perhaps he was right, but that still didn't solve the problem of Yara. She didn't know what Cyn was capable of, but she knew what Yara was capable of. She didn't want to think of what would happen if the two ever met. "The Grand Sister will send a bloodhunter after you." Cyani reminded him as she rose to her feet as well.

"Let her come." Cyn placed the vessel back on a shelf, confirming her suspicions. Cyn wanted the fight. "Even if you go back to the high cities, I'm not coming with you. You think I'm going to stand by and be our dear aunt's breeding stud? I don't think so. She's not getting her legacy from me. She doesn't control me, and she never will."

"I just want you to be safe," Cyani argued.

He hung his head. "I thought you were dead. They say a twin is supposed to know if the other dies. I felt it, Cyani. We were born together . . ." He paused and looked away, as if he couldn't finish that thought, but Cyani knew what he was trying to say. He didn't want to live if she was gone.

"I found out you were alive," he looked back up at her. "For five years I've been fighting to find you. I couldn't handle the thought of losing you before I found you again."

He uncorked a flask and poured another drink. "If you want to be noble and selfless, stop trying to protect me and give me the only thing I've ever prayed for."

Cyani stared at him. "You pray? To whom?"

"To anyone who'll listen." He glared at her. "Be safe, free. God, Cyani, be happy." His expression turned wistful as his foxlike smile slid back across his face. "And if you can work it in, I wouldn't mind being an uncle."

Cyani stood in the center of the room as waves of shock pulsed through her numb fingers. Without the certainty of her duty, her future stretched out before her like a large void. Did she really have a choice?

"It's your future, sis. Go back to Azra, trust your Elite *sisters*. Maybe I'm wrong—maybe they won't blame you when the ground and the seas finally rise up against them. Or you can stay here, hidden and safe with a man who loves you. What do *you* want?" Cyn asked.

The words echoed in her mind, her heart. She had heard them before.

"If I become the Grand Sister, you won't need your revolution. I can make things better," she reasoned.

"Damn it, I can't turn back now. The islands will erupt with or without me. I'm going to stand for what I believe in. I'm a soldier, and I've made my choice. I will fight. I don't want to fight you. Stay, Cyani. Please. Do what makes you happy."

A fluttering feeling started in her numb toes and rushed up her legs. The release was intense as she felt hot tears on her cold cheeks. She could have a life of peace. She could have love. She could have babies of her own raised in safety with a strong and noble man as their father. Joy rushed through her. She threw herself into Cyn's arms.

He laughed as he caught her.

"I love you, sis," he confessed. "Mom and Dad will be thrilled."

"I love you, too, Cyn, even though I hate you right now." She squeezed him tighter. "I swear, if you get yourself killed, I'll kill you."

"Don't worry about me. I've learned a thing or two in the last few years. I'll be fine."

The door slid open and Nu stood in the corridor with her arms crossed.

"I swear, Smith, you are a menace. Fenril help the woman who ends up with you," she scolded.

Cyn let go of Cyani as she tried to stifle a chuckle.

"Aw, Nu. Are you saying you don't want to spend the rest of your days with me?" he teased.

"I'd rather tie myself to the foul end of a mammoth with a digestive virus," she grumbled. "The sooner I get you off this ship, the better. Are we leaving?"

"Wait," Cyani burst out. "I need to stay."

Nu's hard eyes softened. She placed a hand on Cyani's bicep and gave it a squeeze. "Good. Take Skitter with you, and the translator. Skitter will be able to communicate with Bug. You can contact your family secretly that way." Nu winked. The orange A.I. floated up and the light around her swelled with what could only be pride.

Cyani's shock nearly stole her speech. "Why?"

"Cyn here isn't the only one capable of spying," Nu stated as she poked him in the chest. "I'll monitor any communication between the two of you. You are not to mention the Yeshulen or Byra's location. Keep it to family. And when you do speak, know this, I will know exactly where you are."

Cyn nodded, but his face turned contemplative, like he was trying to figure out a way around the tech-leash.

"Why would you do this for me?" Cyani asked.

Nu shook her head as she exhaled. "Azralen, you know nothing of the Yeshulen. *Nothing* is more important than family."

Cyani reached out and gave the woman a hug, then gave Cyn another hug.

"Get out of here," Cyn ordered. "Go be happy."

Cyani smiled. The smile grew, starting in her heart and spreading out until the euphoric feeling surrounding her felt like it radiated around her.

She followed Skitter through the ship and out through the shield.

Heavy rain drenched her as she tucked her head and ran for shelter at the far end of the market. The drops of water felt warm and fresh. Her whole body seemed lighter somehow.

She loved Soren.

They could be together.

As the rain pounded her shoulders, she ducked under an old awning in a dark alcove and hugged her arms around her chest to ward off the lingering cold from the Yeshulen ship.

The hatch door closed, and with a smooth gliding motion, the enormous ship rose into the air.

Cyani watched it go. She sent a quick prayer for Cyn's safety, and that he would be the spark that started a firestorm of change for her people. He was truly of the blood of Cyrila and Fima. She hoped that the knowledge that she was safe would temper his recklessness. If anyone could change their world, and make it out alive, it was him. She had faith in her brother.

Maybe there was hope for Azra after all.

She pressed back deeper into the alcove. The empty market was completely deserted. She watched the heavy drops of rain splash into the puddles on the worn stone, sending a spray of water back up from the ground.

This was her home.

No more whips, no more weapons. She could spend her days using her hands to nurture life instead of taking it. She took a deep breath. Perhaps her nightmares would fade, replaced by dreams of light bugs floating near a clear stream.

She heard a galloping in the distance, a lone Byralen caught in the storm.

It was coming toward her, not back to the lifegardens.

Soaked and muddy, a silka raced into the market. A cloaked woman threw herself from the beast's back and ran to the landing area.

"No!" she screamed at the sky with chilling agony in her voice. "No, come back. Come back!" She collapsed into a puddle in heart-wrenching sobs.

"Rensa?" Cyani called, leaving her shelter in the alcove. She ran to Soren's sister and took her by the shoulders. She tried to lift Rensa up to pull her out of the storm. Rensa lifted her face to her. Her wet hair hung limp across her pale face, framing deep black eyes brimming with unshed tears.

"Cyani?" she choked out. Rensa threw her arms around Cyani's neck, throwing them both back into a puddle. "You didn't leave!"

Cyani wanted to laugh as she felt the cool water soak up into her robes on her backside. Why was Rensa crying?

"I couldn't leave," she told the girl in an attempt to calm her down. A flash of lighting ripped through the sky and thunder boomed overhead with such force Cyani could feel it in her chest. The silka screeched and galloped off the way it had come. "We have to get out of the open. This is dangerous."

Rensa clung to her as she dragged the girl into the alcove. They ducked under the fall of water sliding off the canvas awning. Rensa stumbled and knocked over a stack of empty woven baskets. Cyani tried to pick them up, but Rensa caught her by the arm and pulled her back toward the storm.

"Cyani, you have to get back to the garden right now," she pleaded.

"We should wait out the storm," Cyani reasoned.

"Don't you love him?" Rensa asked, her voice hard with accusation. "Don't you want to be with him?"

"What are you talking about? We'll get killed if we go running out there. As soon as the storm clears, we can go back." What was wrong with her?

"Soren is dying." Her voice broke into a sob.

"What?" Cyani's knees buckled as she stumbled sideways. She caught one of the supports of the awning and clung to it while she tried to breathe. How could that be? He hadn't bonded with her. He told her he hadn't. He promised she would have a choice, that he wouldn't chain her.

He let me go.

Thunder boomed again as another strike of lightning hit close by. Suddenly the truth threaded itself through her memories of the last few days. His eyes were blue.

He was bonded to her, and he let her go.

"*Shakt*," she whispered. "How bad is it?"

"He's not fighting." Rensa collapsed against the wall.

"I don't understand—he can live a couple of weeks, right?" She had time. She had to have time.

"No, Cyani. He's bonded. It changes our blood. The longest anyone has survived the loss of a fully bonded mate is a day. If he doesn't want to live, he won't last the night."

22

SHE HAD TO GET BACK BEFORE—NO, SHE COULDN'T EVEN THINK IT. A SEARING flash of lightning slammed into a towering oak. The air crackled as a heavy limb creaked and fell, shattering the roof of a nearby building. The ground beneath Cyani's feet shook with the force of the impact.

"How do I get back?" Cyani shouted over the roar of the storm.

"Follow the disc," Rensa yelled. "For the love of the Grower, hurry!"

Cyani threw herself into the slashing fury of the rain. Skitter rocketed ahead until she became nothing more than a glowing dot of orange. Cyani nearly lost sight of her.

No.

Shakt.

She had to keep up. Cyani pushed her body harder than

she ever had, harder than the long battles against the Garulen on Felli. Harder than the endless hours spent in training under the threat of the whip or death. Harder than the nights she ran from the flesh traders in the shadows as a child. Her muscles burned as the rain flooded into her bleary eyes. She did her best to control her breathing, to draw from her endurance, but her heart pounded so fast, so loud in her ears it rivaled the thunder.

Her feet sank into the sticky mud as the cold rain splashed up her legs and thighs. The fabric of her robes clung to her skin as she pushed relentlessly into the darkness.

Please don't die.

Lightning struck, illuminating the walls of thicket on either side of the road.

It'll be my fault.

He loved her.

She was such a fool. Why didn't she see it?

I didn't want to see it.

He had done what he promised. He'd given her a choice. He was willing to give his life for her freedom. He couldn't die.

I love him.

She would love him the rest of her life.

No matter how hard her panic pushed her forward, she felt like she was crawling through the thick mud, wasting precious time. Her shoes had fallen off. Her hair clung to her neck and shoulders, but it didn't matter. She pursued the tiny glowing orange orb, the lingering hope on the horizon.

Until Skitter stopped. The orb started spinning in frantic loops in a wide spot in the road.

What was wrong?

The road split into five different routes. Skitter flew around in wild circles, screeching a panicked "*EEEEEEEEEeeeee.*"

"Skitter, find the vine that looks like this," she commanded as she held up her wrist. Skitter zoomed down, flew slowly around her hand, then zipped off through the pounding rain.

Shakt. She planted her muddy hands on her thighs and bent over, fighting for breath as she waited at the crossroads while the orb flew in and out of the darkness. She looked at the imprint of her muddy hand on her once pristine robes. Sodden and dripping with dark black mud, they weighed her down.

She had no time for this. She had no time left.

A loud victorious whistle pierced the fury of the storm.

She had found him.

ANOTHER FEVERED CHILL SHOOK HIM AS THE THUNDER ROLLED OVERHEAD like K-bombs in the distance. He'd stripped off his clothing. He felt so hot and so cold at the same time. He couldn't stand the feel of soft cloth on his skin, but when he tried to stand, to walk, he passed out.

So he leaned his head against the wall while Vicca placed her paws on his knee and let out a whimper.

He stroked her soft ears.

"It's okay, little girl," he whispered. "It's going to be okay."

It wouldn't be long, and it would all be over.

None of it would touch him anymore. None of the pain, none of the terrible darkness. He'd finally be free. His spirit would linger here, and sustain his garden for his brother's son, his namesake.

His only regret was the pain he'd caused his family by allowing them to hope.

His father had to carry his mother out of the garden when Soren told them what he'd done. He could still hear the echoes of her cries in the wind.

He didn't want to think about the look on Rensa's face when he told her that Cyani had chosen to leave.

"How could she do that to you?" she pleaded.

"She doesn't know." The simple statement had crushed Rensa. It was as if he had killed a part of his sister's spirit. She ran, leaving him to die alone.

Soren scooped up Vicca and held her to his bare chest. He didn't want to bear the guilt anymore.

It would all be over soon.

Vicca wriggled out of his grasp and bounced toward the door. It crashed open, knocking her backward.

Time froze.

Cyani stood in the doorway, drenched and covered with mud. Her chest heaved under the transparent fabric of her filthy robes. He'd never seen anything more beautiful.

"Soren?"

Cyani tried to swallow her panic. He crouched naked against the far wall, a sheen of sweat covering his strong shoulders while his streaked hair clung to his damp skin. His eyes were glazed, his brow knit in pain, but he was alive. Vicca barked and leapt around the room in crazy spinning circles.

"Soren?"

His eyes blazed with blue violet. The light filled the room as he lunged toward her.

He crashed into her, throwing them both back against the

far wall. He crushed her as his mouth took hers, feeding off her. She knew what he needed. She knew what she had to do to save him. She embraced it with a rushing sense of joy and frantic relief.

Feed from me, devour me. Take what you need to live.

She wrapped her arms around his neck and pulled him in. The burning heat of his skin eased the terrified chill coursing through her body. She sent a grateful prayer to the Creator that he was alive.

His frantic hands ripped through her robes. She tore at them—she couldn't get them off fast enough. She had to feel his skin against hers. Her whole body shook with exhaustion, burning pain, and the electric pleasure of his touch. His hand pressed into the small of her back until her naked skin met his. She could feel his engorged flesh hard against her abdomen. She brushed her hand over its length and he stiffened.

"Cyani," he growled, but his voice cracked with emotion. He scorched a trail of kisses down her neck, feasting on her skin.

"I'm here." She wound her fingers into his silky hair. "And I'm never leaving you again."

He captured her in a devastating kiss as his strong hands gripped her hips and lifted her off the floor. She wrapped her legs around his waist and moaned into his relentless kiss as his body slowly sank into hers, stretching her, filling her.

She clung to his shoulders and hung on as he thrust into her with fierce desperation. It was all she could do to remember to breathe as the burst of color from his touch painted the room in a cascade of flowing light.

"Soren," she begged. She kissed his neck as his body

pumping in her drove her to such frantic ecstasy she could barely hold on to him.

His whole body shook as he clung to her. The rhythmic slide of his flesh entering her over and over drove her mad as the tension in her body wound to the breaking point.

It shattered, and she screamed as he thrust into her. His muscles tensed. He pushed harder. Deeper.

She couldn't breathe.

She heard him roar, then sob.

And then peaceful darkness embraced her.

SOREN STRUGGLED TO COMPOSE HIMSELF. HE PULLED AIR INTO HIS BODY IN forced gasps as the rush of pleasure and relief still gripped him.

She came back.

With his muscles taxed and shaking, he gently eased them both to the floor. He buried his face between her damp breasts. With each breath, he felt himself grow stronger, his heart lighter. She came back to him. In spite of everything, she chose him.

He would spend the rest of his life worshipping her.

He lifted her hand. Mud caked her arms. The time to begin his adoration was at hand. She needed him now.

Gathering his strength, he embraced the cool touch of the night air as his fever receded. She moaned as he lifted her into his arms. She must have run through the storm from the market.

Astonished by her endurance, she had pushed herself past her body's breaking point and passed out again. Her head lolled against his arm, the way it had when he had lifted her out of the stingship on Makko. She had saved him then, and now again. In the years of his life that stretched before him, he would never be able to repay her, but he would certainly enjoy the attempt.

In awe of her strength, he carried her out of the house to the bath pools near the edge of the vineyard. Warm water fell over the edge of a smooth, flat black stone into the dark pool. The soft rain fell in gentle waves, making the water dance. The fury of the storm had passed.

He lowered them both into the pool. She still didn't wake, but he wasn't concerned. They had both been through too much, and the intensity of his hormones entering her must have been difficult for her to absorb after her exhausting run.

He settled her in his lap, and with careful attention, he bathed her exquisite body. She would wake in comfort, clean and pure. This would be a new beginning for both of them. He paid careful attention to her hands, stroking her long fingers, and kissing the tattoos circling her wrists.

She sighed as he gently washed her hair, then lifted her back out of the pool. Carefully he cradled her as he brought her back into the house. With loving attention he dried her and settled her into the bed.

He had work to do.

Hours later as the dark exhaustion began to lift, Cyani turned, and tried to wake. *Shakt*, she had passed out. She'd always found that trait of her species a bit annoying.

"Cyani?" Soren's soft voice murmured in her ear.

She felt his fingertips feather down her temple and across her cheek. She took a deep breath and opened her eyes.

Soren lay beside her in an enormous bed. Four intricately carved posts of a warm red wood rooted into the floor and grew up through the ceiling. They had been adorned with flowing garlands of violet and white flowers cascading down the posts and over the edges of the bed. Exquisite woven blankets in cool shades of green and blue draped over them as her head sank into a fluffy pillow.

She had died and gone to heaven.

"Cyani, are you okay?" he asked, tenderly kissing her on the forehead.

"I'm wonderful." She smiled in spite of the aching pain coursing through her whole body. She'd probably be sore for a week after that run, and the other things.

Cyani stifled a giggle as she thought about the frantic passion of those other things. How long had she been sleeping? She was clean. Her hands gleamed in the soft light. He had bathed her while she slept. A shiver of excitement blossomed in her belly. No one had ever given her such tender care.

She breathed in the sweet perfume of the flowers filling the room. The walls of the room seemed to be carved from seamless wood. Relief sculptures of different animals and plants surrounded them in beauty. Clusters of flowers adorned the walls. Draperies similar to the ones she had seen in Nu's quarters covered the window, while a soft white light glowed from two golden sconces on either side of the bed.

"Are you okay?" Soren asked, concern seeping into his voice. Vicca leapt onto the bed, turned a quick circle on Cyani's feet, and plopped herself down. Cyani chuckled but her abdomen hurt from the strain of the run.

"I'm fine. All Azralen pass out when their bodies need to

recuperate from something. It keeps us from falling out of the tree if we're wounded enough to compromise our balance." Suddenly her mind cleared. "How are you? Are you still ill?" She pressed her palm to his forehead. His skin felt warm, but not feverish.

"I've never been better," he admitted as he pressed a loving kiss to her lips.

"Good, because I'm going to kill you." She grabbed a pillow and whapped him across the head with it. "You lied to me."

He laughed.

"Damn it, Soren. You knew you had bonded to me, and you didn't tell me." She drew the blanket up over her breasts. "You were going to die because of me."

"I kept my promise. I gave you a choice." He planted a soft kiss on her collarbone, right beneath the edge of her necklace.

"You are too damn noble," she grumbled.

"No, I just love you." He plucked a deep violet blossom from the post of the bed and offered it to her.

Cyani's heart fluttered and her hands trembled as she took it. He smiled at her, his eyes glowing a clear bright blue, the exact color of hers.

He gathered her hand in his and planted a soft kiss to her knuckles. "Will you stay here with me? Will you make this your home?"

"Yes," she whispered. "I love you, Soren."

"What about Azra?" he asked, his tone still doubtful.

"As my brother so eloquently put it, it's not my fight." She looked down and smoothed her hand over the blanket.

Soren slid his hand up her thigh and began a delicious massage of her taxed muscles.

"Cyn will be fine. He's too much like you."

"I hope so . . ."

He captured her words in his kiss as his hand brushed over her abdomen.

She smiled as she relaxed back into the soft bed. She wouldn't deny him, not now, not ever. She was addicted to him, too.

She reached for his shoulder, and pulled him on top of her. He slid into her sore and grateful body, soothing the deep ache and creating a new one.

Slowly he made tender love to her until a new dawn touched the sky.

SOREN'S MOTHER CHUCKLED AS CYANI PICKED AT THE HOPELESS TANGLE OF yarn in her lap. The elder woman's fingers flicked and spun a hooked needle, creating a soft cushiony fabric. Cyani hadn't mastered the art of untangling the thread.

"Patience, Cyani. It will come to you," she encouraged.

"I was much better at shearing the silkas," Cyani grumbled.

Soren's mother laughed. "I've never seen anyone immobilize one in such a hands-on manner."

Soren entered the house with a laden basket slung over his shoulder.

"Cyani, come with me," he urged, pulling her up from the wild tangle of yarn threatening to swallow her. "I have something to show you." He led her outside.

They crossed the vineyard and entered the forest on the other side. She hadn't explored the forest yet, and didn't want to get too distracted by Soren's hungry looks. She wanted to know the garden the way Soren did, every creature, plant, and insect. She wanted to care for it and watch it grow. It was her home, a place of acceptance and peace.

She finally gave up her fight against his amorous hands as Soren kissed the back of her neck and pulled the edge of her skirt up her thigh.

A flash of white caught her eye.

"Soren?" She turned to him, but his gaze was locked on a glade in the distance. He waved at her to be quiet as they crept closer.

"I saw them earlier. I was hoping they hadn't left," he whispered.

Cyani couldn't speak as she peered into the glade. Two pure white horses, each with a single horn in the center of its forehead, stood in the clearing. The bigger male arched his neck as he touched his nose to the female's in a loving gesture.

"They're fragile creatures, very rare. They only come to gardens that are perfectly balanced and truly blessed," Soren whispered. "If they choose to foal here, we'll have many children."

"We are blessed," she murmured as his strong arms closed around her shoulders.

The beautiful creatures whinnied then chased each other through the woods. They seemed to bring with them a promise of joy, love, hope, and peace.

Epilogue

CYN HID HIS SMILE BEHIND HIS RELAXED HAND AS HE LOUNGED IN THE PILOT'S seat. Cyani's image floated in the holo-screen above Bug. She beamed with pride as she held up a lumpy mass of cloth that looked like a crump fungus.

"It's lovely, sis, really," Cyn encouraged. "How's the cooking coming?"

He kicked his feet up on the controls as he leaned back in the seat. He played with a lock of his hair behind his ear. He hadn't had his hair this long in years. It was good to be free of the Union.

"Soren isn't allowed to complain. He's worse at it than I am," Cyani responded.

She glowed. Her eyes shone with laughter, love, and a good bit of frustration that was healthy for her. She needed the challenge.

Nothing could have made him happier.

"Perhaps Nu will let me stop by in a month or two, and I can help with the cooking. At the very least you both deserve one good meal this year," he taunted.

"Hey," she protested, but she brightened with excitement. "We'd love to have you stay. Vicca should have had her pups by then."

"And what about you?" he asked.

"We'll see."

Someone shouted in the background, and Cyani looked behind her. "I've got to go. Vicca just got stuck in a vat of blackwine. She'll be purple for a month. Stay safe."

"I will," he promised.

With a flick she disappeared.

Suddenly the ship seemed very quiet and empty.

He couldn't think about it. If he did, it would distract him. He had work to do.

Static buzzed in the com. Cyn glanced at it. Who would be calling him?

"Cyrus, you there?" Xan's voice boomed through the com. "I've got something for you."

Cyn brought his image to the screen. "What's up?"

"Take a look." The image of Xan flashed off, and in its place a picture of a tall Azralen woman filled the screen. Cyn felt his pulse quicken as he looked at her. She had light hair, bright lime green that flew in a haphazard array of short wild wisps around her face. Her burning gold eyes were focused, intelligent, and there was something else in them. Something that drew Cyn closer to the screen.

"So this is Yara." Cyn couldn't stop looking at her eyes. "She's pretty."

"She's a Union commander and an Elite bloodhunter, so don't get any ideas. I intercepted a communication to the Union calling her back to Azra. She's been ordered to hunt down Cyn of Cyori."

Well then, I'll make sure she finds him.

"Thanks Xan." He tapped his finger on the edge of the control screen. Xan's image blinked off.

Cyn smiled as he set his course.

There was an old saying on Earth. Keep your friends close.

And your enemies closer.

Printed in the United States
by Baker & Taylor Publisher Services